She blew out a hard breath.

"That is the worst idea in the history of bad ideas."

"Sadie, it's not. It's the best way to deal with a problem like ours."

"For you, maybe. Not for me."

"Nobody ever has to know."

"Sneaking around, that's what you're suggesting. That's all you've ever suggested. I keep telling you it's not happening and yet you won't stop pushing me."

"Sadie, just—"

"Nope. Uh-uh. Not. Going. To happen."

He picked up his drink, swallowed the last of it and set the glass back down hard. "I should go."

No kidding. "Yeah. I guess you should."

"If I stay, I'm only going to try to change your mind. I really want to kiss you..."

"Don't."

A muscle twitched in his sculpted jaw. "Fair enough. Think about what I said."

No problem. She would have trouble thinking about anything else.

Dear Reader,

Rivals to enemies to friends to...so much more?

Ty Bravo and Sadie McBride have a rocky history together. As children, they were rivals at school, always trying to top each other in every way. Then Ty married Sadie's best friend, Nicole. It was a troubled marriage from the start and Sadie was Team Nicole all the way. Now Ty and Nicole are divorced. Sadie and Ty have slowly become good friends, and Nicole is about to marry again—this time to the love of her life in her dream Christmas wedding.

Sadie's the maid of honor and Ty is the best man. The two of them are beginning to see each other in a whole new light. But Sadie is looking for a lifetime love. And Ty? He's never going to the love place again.

Plus, there's Nicole, who is something of a diva and a bit of a drama queen. There's no way to say how she'll react if her best friend falls for her ex. Sadie knows she should stay away from Ty romantically. He's a bad bet on more than one level, but her yearning heart has other plans.

I hope Ty and Sadie's story gives you everything you're looking for in a Christmas romance. And I'm wishing you fun, family and joy this holiday season.

Happy reading, everyone!

Christine

Her Best Friend's Wedding

CHRISTINE RIMMER

HARLEQUIN

SPECIAL
EDITION

Recycling programs for this product may not exist in your area.

ISBN-13: 978-1-335-59439-6

Her Best Friend's Wedding

Copyright © 2023 by Christine Rimmer

For questions and comments about the quality of this book, please contact us at CustomerService@Harlequin.com.

Harlequin Enterprises ULC
22 Adelaide St. West, 41st Floor
Toronto, Ontario M5H 4E3, Canada
www.Harlequin.com

Printed in U.S.A.

Christine Rimmer came to her profession the long way around. She tried everything from acting to teaching to telephone sales. Now she's finally found work that suits her perfectly. She insists she never had a problem keeping a job—she was merely gaining "life experience" for her future as a novelist. Christine lives with her family in Oregon. Visit her at christinerimmer.com.

Books by Christine Rimmer

Harlequin Special Edition

Wild Rose Sisters

The Father of Her Sons
First Comes Baby...
The Christmas Cottage

Montana Mavericks: Brothers & Broncos

Summer Nights with the Maverick

Montana Mavericks: The Real Cowboys of Bronco Heights

The Rancher's Summer Secret

Montana Mavericks: What Happened to Beatrix?

In Search of the Long-Lost Maverick

Montana Mavericks: Six Brides for Six Brothers

Her Favorite Maverick

Montana Mavericks: Lassoing Love

The Maverick's Surprise Son

Bravo Family Ties

Hometown Reunion

Visit the Author Profile page
at Harlequin.com for more titles.

A big shout-out to Christina Helin and her cats,
Boo and Olive, who are the inspiration for
Sadie's cats in this book.

"My two cats are soul sisters," Christina says.
Boo got her name because she's pure white,
a stray found right before Halloween. Olive, a calico,
was found a year later, an abandoned kitten
on a cold November night in the middle of
Mt. Olive Road. Christina explains that the moment
Boo met Olive, it was love at first sight.
The two have been inseparable for almost ten years.

Thank you, Christina, for allowing me to use their
names and likenesses in *Her Best Friend's Wedding*.

Chapter One

"Wait. Don't tell me," Ty Bravo teased as Sadie Mc-Bride set his usual breakfast in front of him. "You like him." Ty tipped his head at the big guy just going out the door. "He gets a date."

"I do like him," she replied. "He's really nice."

"Nice." Ty made the word sound boring in the extreme.

"Yeah. Nice is a good thing. And some of us still believe in love and won't quit till we find it, so you can wipe that know-it-all grin off your face."

Ty scoffed. "Never seen him before." He stared out the front window as the big guy passed under the Henry's Diner sign and disappeared down Main Street. "Who is he?"

"He's Mrs. Lamont's nephew." Martha Lamont had been teaching third grade at Medicine Creek Elementary for more than thirty years. Twenty years ago, she'd taught both Ty and Sadie—as well as Sadie's best friend, Nicole, who was also Ty's ex-wife.

Ty turned his piercing blue eyes directly on Sadie. "Mrs. Lamont's nephew got a name?"

"Deacon Lamont. He's just moved to town from Billings and he's planning on opening a landscaping business here. Friday night we're having dinner at Arlington's." Arlington's Steakhouse had been a Medicine Creek, Wyoming, landmark for as long as Sadie could remember.

"You're meeting him at the restaurant, right?"

"Of course." Sadie refilled his coffee cup and the cups of Lester Biggs and Bob Early, who sat on either side of him.

"Good."

Annoyed at his domineering attitude, she turned and set the coffeepot back on the warming ring. "I'll say it again, he's nice and he's Mrs. Lamont's nephew."

"Nice or not, you can never be too safe."

"That's true. And I've been doing this for a while now, you know." Sadie always set up a coffee date to start, or she had the guy drop by the diner while she was working. Then, if she liked him, they met somewhere for lunch or dinner. And for the first actual date, she drove her own car.

"Hey. I just want you to be safe," Ty said almost gently.

Her heart kind of melted. She and Ty had a lot of history, much of it rocky. But all in all, she considered him a true friend, someone she could count on, someone she trusted. "And I *am* safe, Ty, I promise you."

He sipped his coffee, a thoughtful look on his chiseled face. "How many guys you been through now?"

That melty feeling? Poof. She glared at him. "*Been through?* Like I chew them up and spit them out?"

"Oh, come on, Sadie. You've been on a lot of dates in the past few years. I can't ask how many?"

She refused to dignify that with an answer. Instead, she threw him a withering look and headed off to take breakfast orders from a table full of ranch hands.

As she left the counter behind, she heard Lester Biggs mutter, "Damn, bro. Death wish, much?"

Once she'd taken the orders, she made the rounds with the coffeepot.

When she finally circled back to Ty, she picked up their conversation right where they'd left off. "Yes, I have been on a lot of dates with a lot of guys. That's kind of the point when you're looking for someone special, which means that the exact number of guys I've been out with is not the issue. It only matters that I don't give up—and what's it to you, anyway?"

"Well, Sadie Jane, have you noticed that your prince is taking a long-ass time to come riding in on his big white charger?"

The look she gave him then should have seared him to a cinder, leaving nothing but a tiny pile of ash in the middle of his stool. Too bad he only kept on smirking at her.

She seriously considered giving him a large piece of her mind. Instead, she spoke to him sweetly. "Yes, Tyler Ross, I have kissed a lot of frogs and I will keep right on kissing them until my prince appears, thank you very much." And then she couldn't resist a little dig at Mr. Cold, Hard and Cynical. "So, what about *your* plans for the weekend? Wait. Let me guess. You'll be off somewhere doing your hound dog thing, am I right?"

He had the nerve to look hurt. "Come on, Sadie. You don't have to put it like that."

"Yes, I do."

"Why?"

"Because 'So will you be flying off to LA or Dallas, where you'll meet a woman, romance her and have sex with her for the weekend?' is too long to say." She slapped down his check as Lester and Bob snorted with laughter and Ty shook his head.

Adding a giant tip as always, he paid in cash. "See you tonight." His voice was fond.

She gave him a real smile in return. "I'll be there."

Ty resettled his buckskin felt hat on his head, slid off his stool and headed for the door, where he grabbed his shearling jacket off the coat tree and shrugged it on.

Outside, the sky was overcast, the temperature in the midforties. He went on down the street, waving and nodding at friends and neighbors as he passed them. Rounding the first corner, he entered the two-story brick building that housed Cash Enterprises on the ground floor, with Bravo Real Estate above. Cash was Ty's dad's name—well, technically it was a nickname. Cash's given name was John, but he'd always had a knack for making money. He'd acquired the nickname early and it had stuck.

In the open reception area seated behind her tidy desk, Ramona Teague, their longtime secretary, greeted Ty with a prim smile and a reminder that he and his dad had lunch scheduled for noon at the Stagecoach Grill with a couple of land speculators from Idaho Falls.

His phone rang as he entered his office. He took it from his pocket and checked the display.

Madeline.

Sadie liked to give him a bad time about being a player. He wasn't, not really. Not currently, anyway. He just had zero interest in falling in love with anyone. His seven-year marriage had taught him one great lesson: a committed relationship was a lot more trouble than it was worth.

So no, he never got serious with anyone. And he always made himself clear from the start. If a woman wanted love and a ring on her finger, he was not her man. Ty kept his dealings with women simple and straightforward. A few drinks, a few laughs, a night or two in bed together.

And yeah. Now that he thought it through, maybe that made him exactly the hound dog Sadie had called him.

Just not so much lately.

He and Nicole had not been happy together. Still, he'd honored his vows and never cheated on her—though he'd wanted to. After the divorce, he'd gone a little wild for a couple years.

In the past year, there'd been exactly three women. Madeline Leroy was the most recent of the three. Back at the first of August, he'd spent a weekend in Denver with her. He hadn't seen Madeline since.

Did that make him cold, hard and cynical, just like Sadie had said? Maybe. But the way he saw it, he had two kids, an ex-wife he tried hard to get along with and a job he enjoyed. He and his dad were mostly in property and land development now. The work was both satisfying and demanding. Not only did sleeping with strangers get old after a while, he didn't have a lot of time for it. Work and the kids kept him plenty busy.

The phone was still ringing.

He gave in and answered it. "Hello, Madeline."

"You're not dead."

"Nope. Still breathing."

"It's good to hear your voice. How've you been?"

"Madeline, I…"

She made a small, thoughtful sound. "Not happening, huh?"

He winced. "I guess that's the simplest way to put it."

"I was just going through my contacts, cleaning things up."

"I hear you."

She said nothing for several seconds. "I'll delete your number, then."

"Fair enough." What else was there to say? "You take care."

She disconnected the call. He tossed the phone on his desk and dropped into his chair. Leaning back, he laced his fingers behind his head, stretching a little, thinking of Sadie again.

The woman had one gear—full speed ahead. He knew her so well. Today, she would work until the very last minute and be late to the family meeting at Nicole's. She loved her job as much as he loved his.

He frowned as he thought of the curly haired landscaper she was meeting for dinner Friday night. The guy wasn't the one for her. Ty could tell just by looking at him. Too…unsurprising. Too nice.

Sadie needed someone sharper, a guy who could take it when she got sassy. A guy who could give it right back—but with respect and a decent sense of humor.

He made a mental note to check in with her Friday

night, just to make sure Mrs. Lamont's nephew was as nice as she'd made him out to be.

For Sadie, the day flew by—but then, it always did. Her mom, Mona, came in at ten to manage the counter and tables. That freed Sadie up to stay on top of ordering, inventory, bookkeeping and payroll—and, weather permitting, to pay visits to their other two Henry's locations.

Her dad had opened the original Medicine Creek Henry's back in the eighties. It had provided a comfortable living for their small family. Her dad and mom never planned to expand. It was Sadie who'd wanted that.

And she'd made it happen, too. After high school, she'd gotten a two-year business degree and set out to open more diners. Now they had a Henry's in nearby Sheridan and another in Buffalo twenty miles to the south. Overseeing three restaurants kept her busy.

Sadie loved Henry's. She felt great pride that the family diner was a home away from home for a lot of folks in Medicine Creek. And it was doing fine in the newer locations as well.

That day, the cook up in Sheridan had to clock out early. Sadie took over for him. She didn't get back to Medicine Creek until almost six and ended up fifteen minutes late for the family meeting at Nicole's.

Her best friend answered the door. "You're late," Nicole accused with a pout.

Sadie gave a regretful shrug. "Sorry. Work."

Nicole looked gorgeous as always, all that pale blond hair flowing like a silvery waterfall down her back, her blue eyes enormous in her delicate face. Nicole was one of those women men stared at on the street.

Back in school, she and Ty had been the two best-looking people at Medicine Creek High. They were prom king and queen and shared a passionate, volatile relationship.

Sadie had always found the two of them exhausting as a couple. In high school, they were constantly breaking up and then inevitably getting back together.

And then they got married the summer right after senior year. When their stormy marriage finally ended, the whole family was relieved. Ty was happier on his own. Surprisingly, so was Nicole. As a rule nowadays, the two of them got along just fine.

Even their kids, Emily and Drew, had quickly adjusted to going back and forth between the big house where they'd lived when their parents were together and the roomy place around the block that Ty had bought when he moved out.

Best of all, now Nicole had Gavin. A lawyer from San Antonio, Gavin Stahl was a calm, easygoing man. He adored Nicole. Everyone agreed that Nicole had finally found the worshipful, unwavering love she craved.

Nicole pulled Sadie into a hug right there at the door. "Get some food so we can start."

Sadie greeted them all, including her parents and Ty's mom and dad. No, they were not all related by blood. But they were a family at heart. They loved and counted on each other.

Nicole's mom, Brenda, had been Sadie's mom's life-long best friend. The two besties made sure their daughters were like sisters, too. When Brenda died suddenly, she'd left custody of her only child to Sadie's parents.

Thirteen-year-old Nicole had moved in with the Mc-Brides. She and Sadie had shared a room until the summer after high school when Nicole married Ty.

Sadie filled a plate with lasagna and Caesar salad, and the meeting got under way. There was a lot of ground to cover. They all needed to agree on who would do what for November and December.

Both months were jam-packed. Sadie was handling all the arrangements for Nicole's weekend-in-Vegas bachelorette party coming up a week from Friday. Ty, the best man, who'd met Gavin in college at Texas A&M, was in charge of the bachelor party, which wouldn't be a big deal. Probably just him and Gavin on a guys' night out.

Both Nicole and nine-year-old Emily were bouncing off the walls with excitement—Nicole, because she would have the perfect wedding this time. Back when she'd married Ty, the whole thing had been rushed what with Emily on the way.

This time, Nicole intended for her big day to be perfect. And the family supported her in that. They all wanted Nic to have the wedding of her dreams.

As for Emily, she'd insisted on being a junior bridesmaid. Not a flower girl, no way. She'd also begged to go to Vegas with her mom and Sadie and the three other bridesmaids, but Nicole had held the line on that. Almost ten was far too young to join in on a bachelorette weekend in Sin City.

Instead, Grandma Abby, Ty's mom, would take Emily and Drew out to the Bravo family ranch, the Rising Sun, for the weekend. When Emily whined that a visit to the ranch just didn't stack up to a trip to Las Vegas, everyone reminded her that the *next* weekend she would be the birthday girl.

Emily clapped her hands when they ran through her birthday-party plans. "It is all going to be perfect," she declared, looking so much like her mom with her cornflower blue eyes and *Alice in Wonderland* hair. "I just can't wait!" Emily and five of her closest friends would be treated to mani-pedis and facials at the best salon in town, followed by a princess party complete with a sleepover in a pink-and-gold princess tent.

Next up on the packed agenda was Thanksgiving. It would be happening out at the Rising Sun.

And after that, on the second Saturday in December, Nicole and Gavin would share their vows at a beautiful resort in Breckenridge, Colorado. Then the newlyweds were off for a two-week honeymoon, returning home just in time for Christmas.

Emily sighed and flicked a lock of hair back over her slim shoulder. "I wish there could be a wedding every week—or at least, every month. I can't wait to walk down the aisle in my beautiful dress." She gasped and her eyes lit up. "I know! Sadie, why don't you marry Daddy? We could give you a really good wedding, as good as Mom's! I could be a bridesmaid, just like for Mom, but when you and Daddy get married, I could go to the bachelorette party, too."

Sadie almost choked on her lasagna at that suggestion. She knocked back a gulp of water to get the bite of pasta to go down as Nicole let out a disbelieving trill of laughter.

"Sweetheart," Nic said to her daughter, "there is no way your father will ever get married again—and if, somehow, the stars aligned and he did, it would not be to Sadie."

"Yes, it could be to Sadie," argued Emily. "Daddy and Sadie are friends. Friends can get married."

Ty's dad and mom were sitting directly across from Sadie. They exchanged the strangest glance right then— a knowing sort of glance, a glance full of mutual understanding.

About what, Sadie had no clue.

Nicole scoffed. "Honey. Really. Sadie and your dad? Please. They just aren't couple material. Back when we were your age, your dad and Sadie were always in competition. They both wanted to be the best—at math, at science. Then in high school, they ran against each other for student body president."

"I won," Ty announced way too smugly.

"Just barely," Sadie reminded him.

"Even now," Nicole added, "they sometimes get on each other's last nerve." Nicole had it right on all counts. The chance of Ty Bravo ever remarrying was slim to none. And if by some impossible miracle, he did, it wouldn't be to Sadie.

Sadie slid a glance in Ty's direction and found him staring right at her. He winked. And then he clapped a fist to his heart. "Sadie Jane, should we break the big news now?"

She looked at him sideways. "I have no idea what you're talking about."

He was grinning. "Don't be shy. It's okay. I'll tell them. It just so happens that Sadie and I are already together." Nicole groaned at that one as Ty went on, "God's honest truth. It's real love for Sadie and me. As soon as the holidays are over, I'm sweeping her off to Bali for a long, romantic weekend."

Now everyone looked confused—except for seven-year-old Drew. Stretched out on the floor playing with his Halo soldiers, Drew was oblivious.

Sadie had no idea what Ty thought he was up to. Probably just yanking a few chains, as usual. Well, two could play that game.

"You can't just zip off for a weekend in Bali," she argued. "It takes days to get there. And days more to fly back. Even if you chartered a private jet for the trip, you couldn't fly direct. You'd have to stop to refuel. Uh-uh. No way. You just can't take off for a quick trip to Bali."

"Hear that?" Ty raked his fingers through his blond hair and heaved a heavy sigh. "Sorry, Em. Sadie and me, we're not going to happen. If I tried to sweep her off her feet, she'd order me to put her right back down on solid ground."

"Yes, I would," Sadie agreed, suddenly feeling sad—and for no reason she could put her finger on. A little for herself maybe. All she'd ever wanted was the right man to build a life with. And she kept trying, kept looking, but so far, no luck.

As for Ty, she did honestly hope that the strangers he spent his weekends with were good to him. He could smirk and talk trash all he wanted. But deep down, she believed that Ty's bad attitude toward love and marriage would forever stand in the way of him going after someone who could make his life richer, someone who would change his world for the better.

Emily pouted. "Well. If Sadie doesn't marry Daddy, who else is going to do it?"

They all laughed at that.

Sadie said, "You never know, Em. One of these days, the exact right woman for your dad might come along." Okay, that seemed highly unlikely. Ty was so entrenched in his love of the single life. But why shatter all of Emily's illusions? "However, the right woman for your father isn't me. We aren't suited to each other, your dad and me. I'm a practical person. Your dad is adventurous. He's always ready to try something...new and different."

"Got that right," Ty agreed with a wicked gleam in his eye.

Sadie didn't know whether to smack him or hug him, so she simply moved on. "All right, then. Let's finish up here. Christmas and New Year's. We still need to agree on who's doing what..."

Chapter Two

Deacon Lamont was waiting at the table Friday evening when Sadie arrived at the restaurant. He looked up with a smile when the hostess led Sadie to where he sat.

They ordered drinks and appetizers and talked about his aunt Martha and the landscaping business he was starting, about how much he liked living in Medicine Creek. She said she loved it here, too, and would never live anywhere else. Their server whisked away the appetizer plates. They ordered steaks.

By the time the steaks came, the conversation had flagged. She found herself wondering, *What am I doing here?*

Sadie liked the guy. She did. But after twenty minutes in his company, she wanted…

What?

Something different.. Something *more*.

Really, what was the matter with her?

She reminded herself that it took time to get to know a person, that she needed to give Deacon a break. He was nice to look at, with kind brown eyes and broad shoulders. He seemed interested in her, in what she had to say, in getting to know her better.

But she knew already that she wouldn't be going out with him again.

Because there had to be that *something*, didn't there?

She needed to feel at least a hint of a thrill. She wanted those flutters down low in her belly, the ones that had her longing for the moment when their lips met for the first time.

And beyond attraction, there had to be that hope welling inside her, that sense of potential, the shivery premonition that, at some point in the future, there might be a real connection between them, something deep and true that could stand the test of time.

But none of that was happening. She felt no hint of a thrill and not the slightest premonition of a possible forever.

When the check came, they split it. Neither of them mentioned a next time. Deacon seemed to know as well as she did that there was nothing more to say—except good night.

They walked out the door together. He turned right and she went left. She didn't look back.

The night was overcast. A light snow drifted down out of the ashen sky. She drove home to her pretty white house in a new development on the eastern edge of town.

Inside, her place was cozy and inviting, mostly in soothing grays, whites and browns, but with fun pops of color here and there—the green velvet easy chair, the jewel-blue silk throw pillows on the oatmeal-colored sofa where her cats, Boo and Olive, were sound asleep all curled up together. Best friends forever, those two. As long as they had each other, they didn't need anything more.

Which was good. It meant that Sadie didn't have to feel guilty when she got home late. As long as someone cleaned the litter box and dished up the cat food, Olive and Boo were happy together whether she paid enough attention to them or not.

Sadie sat down beside them. Neither moved, but they both started purring. She petted them, smiling to herself, feeling a little less disappointed about the evening, especially when they finally raised their heads in unison and looked up at her through lazy, contented eyes.

She was in her pj's and in bed at nine and about to explore her streaming options when Ty called.

"What?" she demanded by way of a greeting.

"Just thought I should check on you, make sure that buff landscaper didn't kidnap you and drag you off to his sex dungeon."

"No way Mrs. Lamont's nephew has a sex dungeon." And why in the world did that make her feel gloomy all over again? "Don't worry. I'm home safe and sound." She could hear noise in the background, people talking, soft piano music. "Where are you?"

"A restaurant up in Sheridan. Dinner meeting. I'm just heading home now."

She heard him moving, a door opening. The music and voices receded. "You're going to be driving home?"

"Yeah, so?"

"It's snowing. You shouldn't be distracted behind the wheel."

He chuckled, a low, warm sound. "What are you, eighty? I have Bluetooth, you know." She heard a beep, the sound of a car door opening, rustling noises and the door closing. He started the engine.

"Hanging up now," she said. "Call me back when you're not behind the wheel." She disconnected before he could argue with her some more.

Twenty minutes later, he texted, Home now.

She turned off the movie that hadn't thrilled her much anyway and called him.

He answered with, "So, the landscaper?"

Plumping two pillows at her back, she relaxed against the headboard. "Deacon is a really nice guy."

"Ouch." How did he know exactly what she meant? "Boring, huh?"

"Just, you know..." She let her silence finish that sentence.

"You're going to need to be a little more specific."

"It's just not there, with him and me. I mean, I like him. He's nice. But I honestly can't see it going anywhere. Do you think I'm too picky?"

A silence, then, "Sadie Jane. You don't really want me to answer that."

"So yes, I am too picky." A heavy sigh escaped her. The cats had jumped up on the bed with her. She petted Olive and then scratched Boo behind her ear.

"You have very high expectations," he said.

Was that a dig? Probably. And right now, she was too discouraged to care. "At least I have Olive and Boo. Cats are independent, but nice to cuddle with when you get home."

"Clearly your cats are all you need."

"Spare me the sarcasm—and what are you doing home alone on Friday night?" *Shouldn't you be off to Denver or Seattle for some quality time with a woman you'll never see again?* she thought, and then instantly felt guilty. Really, she was grateful to have a friend like him. Ty Bravo was a fine father, a supportive ex-husband and an all-around stand-up guy. He might be allergic to romantic love, but he was always there when you needed him.

"Busy week ahead," he said. "Nicole asked me to take the kids tomorrow. They'll stay at my place all week."

For years Nicole and Ty had searched for the right nanny, but it never seemed to work out. Finally, they'd just quit looking. Since the divorce, Ty had the kids at his house almost as much as Nicole had them at hers. And they could always stay with Sadie, or with Sadie's mom and dad—or Abby and Cash.

She asked, "Your mom's taking them next Saturday, as planned?"

"Yeah." Sadie, Nicole and the other bridesmaids would be off to Las Vegas first thing Friday morning. Ty and Gavin would be having their two-man bachelor party the following night.

"I still have no idea what you're planning for that. Where are you and Gavin going on Saturday night?"

"Who knows? I've made suggestions. Gavin keeps putting me off. I'm guessing we'll end up right here in town, having a drink and a steak at Arlington's."

"Bor-ing."

"Tell me about it."

"Take him to Mustang Sally's. You can play pool, maybe get in a bar fight."

"Bar fights are not Gavin's style—nor mine, for that matter."

"I know, but still. Going somewhere minimally exciting wouldn't hurt the guy. The girls are going to Vegas. We're staying at the Venetian, seeing the *Magic Mike* show *and* getting pole dancing lessons."

"Noted," Ty replied in a patient tone.

"Okay, okay. Enough about your boring bachelor party…" Sadie readjusted her pillows, getting more comfortable as she settled in to talk for a while.

In the next hour, she and Ty covered a variety of topics. They discussed the busy upcoming holiday season, his latest property deal—brokered by Nicole, who owned Bravo Real Estate—and the horse he was giving Emily for her birthday.

By the time they said goodbye, Sadie had forgotten to be depressed about her lackluster dinner date. Life could be worse, she reminded herself. No, she didn't have a man of her own, but at least she had Ty to talk to after yet another disappointing Friday night.

Seven days later, first thing Friday morning, Sadie, Nicole and her three other bridesmaids piled into Nic's Lincoln Navigator and headed for Sheridan where they caught a short flight to Denver. From there, they boarded a plane to Las Vegas.

Neither Sadie nor Nicole ordered drinks on the plane from Denver. But that didn't stop the other women from getting the party started.

Cindy Hubert, Nicole's assistant at Bravo Real Estate, kept ordering vodka tonics and gulping them down as fast as the poor flight attendants could deliver them. The more vodka Cindy drank, the more vocal she got. She way overshared the details of her issues with her husband, Brad, who owned a tractor dealership in Buffalo.

Erin Vega, Cindy's bestie since high school, wrapped an arm around her. "Cin, don't be sad. Brad loves you to the moon and back and everything is going to be okay."

"But what about *oral*?" Cindy cried. "Is that so much to ask?"

At that point, Nicole leaned close to Sadie and whispered, "How can Cindy be drunk already? We're not even in Vegas yet."

"What can I tell you?" Sadie whispered back. "Sometimes a girl just has to let it all out."

"But why does she have to let it all out on the plane ride to *my* bachelorette party?" Nicole rarely drank. Her mom, Brenda, had battled alcoholism and prescription drug dependence for years. Technically, Brenda had died from a fall when she tripped over her own feet and hit her head on the corner of her coffee table one night. But the sad fact remained: Brenda was not only drunk at the time, she'd also taken way too many of her prescription meds.

"We'll be at the hotel before you know it," Sadie soothed her friend. "Cindy can take a little nap, sleep it off."

"I might have to fire her."

Sadie shook her head. "Don't be vindictive. You love Cindy, she loves you—she loves her job with you *and* she's good at it. You two are a great team. You're always saying so." Nicole took a lot of satisfaction in her work. She used to regret not going to college, but after getting her Realtor's license and creating Bravo Real Estate with the help of Ty and Cash, she'd come into her own career-wise and stopped complaining that she'd missed out on college.

"You're right," Nicole agreed. "I do love Cindy and she's damn good at her job." She gave Sadie a proud smile. "And would you look at me? Taking Cindy's meltdown in stride. Wouldn't Joanna be proud?"

Sadie gave her friend a side hug. "Oh, yes, she would."

Joanna was Nicole's therapist. A self-described "born drama queen" whose father had deserted her and whose alcoholic mother was prone to depression and then died when Nicole was barely a teenager, Nic had come a long way since high school. Back then, everything was about her and you risked Nicole's fury if you messed with her plans or refused to do things her way.

Right now, though, Cindy didn't seem the least bit worried that her boss might be unhappy with her rowdy behavior. Through the remainder of the flight, she kept right on oversharing all of her and Brad's intimate secrets. More than once the flight attendant asked her to please lower her voice.

But then, by the time they got off the plane at Harry Reid International, Cindy had settled down. Everyone breathed a sigh of relief—until she disappeared while they waited for their luggage to roll down the ramp from the baggage carousel.

Erin set off to find her, leaving Nicole, Sadie and Astrid Chen to wrangle their bags with the help of the limo driver, who'd been waiting for them in baggage claim.

Erin did find Cindy—in line at the cabstand, for no reason anyone could make sense of. The two rejoined the rest of them by the door Sadie had designated as their meeting place. Cindy was teary-eyed but subdued. There were hugs and reassurances, and then, finally,

Sadie signaled the driver who'd already loaded all their bags into the limo. Off they went at last.

Twenty-five minutes later, the limo rolled to a stop at the Venetian's main entrance, where the porte cochere's ceiling was covered in fresco paintings inspired by Renaissance artists.

And it might only be the second Friday in November, but the resort was already dressed to the nines for the holiday season. Glittery Christmas trees made completely of lights flanked the ornate entrance. Through the gilded double doors, giant ornaments in gold and red and snowflake white hung from the high, coffered ceilings.

Sadie herded everyone to the front desk and got them checked in. By midafternoon, they'd settled into their suites to unpack, decompress and get ready for the evening.

Cindy, Erin and Astrid were sharing a suite. Nicole had wanted one all to herself, which Sadie didn't really get. Nicole had always loved sleepovers and the suites, which could sleep four, weren't cheap.

On the other hand, it was only two nights. And it was Nicole's special party. She should have things the way she wanted them.

So Sadie got her own suite next door to the bride. And after the show Cindy had put on during the flight from Denver, Sadie found she didn't mind at all having her own space.

That night, they had dinner at a great Italian place a mile up the Strip from the Venetian. From there, they moved on to the Sahara to catch the *Magic Mike* show.

Nicole loved it. She boogied in place, whistling and catcalling, having the time of her life. When one of the dancers pulled her up onto the stage for a lap dance, she went eagerly, not even pretending to hesitate.

Everybody hooted and clapped for her. Another impressively limber guy joined the first guy and Nicole laughed, egging both of them on. She had a handful of the fake Magic money the show provided because no tipping was allowed. Nic tucked a few bills in both dancers' jeans and then made it rain, flicking bills at them fast and furious as they showed off their moves.

Back at the Venetian, Nicole led the way to the casino. They played the slots. Sadie was the lucky one that night, winning a five-hundred-dollar jackpot. They didn't go back up to their suites until a little after three in the morning.

Saturday began with brunch at noon. And then off they went for pole dancing lessons followed by a return to the Venetian and a long, luxurious visit to the Canyon Ranch Spa.

Cindy sighed in contentment under the expert hands of a spa massge therapist. "I feel terrific, ready to take on the world. I'm gonna win big when we hit the casino tonight."

Erin grinned at her from the next massage table over. "See? This trip to Sin City was just what we all needed. A chance to get out with our girls and leave all our troubles at home."

Cindy grinned back. "Brad, who?" She stretched out a hand palm out.

Erin high-fived it. "Never heard of him."

Astrid concurred, "This party is for our favorite bride-to-be—and isn't it nice that it's also just what the doctor ordered for the rest of us?"

"Yes!" they agreed in unison.

As for Nicole, during their long, lazy pedicure session, she announced, "I love you all so much. You've given me the bachelorette party of my wildest dreams!"

Everybody clapped at that—and then Astrid teased, "If it's all so perfect, why are you constantly texting Gavin?"

Nicole blushed and fluttered her eyelashes. For a moment, Sadie just knew she was hiding something. But then Nic sighed, "I can't help it. I'm not used to being apart from him. It's been more than thirty-six hours since I've seen his beautiful face." She put a hand to her forehead as though checking for a fever. "I think I might be suffering from Gavin Withdrawal—and don't you dare laugh." Nicole blushed prettily. "It's a real thing."

Sadie forgot her suspicions in her happiness for her best friend. Nicole could be a handful. She and Ty had tried to make it work, but they'd married so young, and mostly because Emily was on the way. There'd been a lot of mutual resentment. But now Nicole had Gavin, who thought the sun rose and set with her. Even better, Nic felt the same way about him.

After Nicole's declaration in the spa, she continued to whip out her phone at random intervals, to smile and sigh dreamily as she typed out a response. Nobody remarked on it again—until she did it at dinner right there at CUT, the Wolfgang Puck restaurant in the Palazzo.

Sadie groaned at that one. "Nic, come on. Show some respect—if not for the rest of us, then for that gorgeous Wagyu filet in front of you."

Nicole batted her big eyes and announced, "I've had the best time ever, guys. I love you all more than words can express. And I'm really sorry, but I just couldn't help myself..." She seemed to be talking about more than texting at the table.

That was when Sadie spotted the host leading two men in their direction. Gavin went straight for Nicole, who jumped up and ran to his open arms. Sadie and Ty shared a look. He shrugged as if to say, *What could I do?*

The table was big enough to fit two more chairs. Gavin squeezed in between Nicole and Erin. Ty sat with Sadie on one side and Astrid on the other. The guys must have slipped someone a generous tip because the restaurant staff rushed to accommodate them. Drinks and appetizers appeared. The men dug in. Gavin ate most of Nicole's filet.

Sadie leaned close to Ty and accused, "You knew when we talked last Friday night that this was happening, didn't you?"

"I swear to God," he whispered back, "I didn't know."

"Yeah, right..."

"No. Honestly. Gavin showed up at my door last night to tell me the plan. He'd already made plane and room reservations. I tried to talk him out of it at first, but then I thought, hey. If the bride and groom want this, who are the rest of us to say no?"

"Right," she muttered. "After all, they've been apart all day yesterday and last night, too. I'm shocked she's survived this long without him."

Ty leaned even closer. His warm breath brushed her cheek. "And you call *me* cynical. They're in love, remember?"

He had a point. She wrinkled her nose at him. "You're right. More power to them."

Astrid picked up her drink and offered a toast to the bride and groom.

After dinner, they all hung out in the Palazzo casino together. For a while.

But then Nicole and Gavin vanished. At that point, Erin, Cindy and Astrid had said yes to more than a few complimentary cocktails. Ty was trying to explain craps to them without much success. They were getting down-right rowdy, shouting in triumph at every throw of the dice and giggling together uncontrollably for no reason whatsoever.

Then Cindy grabbed Ty by the arm and confessed, "Y'know, Ty. I've always had somethin' of a crush on you…"

Erin spoke up. "Me, too. If I ever leave Roger, I'm givin' you a call."

"I bet you give great oral." Cindy looked up at him through big, hungry eyes.

Astrid, who was recently divorced, said, "I haf t' tell you guys. For the longest time, I really hated sex and hoped never ever to have to have it again. But some-times lately, I do get the itch, y'know?"

Ty had Cindy on one arm and Astrid clinging like a barnacle to the other. He looked at Sadie with despera-tion in his eyes.

She came to his rescue, wrapping one arm around Cindy and getting the other around Astrid, she gently pulled them off poor Ty. "Come on, you guys, let's head back to the Venetian. A good night's sleep will—"

"Sleep?" brayed Erin. "It's not even eleven yet. Sleep is the las' thing anybody needs right now."

"Sing it, sistah!" shouted Cindy. She ducked out of Sadie's hold to high-five her bestie as Astrid laughed so hard, she almost slithered to the floor from under Sadie's arm.

"I know!" Cindy shouted, her eyes were wide as soup bowls. "Blue Man Group…"

Erin frowned at her woozily. "Blue who?"

"I've always wanted t' see the Blue Man Group! Did you spot that big video billboard at the airport? They're at the Luxor…"

"But what time? Do they have a late show? Can we get in?" Astrid pondered aloud at full volume.

"We c'n do anything!" Cindy shot a fist skyward. "But only if we really try…"

Astrid's eyes lit up. "Le's get a cab or maybe an Uber and get over there."

"A cab or an Uber! Yes!" shouted Erin like she'd never before realized such wonderful things existed.

"You mean it?" cried Cindy.

Astrid nodded. "Let's go."

"Guys," Sadie tried hopefully. "Come on. It's too late for that show."

Not one of them acknowledged her suggestion. They turned without another word, linked elbows and headed for the exit to Las Vegas Boulevard.

Sadie called, "Hey! Come on, you guys! Don't leave!" They kept right on walking, stumbling a little, not giving Sadie so much as a backward glance. She frowned at Ty. "Should we stop them?"

He backed away a step, both hands up. "Are you kidding? I'm afraid to try." The three bridesmaids were already halfway to the exit, arms around each other, laughing as they went.

"They do look like they're having a great time," Sadie offered sheepishly.

He gave her a look—half amused, half terrified. "I have to be honest. I don't want to be anywhere near them right now."

They stared at each other. He wasn't budging and she had no idea how to save the drunk bridesmaids from their own poor decisions.

By the time Sadie looked around again, the women were long gone. "I should have stopped them. I'll never forgive myself if anything happens to them."

He was looking at her so strangely.

"What?" she demanded.

"You." Was that a criticism?

"Me, what?" She stuck out her chin at him.

He put up both hands again. "Don't get on me, okay? I'm just saying that you can't fix everything, you know? You can't save everyone from themselves. Sometimes people are just going to do what they want to do."

They stood a few feet from the craps table. People milled around them, looking for the next game to win.

"Okay." Sadie drew a slow breath and confessed, "You just might have a point."

He gave her that stunning smile of his. "Let's get a drink. Regroup."

"Good idea." She took his outstretched hand.

Ty probably shouldn't have been so grateful that the three drunk bridesmaids had left them behind for an impossible shot at the Blue Man Group. But he was grateful. They made him really nervous, those women. He didn't know what kind of stunt they might pull next.

And did they have to be so grabby? Tonight, because of them, he'd gotten a real taste of what women hated about men with roving hands.

But now it was just him and Sadie, her smaller hand in his. Happy it was just the two of them now, he followed where she led. She walked with purpose, focused on the way ahead. He'd always admired that about her. Sadie was smart and she had a lot of heart. Tough, too. A man had to get up pretty early in the morning to keep up with her.

When they were kids, Ty always felt that Sadie could best him at just about anything without hardly trying. Looking back, he sometimes thought all those straight-A report cards he got in elementary and middle school were mostly due to her. Because of Sadie, he'd tried harder. He'd gotten a lot of satisfaction out of competing with her.

Together, they made their way back to the Venetian, stopping first to admire the giant gold ironwork tree that hung from the ceiling in the Waterfall Atrium just off the Palazzo's casino floor. From there, they went on past the famous *Love* sculpture to Restaurant Row, where they decided on Yardbird, which served Southern food and a variety of drinks. They split a fried green tomato BLT. Sadie had a glass of prosecco and Ty ordered a scotch.

The time kind of melted away. They had a small table and he enjoyed just sitting there across from her, sipping his scotch, listening to her laugh and complain about Nicole in a good-natured way.

"I mean, I knew something was up with her," Sadie said. She stuck a fry in her mouth and chewed it thoughtfully. "I swear, she had her phone in her hand eighty percent of this trip—either reading a text from Gavin or writing one to him. And she wanted her own room.

That should have clued me in. I've known her all her life and never until this trip has Nic wanted her own room. When she moved into our house after we lost Brenda, Nic loved sharing a room with me, having me right there to listen to whatever was on her mind…"

"She loves you," he said. "You know that, right?"

"Yeah." Sadie's voice was soft. "I know. And I love her—and I'm glad for her."

Ty nodded, sipped more scotch and admired Sadie's green eyes. She had one of those smiles that could light up a room. She wasn't the kind to make a man walk into a lamppost while staring at her the way Nicole could.

No. Sadie was one of those women you could talk to all night. She was funny and she didn't take any crap, so a man had better be on his toes around her. At the same time, you knew you could count on her to pitch in if you needed a hand. There was no drama with Sadie. He liked that a lot.

And she was so pretty, with acres of wavy caramel-colored hair falling past her shoulders, with round cheeks and soft lips. Tonight, she wore one of those little black dresses. It was short and satiny, with a flared skirt and spaghetti straps on her creamy shoulders. He couldn't help picturing himself slipping a finger under one of those straps and very slowly guiding it over to the curve of her shoulder until it dropped down her smooth arm.

She ate the last of her half sandwich. He'd finished his long ago. "You ready?" she asked.

He'd already picked up the tab. "Yeah. Let's go."

They left Yardbird and he caught her hand again. She pulled him back.

"What?" he asked.

Her cheeks had flushed pink. She suggested almost shyly, "Let's try our luck here at the Venetian."

Sounded like a plan to him.

For three hours, they gambled, playing blackjack, then roulette, and then, after they both lost several hands of pai gow poker, she informed him that she was lucky at the slots.

He couldn't let that pass. "Yeah? Show me."

For two more hours, he stood beside her as she sipped Diet Dr Pepper and fed coins into different machines. He had fun because he got to razz her the whole time about when, exactly, her great luck would kick in.

She gave as good as she got, putting her money in as she laughed and assured him that her big jackpot was coming right up.

It shocked the hell out of both of them when, at a little before six in the morning, she slapped the spin button same as she had a hundred times before and hit the jackpot.

The machine went off like a rocket, every light pulsing, horns and whistles blowing.

Sadie let out a shriek of pure joy, clapped her hands, jumped up and down—and then threw herself into his arms.

One second, she was shouting and clapping, the next, she was all over him, her bare arms tight around his neck, her silky hair brushing his cheek. "What'd I tell you, Ty Bravo? Who's the winner now?"

She pulled back enough to meet his eyes.

And the whole world slammed to a stop.

Damn. Her cheeks were pink, and those green eyes really sparkled. Her mouth was a soft O of pleasure and surprise.

So pretty.

"Sadie…"

"Yeah?"

He couldn't stop himself. He wrapped his hand around the back of her head, pulled her closer and swooped in to capture her lips.

Chapter Three

She gasped when his mouth covered hers.

For a moment, he was certain he'd blown it, that she would jerk back, maybe haul off and slap him silly for daring to make a move on her.

But then…

She went soft, pliant in his arms.

And then she sighed. She wrapped her arms a little tighter around his neck and kissed him back.

He dared to touch her plump lower lip with his tongue—and she didn't even hesitate. She let him inside.

With a low groan, he pulled her even closer as he kissed her long and thoroughly, drinking in the perfect sensations—her scent, clean and light. Not perfumy at all. Her round breasts pressed into him, soft. Beyond tempting.

The curve of her waist seemed made to fit his hands.

Enticing. She really was.

She always had been, though usually he tried his best not to think about that. Not to remember...

A decade since that one other kiss they'd shared—the forbidden one they'd both pretended later had never happened.

But it had happened.

And right now, with her in his arms, that other kiss seemed like yesterday. Like some corner of time had stood still somehow as the rest of their lives rolled on by—stood still and waited, for this moment by the blaring slot machine in the casino at the Venetian.

When he finally let her go, she pulled away slowly, her arms slipping down so she could rest her hands on his chest. She stared up at him, dazed. He figured he probably looked about the same.

Gently, she pressed her palms against his chest.

He took the hint and let her go.

That was when he noticed the guy from the casino standing right there beside them. Smiling, the man offered congratulations.

Half an hour later, Sadie was fifteen thousand dollars richer—and she hardly even cared.

She'd kissed Ty. Again. She couldn't believe it.

She'd kissed Ty again—and it was so good.

Like really, really good. Stupid good. Head-spinning good.

Even-better-than-that-one-other-time-back-in-high-school good—*that* kind of good.

She wanted to do it again.

But she wouldn't. Oh, no. Doing it again would be beyond unwise. Doing it again would be nothing but trouble just begging to happen. Trouble she longed for at this particular moment, trouble she *ached* for. Trouble that felt utterly irresistible.

They left the casino side by side. He didn't try to take her hand. And that was good—perfect. Exactly as it should be. She couldn't deal with any casual touching right now. If he touched her right now, anything could happen. She could yank him close and climb him like a tree. She felt that unsettled, that dangerous. She hung on the verge of a leap from a dizzying height.

They'd almost reached the escalator leading up to the bank of elevators that would take her to her suite. Was he staying at the Venetian, too?

She had no idea. And she didn't dare pause long enough to ask him. Uh-uh. To face him seemed perilous, an invitation to behave badly. She kept walking.

And then his hand brushed her arm, sending an electric current zapping upward straight to her racing heart. Before she could jerk away, his fingers closed around hers.

She should tell him to let go. But she didn't. He pulled her away from the escalator, over to a potted palm by the nearest wall.

"Sadie…" He whispered her name.

She heard a moan of pure longing—her own. And all of a sudden, she was in his arms, reaching up, offering her mouth, which he covered with his.

That kiss?

Better than the last one. He took her by the waist, lifting her. Her shoes left the floor, and she was above him, her hands grasping his wide shoulders, holding on tight as she kissed his upturned mouth for all she was worth.

Slowly, he let her slide down his body. That was exciting. She could feel everything, his broad chest, his hard belly—and how much he wanted her, too.

And then he was lifting his head. She almost reached up and yanked him back into the kiss she wasn't ready to end.

But a small sliver of sanity remained. She opened her mouth to say, *This has to stop.*

Except she didn't want it to stop.

"You're here, in the Venetian Tower, right?"

"Uh, yeah."

"Come on." He had her hand again and he was pulling her to the escalator and upward. Not patient enough to let it carry them, he pulled her up the steps as they moved toward the next level. She followed, unresisting.

"Which elevators?" he demanded.

She told him, her voice weirdly desperate sounding. He led her to the bank of elevators that would take them up to her suite. They got on the car alone. She pulled her key card from the pocket of her skirt and waved it over the control panel.

As the doors slid closed, he reached for her again and pulled her tight against his broad, hard body. For a moment, pressed to his heat and hardness, she stared up into those gorgeous blue eyes.

And then he was kissing her. Until the elevator stopped. She pushed him away. They faced front and she tried to look normal, unruffled and calm, as two other couples got on.

Breathless, not daring to glance at the man beside her, feeling oddly disembodied, she stared straight ahead until they reached her floor at last. The doors slid wide, and they got out.

"Which way?" he demanded.

She pointed. About then, she remembered that they had a problem. "My suite's next to Nic's," she warned. "We can't—"

"It's okay." He had her hand again and he was pulling her down the long hallway toward her door. "Gavin got a great suite in the Palazzo Tower. He mentioned that he planned to take her there."

"Oh," Sadie heard herself reply, a breathy little sound, not like her at all. He kept pulling her onward. They were going to her suite. She should probably object.

But there was a problem with objecting. She didn't want to do that.

Just like she didn't want to talk about this. If they talked about it, they would end up agreeing what a bad idea it was.

And she didn't want to make that decision, or to give *him* a chance to make it.

She just wanted to...

Not think.

Because thinking would no doubt have them calling a halt to this beautiful madness.

"Which one?" he asked.

She rattled off her suite number—and when she did, he stopped in the middle of the hallway and wrapped those hard arms around her all over again.

They kissed some more. Her lips were on fire, the rest of her body consumed in flames. It was glorious.

That time, when he lifted his head, she took the lead, grabbing for his hand, guiding him the rest of the way to her suite.

"This is it," she said breathlessly, letting go of his hand to fish her key card out of her pocket again.

He reached for her.

She laughed and pushed him away. "I need to get my key card out…"

"I know, but I just can't stop kissing…"

A sound from the suite next door had them both freezing stock-still. Sadie heard the door guard flip back and the bolt click.

The door opened just enough for Gavin to stick his head out—Gavin in a white robe, his hair standing up in all directions like he'd put it through a blender.

Apparently, he and Nic had been having a great time—in *her* suite, not his. "Hey, guys," he said, equal parts cheerful and worn-out. "Win big?"

She realized that Gavin was completely clueless. And why wouldn't he be? Not in their wildest dreams would anyone they knew believe that Sadie and Ty would ever end up in the same bed together.

"Oh, yeah," Ty answered Gavin's question with a wink.

She pulled the casino's check from her pocket and waved it at him. "Jackpot."

"Good for you! Congratulations." Gavin bent and grabbed the free newspaper waiting at his feet. He saluted them with it. "Later…" And then he shut the door.

She turned to Ty. For a minute or two that lasted a lifetime, they just stared at each other.

Finally, Ty winced. "Sorry." He kept his voice low, so they wouldn't hear him in the suite next door. "Gavin was all excited about the suite he booked at the Palazzo. He said he couldn't wait to take Nicole there."

Sadie shrugged. "She must have overridden him. All her things are here. And Nicole never goes to bed without her own face wash, toner and night cream."

"Tell me about it." He swore under his breath. "I should've remembered that."

Because they'd been married for seven years.

Sadie shut her eyes and drew a slow breath through her nose.

Ty said, more softly than before, "Sadie…"

It was no good. They both knew it. Gavin's sudden appearance had brought sanity roaring back.

Sadie did care for Ty—hey, next to Nicole, he was her best friend. But this was a bad idea. Too many family connections, too much water under the bridge.

It would be too weird for them to fall into bed together—plus, friends mattered, especially the good ones. She could lose him over something like this. Their friendship could be ruined.

Because Ty could so easily have a fling and walk away. He did it all the time.

Not Sadie, though. She had to get real here. She just wasn't up for a onetime thing. Especially not with Ty. Not given their history, given the family dynamics, given…everything.

Ty read her thoughts as though she'd said them aloud. He pushed back the sides of his black Western jacket and stuck his hands in his pockets. "Okay, I get it. Bad idea."

She nodded and whispered, "Come in, though. Just for a minute or two. We'll talk this out." Unlocking the door, she held it wide for him to enter.

He walked by and straight to the living area with her following right behind. Neither of them sat down.

"Tonight was great," she said. "We should agree on what happened."

"So that we'll be telling the same story, you mean?"

"Yeah."

He lifted an arm to rub the back of his neck. "Right. Let's see. So, after the drunk bridesmaids took off for the Luxor, we hung out, you and me. We went to Yardbird, gambled for hours at the casino downstairs. You won a jackpot. I never kissed you."

"I never kissed you back." It made her sad to say it.

"And then I walked you up here to your suite. Gavin stuck his head out as we were saying good-night. I came in for a few minutes..."

"To...use the bathroom?"

"That works."

"And then you left."

He nodded. "Right. What time's your flight?"

"One thirty." She felt so tired suddenly.

"We take off at noon—and we'd better get some sleep, huh?"

"Yeah."

He turned for the door.

She followed. "Safe flight," she said as she ushered him out.

"You, too."

She locked up behind him, turned her back to the door and slid down to the floor. Wrapping her arms around her shins, she rested her cheek on her knees.

Twenty minutes ago, she'd had energy to burn.

Now she felt like a sad, deflated balloon, abandoned on the floor when the party's over.

The three bridesmaids looked a little the worse for wear when they all headed down to the famous French bakery Bouchon for brunch before the ride to the airport.

Cindy grumbled, "We don't want to talk about the Blue Man Group."

It was not a smart thing to say in front of Nicole, who immediately demanded the whole story, which it turned out had included a cab ride to the Luxor, where the nine o'clock Blue Man Group show had ended at ten thirty.

Astrid confessed, "I had a little tummy upset."

To which Erin whisper-shouted, "She chucked her cookies in the Luxor lobby ladies' room."

"Then we couldn't catch another cab," grumbled Astrid.

"I tried Uber," said Erin.

"That worked," added Astrid. "But the car smelled like deviled eggs. I started feeling sick again…"

Cindy waved a hand. "Let's just say it was an experience."

"Well, at least you three are safe and sound this morning," Sadie said.

Nicole sipped her flat white. "What was that this morning—you and Ty outside your room?"

Sadie delivered the agreed-on story, starting with a nod at the three bridesmaids. "When these three took off, Ty and I hung out. It was fun. We went to Yardbird for a snack, then we gambled. When we called it a night, Ty walked me to my room."

"Gavin says you hit another slot jackpot."

"I did. Play your cards right and I'm picking up the tab next girls' night out."

Astrid clapped her hands. "Yay, Sadie!"

Cindy said, "Okay, Nic. Tell us about your hot night with Gavin. I'm talking details. I want to know *everything*."

It was all the encouragement Nicole needed. She talked about Gavin for the next ten minutes.

The plane ride to Denver was mostly quiet. They all napped.

Except Sadie. Every time she closed her eyes, thoughts of Ty assailed her—starting with the kisses they should not have shared in the early hours of that morning, but not ending there.

She smiled to herself as she remembered their fights when they were kids, the way they always tried to best each other. Back then, Ty hardly noticed Nicole. He was all about being better than Sadie.

Until the three of them were well into their teens, Nicole actively disliked Ty. Why wouldn't she? In all the ways that mattered, Sadie and Nicole were sisters, after all. And Nic's first loyalty was always to the sister of her heart.

But then, in their freshman year, Nicole…blossomed. There was no other word for it. Her breasts filled out and so did her hips. Her cheeks got pinker, her blue eyes more jewel-like, her lips plumper. Ty, like every other guy at Medicine Creek High, suddenly couldn't stop looking at her.

And Nicole looked back—not at all the guys. No. Nic looked back only at Ty.

Nic and Sadie had fought about that. Sadie caught her making goo-goo eyes at Ty. That night, in the room they'd been sharing for over a year then, Sadie called Nic a traitor.

Nic let out a cry of outrage at the insult. She threw her hairbrush, bopping Sadie on the shoulder, and swore she had no interest in Ty Bravo and she would never get anywhere near him again.

Two days later, Sadie caught the two of them under the bleachers at school. Kissing. She didn't speak to Nicole for a week, except to say, "Excuse me," or maybe, "Please pass the gravy" at dinner.

But then Nic started begging her to try to understand. Nic said that she and Ty were meant to be. That Nicole could no more imagine her life without Ty than she could bear the thought of a life without Sadie.

By then, well, what could Sadie do? She loved her bestie. She grudgingly accepted that Nicole was gone on Ty. For Nicole's sake, she put up with him, even though he annoyed her as much as he ever had.

And every time he and Nic broke up, Sadie took her bestie's side.

But the breakups never lasted all that long. Nic and Ty always got back together.

Was Sadie a bit cynical about their on-and-off "true" love? If she was, she made sure to keep her opinions to herself. Yes, Ty and Nic were always breaking up. But that never meant it was over. They inevitably made up and the whole cycle started all over again. Sadie put a lot of effort into being supportive of Nicole without saying bad things about Ty.

Near the end of senior year, Nicole and Ty broke up yet again. It was a bad one. Nicole cried all the time. She clung to Sadie and said she didn't know what to do. Ty had said it was over—and this time, she believed him. Ty was through with her. Her heart was broken. She would never recover.

Sadie tried to say the right things, to give Nic what she needed.

And to stay away from Ty, who really had to get his act together and either be with Nic or leave her alone once and for all. But Nic was so sad. Sadie hadn't seen her best friend that unhappy since the year Nic's mom died.

So, Sadie decided to try to talk a little sense into Ty—not the brightest idea she'd ever had. But she wanted to help, she really did.

They had student council together—that year, he was president and she was vice president. She waited till the biweekly meeting finally ended, then hung around feeling awkward till everyone left but Ty.

And then she marched right up to him…

"We need to talk, Tyler Ross. Just you and me."

Ty glowered at her. "Stay out of it, Sadie."

"But you and Nic need to—"

"Sadie, come on. We're done, Nic and me. It's over."

"Oh, please. We've all heard that one before."

He shook his head. "This time, it's for real."

The door to the hallway was wide-open. She heard footsteps going by. Anyone could interrupt them. That couldn't happen. Not till he stopped being an idiot and agreed to reach out to Nicole.

Sadie grabbed his arm. "This way…"

She expected him to pull away, but he didn't. So she dragged him into the supply closet and shut the door.

"This is just stupid," he said.

She looked up into his eyes and willed him to change his mind. "She's miserable. You're miserable."

He scoffed, "No I'm not. I just… Look, it isn't working with her and me."

"What do you mean? You had a fight. Big whoop. It's what you do, the two of you. You fight, but then you get over it and get back together."

"*Oh, come on, Sadie. You know her. There's just never enough for her. I can't deal with her anymore. I really can't.*"

"*So stop fighting with her. Try to make it work.*"

"*Did you hear what I said? It's over. I'm done. There is no making it work for me and Nic.*"

"*That's not true. You'll be back together next week or the week after that. You know you will.*"

"*Wrong.*" *He reached for the doorknob.*

She caught his arm again. "*Come on, Ty...*"

He whirled on her, face grim, eyes flaring. "*Come on, what? What do you want from me, Sadie?*"

"*I want...*" *Something happened to her then. She stared up into his flushed face and his stormy eyes as the world tipped over. All of a sudden, it wasn't about him and Nic at all.*

He said her name, "*Sadie.*" *Said it low and rough and full of something she shouldn't let herself understand.*

And then he reached for her.

She fell against him, into his heat and urgency, into that burning look in those eyes of his.

His mouth came down. She tipped hers up.

And they were kissing—deep and hard and desperately. In that brief, chaotic moment, they were the only two people on earth.

She had no thought for her best friend who loved him, no remembrance of her yearslong, angry rivalry with him. It was just her and Ty, and it was everything she'd never come close to feeling with her sweet and steady boyfriend, Kevin Purdy.

Seriously, what was the matter with her? This was so wrong.

She shoved Ty away.

They faced off in the small space, both of them panting like they'd run a long race.

He said, "Dump Kevin."

She gaped at him. "What? No!"

"Yeah. Break up with Kevin. You and me, we'll go out."

"No way. This is not what I dragged you in here to talk about."

"Just do it, Sadie."

"Forget that. You and me, we are never going to happen. You need to get back with Nicole. You know you do. You know that you will. You always do."

"No. Not this time. We're done, Nic and me. It's over."

She just shook her head. Words had deserted her. Inside this storage closet, the world had turned upside down.

"Just break up with him," Ty said again.

She knew if she stayed in this closet with him, he would kiss her again. And she would let him do it. That couldn't happen.

She spun on her heel and got out of there.

The same night that she'd kissed Ty in the closet, Sadie hadn't found it easy to get to sleep. Finally, she'd dropped off into restless slumber only to wake suddenly to the sounds of Nic sobbing.

When she threw back the covers and went to comfort her, Nic confessed that she'd driven to Sheridan to get a home pregnancy test. She'd taken the test that morning. She was pregnant with Ty's baby.

Holding her, soothing her, Sadie whispered that she needed to tell Ty, that everything was going to be all right.

Nic went to him the next day. He asked her to marry him and Nic said yes.

As for Sadie, a few weeks later, she broke up with Kevin. But not because she intended to go out with Ty, who was marrying her best friend soon after graduation.

She ended it with Kevin because of those moments in the supply closet. Because that day, Ty Bravo had shown her what a real kiss could be. And she knew she'd been kidding herself. Kevin Purdy was a very nice boy, but he wasn't the boy for her.

Chapter Four

Olive and Boo, who must have heard Sadie coming up the steps, were waiting in the arch to the great room when Sadie let herself in the front door.

"Hey, you guys…" She hoisted her suitcase over the threshold and closed the door. "Come here…" She bent to scoop them both into her arms, putting one on each shoulder. They purred as she cuddled them.

"Missed me, huh?" She nuzzled Boo and then Olive. "Did Grandma take good care of you?" Her mom had promised to come by for an hour or two each day while she was in Vegas.

Boo rubbed her wet nose on the side of Sadie's neck. Olive yawned.

"I'll consider that a yes. Grandma was good to you."

Carefully, she set the cats back down and grabbed the handle of her suitcase again, rolling it to her room to unpack.

When she hoisted it to the mattress, unzipped and flopped it open, the first thing she saw was the little black dress with the flirty flared skirt that she'd worn last night while hanging out for hours with Ty, kidding around with him, gambling with him.

And later, kissing him.

Repeatedly.

Staring down at that dress, she could actually feel the way the skirt had dragged against him as she slid down his broad, hard body...

All of a sudden, she just felt exhausted. Wiped out.

Kicking off her shoes, she sat on the bed. Her phone rang in her pocket—it was her mom, just checking in.

Sadie led with her big win. "Last night I won fifteen thousand dollars. Do you believe it?"

"Wow! Congratulations."

"And Friday night I won five hundred."

Her mother laughed and warned her not to spend it all in one place.

Sadie promised she wouldn't. They talked for a few minutes, catching up. It was good to hear her mom's voice. She learned that everything was fine at Henry's.

"Thanks, Mom, for looking after the cats."

"Anytime. I'm so glad you had fun."

"It was great," Sadie said with more enthusiasm than she felt.

When they said goodbye, she dropped the phone on the bed and fell back across it. "I'm just shutting my eyes for a minute or two..." she whispered to the ceiling.

She woke to her phone buzzing. "Huh!"

There was purring from Boo and Olive. They'd curled up close to her on one side. Her open suitcase still waited on the other.

She picked up the phone, which lit up the display. It was seven at night. She'd been asleep for almost two hours.

And she had a text from Ty: You home?

Ignoring the absurd full-body shiver that zipped through her at the mere sight of his name, she punched out a quick reply with her thumb. Yeah.

His answer came right back. Talk?

Really? Did they have to? She'd prefer to shut her eyes and go right back to sleep.

About what? she answered reluctantly.

The phone rang in her hand. She longed to let it go to voice mail. But running away from the problem wouldn't make it disappear. "Hi, Ty."

He didn't bother with a greeting. "We do need to deal with this."

"Why?"

"Damn it," he muttered. "You know why. It's not going to go away just because you ignore it."

That pissed her off. "Ty. Think about it. It went away for ten whole years. We ignored that kiss in the supply closet. We never so much as mentioned it again, not even in passing. We put it behind us and did what we had to do."

"Everything's different now. I'm a free man. Nicole's in love and happy with Gavin."

"Still, we have no idea how she would deal with you and me being suddenly—" how to put it? "—more than friends."

"It's none of her business if you and I—"

"Think about it, Ty."

"Oh, believe me, I am." His voice danced along her

nerve endings, low and deliciously rough. "We could be good together. You know that we could."

"Yeah, and for how long?" That shut him up. While he tried to decide how to answer her question, she reminded him, "Over time, we've built a friendship. A good one. And that friendship matters to me."

"It matters to me, too."

"I'm glad to hear that," she said.

"And as for ten years ago, we had no choice then."

Sadie had the urge to argue that point. But where could such an argument go? They were kids. He'd done his best. He'd stepped up and married the mother of his child.

She said, "What I mean is, we did it then. What happened in the supply closet stayed in the supply closet. We can do the same thing now. We can save our friendship and avoid the risk of causing trouble in the family. All we have to do is forget what happened in Vegas."

He instantly objected, "I don't *want* to forget."

She popped to a sitting position and exerted great effort not to shout into the phone. "Well, that's just too bad. It's not going to work and it's not worth it. I want a real relationship. You just want to…scratch an itch."

"Come on. That's not fair."

"Oh, really? Are you telling me that now you've kissed me in Vegas, you're suddenly ready to consider a future with me?"

His silence said it all.

She answered for him. "Of course, you're not. As I already said, we want different things."

He made a low, unhappy sound. "You know it's more than an itch. You're important to me."

"Well, that's great. Because if I'm important to you,

then you'd better think this through. The way I see it now, you and me scratching this itch is an invitation to disaster."

"Would you please quit calling it an itch?"

"But that's what it is. An itch. A yen. A craving. It's nothing important, Ty. One way or another, it goes away eventually. I'm not giving up our friendship for it. And that's what would happen. Maybe you can enjoy a casual fling. But I'm just not built that way. And even if, somehow, we ended it with both of us happily walking away, I'm not taking the chance of Nicole going full-out drama queen on us. I'm just not."

He was silent. For a moment, she thought he'd hung up on her.

But he hadn't hung up. "It could ruin our friendship, anyway," he muttered.

She answered gently, "Not if we don't let it."

More silence on his end. Then, "I don't know what else to say to you."

"Let it go, Ty. Please."

He was quiet for a full minute, at least.

She couldn't stand it. "Ty?"

"Still here." His voice had changed, turned rueful. "And suddenly realizing I'm hovering right on the edge of being a dick."

She laughed. And that made her feel better about everything. "It's going to be okay. You'll see."

"Good to know. I'll bet you're tired."

"Exhausted."

"I'm out of town for a few days starting tomorrow. Heading to LA for some business meetings."

He would probably meet some pretty woman down there. It hurt to think that. But the pain was instructive.

There would be no happily-ever-after for her and Ty. She needed to keep that firmly in mind.

She said gently, "Travel safe, Ty."

"I will, thanks."

Monday, on the flight down to LAX, Ty thought about making some calls, seeing if he could meet up with one of the smart, gorgeous Southern California women he'd dated last year and the year before.

But he would only be doing that to try to get Sadie off his mind. And that just felt wrong on every level. There was only one smart, gorgeous woman he wanted.

And if he couldn't have her, well, what was the point? Maybe she had it right. If they didn't give in to this craving, it would fade by itself in time, leaving their friendship intact. Eventually, they would go back to being best buddies.

He spent a couple of days taking meetings and firming up deals, then flew back to Wyoming on Wednesday. Thursday, he had breakfast at Henry's—and not because he couldn't wait to see Sadie again.

He had breakfast at Henry's at least three times a week, after all. It was a great little place, welcoming, with the best breakfast in town. He liked the long counter, the classic bolt-down diner-style stools with the green vinyl seats, the big chalkboard next to the service window where Sadie or her mom scrawled the daily specials.

Henry's was everybody's home away from home. And he saw no reason to stay away because of what had happened in Vegas.

He went good and early, too, when he knew Sadie would be there. Because maybe she was right. And they could just go back to being the good buddies they'd always been.

Maybe they really could just put Vegas behind them and move on.

She looked over when he came in.

There was a moment. Her mouth went soft, and her eyes got so wide. It sent a thrill straight through him, made him realize that wanting Sadie when she refused to consider becoming his lover wasn't all bad.

Really, he hadn't felt like this in years.

Like the world just brimmed with promise. Like he could slay dragons and eat them for breakfast.

No dragons on the menu at Henry's, however. Ty sat between Bob and Lester, as usual. Turning his cup over, he watched in satisfaction as Sadie filled it.

"Morning, Ty."

He gave her a nod. "Morning."

She put in his usual order. Through the service window, he could see her dad at the grill. Tall, thin and bald, Henry McBride wore Harry Potter glasses that constantly threatened to slide off the end of his nose. Henry was a happy man, always glancing up to smile at his customers through the window. He loved his wife, and he was proud of their only child, who loved the diner he'd built so much she'd opened two more of them.

Ty had just finished his excellent breakfast and accepted a coffee refill from Sadie, when the bell over the door to Main Street jingled yet again. It was Carolyn Kipp, who ran the front desk at Don Deal Insurance over on Snider Street. Half the customers at the counter gave Carolyn a wave, including Ty. He and Sadie had been a couple of years ahead of Carolyn back in school.

Carolyn stepped up to the POS and cash register,

which wasn't far from the door. Sadie took a large to-go bag from under the warming lights in the window and went to meet her.

They chatted as Carolyn paid the bill.

"So, Don hired another agent, did you hear?" Carolyn asked. Don Deal was new in town. He'd opened his agency just a few months ago.

"Business must be booming." Sadie indicated the card reader and Carolyn waved a credit card over it.

"Yep," said Carolyn. She had a sly grin on her round face. "He's cute, the new agent. Midthirties. Name's Brent Laird…?"

Sadie was nodding. "I remember him. He came in for breakfast Monday—yesterday, too, come to think of it."

Ty carefully set down his coffee cup.

Carolyn gave a shrill little giggle and then leaned across the counter toward Sadie. "Brent thinks you're cute," she said in a stage whisper. "He says he's going to…" Carolyn got right up to Sadie's ear and lowered her whisper so only Sadie could hear.

Everyone at the counter was listening now—and more than a few people seated in the booths. As for Ty's favorite breakfast, it was suddenly a ball of lead in his belly. What did this Brent character think he was up to?

Carolyn sat back on her heels. "The way I see it, a heads-up never hurts."

"Thanks, Carolyn." Sadie pushed the to-go bag across the counter and handed Carolyn a receipt. With a jaunty wave, Carolyn grabbed the bag and strutted out the door.

Grabbing the pot from the coffee station at that end of the counter, Sadie filled some cups and took a couple of food orders.

When she came back around to the counter, Lester just had to open his big mouth. "So you're going out with the new guy at Don Deal Insurance?"

Sadie answered with an easy shrug. "What can I tell you, Lester? I've met the guy twice. We might have discussed the meat loaf special. I think maybe yesterday he asked for extra bread. The conversation was not wide-ranging. As for getting dinner or seeing a show together? It never came up."

"But if he—"

"Lester." She gave him her sweetest smile, a smile that said, *Mind your own business*, in the nicest possible way. "You know everything *I* know. There's nothing more to say."

That shut Lester up. And everyone else in the place, too, for that matter.

Unfortunately, it didn't ease Ty's mind one bit. *Would* that Brent guy ask her out? More to the point, would she say yes?

If she did, well, that should be fine with him. Because they wanted different things from the people they went out with. Because Sadie and him? They were friends, period. Full stop. End of story.

Only now…

Well, he didn't feel like a friend, period. He felt like he wanted to pay the new guy at Don Deal a little visit. And not a welcoming one.

Before Vegas, Ty would have picked up the conversation about the new guy right where Lester left off. He would have found out if she was the least bit interested in this Brent character. If she admitted she was interested, he would have taken way too much pleasure in razzing her for being a hopeless romantic—and then, as always, he would have reminded her to be cautious until she knew the guy better.

But this was not before Vegas.

This was that awful place where suddenly she was all he wanted—but she was looking for something he couldn't give her and that meant that he couldn't have her.

And right now, he really needed to get the hell out of Henry's.

Slipping a fifty under his saucer, he headed for the door.

Sadie felt relief when Ty got up and left.

Relief mixed with misery—because what happened in Vegas hadn't stayed there. Not for her, anyway.

The past few days, while he was off in Los Angeles, she'd had to exert way too much willpower not to constantly obsess over what he might be doing now—and whether what he was doing included a willing woman. More than once, she'd pulled up his number on her phone and barely managed not to give him a call.

Before Vegas, she wouldn't have thought twice about texting or calling just to check in with him, to maybe talk for a while about whatever she had on her mind, to ask him how he was doing and hear about the current deal he was working on.

She ached, she really did.

To hear his voice, to ask him if…

What?

Oh, this was bad.

Already, only four days after Vegas, she found herself thinking of tossing her own romantic goals aside—

just long enough to have a hot, secret fling with her best friend's ex-husband.

The more she thought of that, the more she wanted it.

Especially after this morning, when the bell rang over the door to Main Street. And there he was. Her poor heart had lifted. For a minute or two, she'd dared to hope that maybe everything would be all right.

But it wasn't all right.

He'd said exactly one word to her, *Morning*. After that, he'd hardly looked at her long enough to give her the signal to put in his order. And after he'd eaten, he just got up and left.

No fun banter. No bossy, annoying advice. Not even a How've-you-been-Sadie.

He came, he ate, he left a thirty-dollar tip.

Would he bother to say more than *Morning* to her if she went ahead and had sex with him?

She reminded herself that she really didn't want to know. Right now, she just needed to go about her business and not let him get to her.

On Friday, she had no problem dealing with him—because she had no contact with him. He didn't come to the diner. He didn't call, he didn't text.

Neither did she, for that matter.

That got her thinking that, really, if she wanted to talk to him, she needed to pick up the phone and get in touch.

But she didn't. She hadn't.

She didn't know what to say.

And that made her a little more sympathetic toward him. Hey. Maybe he felt the same way she did. Maybe he was waiting around for her to make a move, to let him know she was willing to put some work into repairing the sudden wreckage of their friendship.

And she *was* willing. Truly.

If only she knew where to start.

At noon, Brent Laird showed up. He ordered the Salisbury steak and asked her out.

You could have heard a feather whisper its way to the checkerboard vinyl floor when that happened.

And Sadie realized two things. One, she really didn't want to go out with the new guy from Don Deal Insurance. And two, she didn't want to turn him down in front of everyone at the diner, either.

She wrote her number on his napkin and asked him to give her a call after six. He smiled and said he surely would.

When he left, she refused to discuss him or their never-going-to-happen date with anyone in the restaurant. And that night, when he called, she explained that she was taking a break from dating, that she just wasn't ready right now to go out with anyone.

He was nice about it, at least. He said he understood. They said goodbye and she felt only relief.

Friday night, Emily and Drew stayed at Ty's house.

Saturday was Em's birthday. Early Saturday morning, all three climbed into Ty's Escalade and drove out to the family ranch.

The Rising Sun Ranch and Cattle Company had been in the Bravo family for generations. Now it belonged jointly to Ty's dad, Cash, and Cash's two cousins, Nate and Zach. Only Zach lived on the property. But at the Rising Sun, the door was always open to family and friends.

Everyone ran out to greet them—Zach and his wife, Tess, their second son, Brody, and Ty's grandmother Edna Heller, who was close friends with Tess.

Years and years ago, Edna had been the housekeeper on the Rising Sun. Edna's only daughter—Ty's mom, Abby—had been raised on the ranch. Now Edna lived in the foreman's cottage not far from the main house.

Jobeth, Tess's daughter from an earlier marriage, had her own house on the property. She, her husband, Hunter, and their toddler, Paisley, came out, too.

As for the birthday girl herself, Emily ran around hugging everyone, loving the attention as they wished her the best day ever.

Finally, Em couldn't stand it anymore. She burst out with, "Please, you guys! Is it what I hope it is?" She grabbed Ty's arm and gazed up at him with pleading, eager eyes. "Daddy, I might *burst* if you guys make me wait one minute longer."

Jobeth spoke up then, her voice calm as always, a big smile on her face. "Fair enough. Let's head on over to the horse barn, shall we?" Zach had adopted Jo way back when he and Tess got married. He'd taught Jo to ride, and she was the best horsewoman in the family.

"Yes!" cried Emily. "Yes, let's go now!"

Jobeth handed Paisley to Hunter, and he turned to take the toddler back to their house.

The rest of them piled into various vehicles and off they went along a snow-dusted dirt road. Emily, buckled up in the front seat with Ty, glowed with excitement and chattered nonstop.

Ty glanced in the rearview to check on Drew. The boy sat calmly looking out his side window toward Cloud Peak, which poked into the sky off to the west.

Drew seemed to sense Ty's glance and gave him a quick, soft smile.

Sometimes Ty marveled at the difference in temperament between his son and his daughter. Emily was a lot like her mother, fluttering around, always on the move, constantly announcing her desires and opinions. She was completely charming and also a handful.

In contrast, Drew had a deep, ingrained stillness. He always seemed to be thinking, studying the way things worked. Even when he first learned to talk, he would think before he spoke.

They topped the next rise and a moment later they were pulling the vehicles to a stop at the horse barn, which opened in back onto a large, fenced pasture.

Several horses waited at the fence.

Emily unsnapped her seat belt and bounced up and down, clapping. "I knew it, I knew it! Oh, Daddy. I'm so happy!" She lunged at him across the console and threw her arms around his neck.

He hugged her back, thinking that fatherhood definitely had its great moments. "Not too hard to guess, huh? Not when I told you to wear your sturdy jeans and riding boots."

"And to bring my riding helmet," she added with a scowl.

"That's right." He'd made it clear to Jobeth that his girl would be wearing a helmet at least for the next couple of years. Yeah, a hat was cooler. But more brain injuries were caused by horseback riding accidents than by football, soccer, rugby, skiing or motorcycle riding. Ty knew because he'd looked it up.

Everyone scrambled out of the vehicles and Jobeth introduced an ecstatic Emily to her first horse.

Quincy, a five-year-old sorrel gelding, stepped right up to nuzzle Em's open palm. For a few minutes, Emily petted him and whispered to him, getting to know him a little. She fed him a couple of small apples, which Jobeth had provided.

Then Jo helped her tack up. The rest of them hung on the fence in their winter coats, warm gloves and wool hats. They enjoyed the show as Emily, who'd been taking riding lessons from Jobeth for several months now, rode her new horse around the pasture.

"Dad?" asked Drew quietly.

"Hmm?"

"Do I have to be ten before I can have a horse?"

Ty glanced down at his son. "Not necessarily. But it's a commitment—you remember what a commitment is?" They'd talked about commitments a few months back. Drew had wanted a newer, fancier tablet. He'd made a commitment to have his chores and schoolwork done before he played on his tablet.

Drew, always the serious one, was nodding. "Commitment is when you say that you'll do something and then you do it. And not just one time, but all the time, whenever it has to get done."

"Exactly. Emily's made a commitment to spend three afternoons a week here at the ranch working with Quincy, grooming and caring for him, improving her riding skills." Ty would not only be making sure his daughter got a ride to the ranch, but he would also pay Jobeth to board Quincy and continue Emily's riding lessons.

"I could come out when you bring Em and learn all that stuff, too."

"Is that what you want to do, Drew?"

Drew's eyebrows bunched up as he considered the question. "Can I try it to see if I like it?"

"I'll talk to your mom and to Jobeth. We'll see if we can make that happen." Ty offered his hand. His son's small fingers disappeared in his grip. Then, together, they turned back to the fence.

Ty waved and shouted encouragements at Emily, whose smile took up her whole sweet face as she rode her very own horse back and forth across the pasture, the hated helmet strapped firmly on her head.

Moments like these, Ty realized he had very few regrets. He hadn't wanted to be married right out of high school and a dad a few months later. But his bad choices had somehow led to good things—like Emily. Like Drew. If he hadn't married Nic, there would be no Drew.

When Ty thought about his life that way, he wouldn't change a thing.

They got back to town at a little after noon. He drove straight to Nicole's.

Inside, it was a madhouse as everyone rushed to get ready for the princess party and the sleepover before heading to Astrid Chen's salon, The Beauty Studio, for an afternoon of pampering that would include Emily and five of her closest friends.

He herded Drew and an overexcited Emily into the kitchen for sandwiches and fruit as Nicole, Mona, Sadie and Abby all bustled around packing goodie bags and putting up decorations, making sure everything was just so for Emily's birthday celebration.

Sadie gave him a nod as he passed her on the way to the kitchen. "Ty," she said.

"Hey, Sadie."

She wore jeans and a bulky sweater, her thick hair anchored up in a sloppy bun. He watched her fine, round ass as she walked away and thought about all the things he would love to get a chance to do to her.

Not going to happen, he reminded himself sternly for the five hundredth time since Vegas. *Bad idea.*

His decision not to go there probably meant she would be spending at least one evening with the new guy from Don Deal Insurance.

Had she talked to that guy since Thursday?

Did they agree on a time to get together—tomorrow night or some night soon?

Well, so what if they did?

It was none of his damn business who Sadie went out with. He needed to quit obsessing over her and the time she spent with other guys.

They needed to talk, him and Sadie. He missed her. He thought about her way too much and most of his thoughts were a lot more than friendly.

Okay, yeah. He wanted her. But that was just too bad because he wasn't going to have her. A man didn't always get every damn thing he wanted.

One way or another, he and Sadie needed to close this distance between them. They needed to get back on track, back to being good buddies the way they'd been for years now. She mattered a lot to him. And if he didn't change his attitude, he would lose her friendship.

"Daddy!" screeched Emily. "Not mustard! I hate mustard!"

Drew, on the other hand, loved mustard. And Ty had been just about to squeeze out a smiley face of it on Emily's ham and cheese on wheat.

"Sorry, Em." He stuck his hand under the squeeze

bottle and caught the glob of yellow goo before it hit the ham.

Emily laughed. "Ew, messy!" But then she fluttered her eyelashes. "But thank you, Daddy. Mayonnaise, please."

"Comin' right up, birthday girl."

Nicole came flying in, cheeks pink, eyes frantic. "Ty, there you are. Can you pick up the cake before five?"

"Sure."

"We'll do the food at six, and then the cake, the candles, all that. And then the presents."

"Sounds good."

"So if you and Drew get here at say, five forty-five, that would be perfect."

"Will do."

"With the cake."

"Understood."

Nic heaved a giant breath. "What were we thinking—the horse, the spa day, the princess party, the sleepover…?"

Em had the answer. "You were thinking that you're giving me the best birthday ever in my whole, entire life!"

"Well, that explains it, then." Ty spread mayo on Emily's sandwich.

By three thirty that afternoon, as the spa day at The Beauty Studio wrapped up and six nine- and ten-year-olds squealed in delight at the butterflies and ladybugs cleverly painted onto their toenails, Sadie had begun to wonder if she wanted children, after all.

The girls were adorable, each one dressed in a princess costume from the rack of them Nicole had rolled out back at her house before she and Sadie ferried the girls over to the salon.

But all that squealing got old fast.

Maybe boys, Sadie found herself thinking. Yeah. She would only have boys.

The girls squealed some more when Nicole passed out jeweled princess slides for their pretty little feet—so they wouldn't mess up their pedicures. Outside, it was snowing, though not really sticking. The girls ran screaming to the cars, trying to get there fast on their nearly bare feet.

Back at Nicole's, Sadie turned up the thermostat to keep all those gorgeous little feet nice and toasty. They played princess games—Stepmother Says and pin the tiara on the princess. They made their own Disney princess stationery, decorated royal cookies, and hunted all over the house to fill Ariel's treasure chest with *Little Mermaid*-themed figurines, jewels and cute plastic sea creatures.

They were all so excited, which led to misunderstandings and overreactions. Sadie and Nicole spent quite a bit of time settling minor disputes and offering hugs. Somehow, they got all the way through to dinnertime without any major meltdowns.

Sadie was so completely absorbed in keeping up with the overwrought princesses, she barely registered when Ty and Drew returned, bringing Gavin along with them.

Around six, she glanced up from praising a handmade princess greeting card and there was Ty, standing in the open doorway from the kitchen, looking right at her, his eyes serious, focused. Full of intent.

For a long, sizzling moment, she actually felt weak in the knees. But then she reminded herself that she'd been so busy, she'd failed to make time for lunch. And therefore, that jittery feeling had nothing at all to do with Ty Bravo standing in the doorway with that dangerous look in his eyes.

Lucky for her, dinner came next. It consisted of a bunch of finger foods from the *Disney Princess Tea Parties Cookbook*. Sadie gorged on Pizza Roses and Belle Mini Quiche Cups.

A little while later, Nicole brought out the princess cake. They all sang happy birthday to Emily. She blew out her ten candles and then Nicole cut the cake.

By that time, everyone was full.

Didn't matter. They all said yes to a slice of that gorgeous three-layer pink cake. Sadie happened to glance up as she stuck a buttercream rose in her mouth—and there was Ty again, standing by the downstairs hallway.

Looking right at her.

All of a sudden, her breath got caught in her throat along with that mouthful of frosting. She knew she would choke.

But then, carefully, she relaxed her throat and drew air through her nose. It worked. That buttercream rose slid down without further difficulty.

Ty still had his gaze locked on hers.

And then, with the slightest tip of his head, he turned and disappeared down the hall.

What the…?

He actually thought she would follow him?

Well, the man had another think coming.

No way was she vanishing down that hallway just because he gave her that look.

Nope. She stayed right where she was and focused on her cake.

But then, well…

What if he had something important that he needed to tell her? What if…?

What?

She had no idea.

But maybe she really ought to talk to him.

She could see Nicole through the archway that led to the kitchen. She stood at the large granite island conferring with Carrie Sloan from the catering company.

It shouldn't be a big deal if Sadie went ahead and found out what Ty so urgently needed to discuss with her, right?

And she could use a bathroom break, anyway.

Setting her half-finished slice of cake on the dining area table, she headed for the hallway down which Ty had disappeared.

Chapter Five

Sadie walked right by the bathroom at the front of that hallway, though the door stood wide-open and there was nobody in there.

Still, she kept going, past Nicole's home office. She was just strolling on by the open door to the craft room Nicole rarely used anymore when a strong hand shot out and closed around her wrist.

No, she wasn't the least surprised.

But she gasped, anyway.

Ty pulled her into the craft room and shut the door.

"This is not okay," she said disapprovingly, pulling her arm free of his grip. "Turn on the light."

"Better not." He kept his voice just above a whisper. He was so close she could smell him—soap and man. Tempting in the most annoyingly elemental way.

She whispered back, "So we're sneaking around now?"

"Why do you say that?"

"Oh, please. We're in Nicole's craft room with the door shut and the light off, whispering to each other so no one will hear. I think that qualifies as sneaking around."

"Look." He leaned a fraction closer. His warm breath brushed her cheek. "I miss you, okay? I don't like this thing we're doing. I don't like feeling like I should avoid you."

"Ty-y-y…" It was only one syllable, but she stretched it out, partly in reprimand, partly in something very close to longing. "Nothing's changed. I still feel the same. I don't want some fling with you. I want at least the possibility of more than a sexual relationship with a ticking clock attached."

"I know you do." He leaned even closer and nuzzled her cheek.

Every molecule in her body melted. She made herself add, "And don't expect me to sneak around, either. I won't. If you've lured me back here to make another pitch for, um, taking it to the next level, Nic would have to be the first to know."

"You don't ask much, do you?" The last two words were velvet soft in her ear.

"It's not funny."

"Do you hear me laughing? I get it, Sadie. I understand what you want."

A small flicker of hope flared to life within her. "Are you trying to tell me you've changed your mind about what *you* want?"

He took several seconds to answer. Sadly, when he finally spoke, what he said was nothing new. "No, I haven't changed my mind. I really don't think I'm cut out for a lasting relationship. As for telling Nic, you must know that wouldn't go well."

She groaned—quietly. "Weakest excuses in the book."

"Oh, come on. You know Nicole as well as I do. She would freak."

"Why? She's totally over you."

"Yeah, but she's possessive—of me *and* of you."

"So, then. All the more reason to tell her what's going on with us right up front."

"Sadie, no."

She accused, "You're afraid of your ex-wife."

"You bet I am."

"As for your other excuse, why *aren't* you cut out for a lasting relationship?"

"I hated being married, okay? It was seven years of misery for me. I'm not going there again. I like being free."

"Please. We both know you and Nicole were not a match made in heaven. That doesn't mean you won't ever meet someone you're more compatible with. Some-day, you'll realize you want more than one weekend fling after another. You'll try again."

"I like my life just the way it is now."

Why was she wasting her breath trying to change his mind about love? "Gotcha. And I need to pee and return to the party…"

He caught her arm. "Damn it, I want our friendship back. I want us to be what we were before last week-end."

Was that even possible now? She doubted it. Then again, she missed him so much. A week without his snarky comments and unsolicited advice, and she just felt so…lonely, somehow.

With a hard huff of breath, she yanked her arm free of his grip and let herself sag against the door. "I want our friendship back, too."

"We need to *take* it back."

"Oh, yeah? Well, to do that, you'll need to start talking to me again."

He narrowed his eyes at her. "You haven't been talking to me, either."

She couldn't hold back a burst of laughter.

"Shh!" he warned.

"Sorry," she whispered.

"And what's so damn funny, anyway?"

"You, Ty. Right then, you reminded me of when we were ten and we had to do that science project together."

"Bottle rockets," he confirmed. "Yeah, I remember."

"For that whole first day of the project, we did nothing but argue."

He looked at her sideways. Probably because the two of them arguing always went without saying. "Yeah, so?"

"Mr. Rafferty told you to get along with me and you piped up with how I wasn't getting along, either."

"Well, you weren't."

She tried really hard not to roll her eyes. "My point being, some things never change, and I find that funny."

He braced a hand on the door just above her head and leaned in. She knew he was going to try to kiss her. *Turn away, tell him no.* But all she did was stare up at him, waiting for that moment when his lips touched hers.

At the last possible second, when she could feel his breath again, sweet and warm on her skin, he pulled back. "Sadie…"

She wanted to grab him, yank him right up against her and smash her lips to his. But she didn't. "Yeah?"

He dropped his arm to his side and stepped away. "I'll call you tomorrow night."

Her pulse went haywire as she sneered, "Fine."

"And I'll see you at the diner on Monday."

"Good—and I need to get back. The presents are next." She reached for the doorknob.

"Wait."

"Ty. We're just asking for trouble here. You get that, right?"

"Yeah, but I need to know. Are you going out with that Brent guy?"

She glared up at him through the shadows of the darkened room. "You've got some nerve."

"Come on. Answer my question. It's making me nuts just thinking about it. I know it's not fair of me to ask, but I have to know."

"Why?"

"I need to stop thinking about it and I don't have a prayer of doing that until I know if he asked you out *and* if you said yes." His eyes burned into hers.

She opened her mouth to explain in excruciating detail what an ass he was—and then thought, why hide the truth from him? Here she was lecturing him about love and honesty and relationships while not being honest about Brent. "Fine. No. I'm not going out with Brent. I told him I need a break from dating."

Faintly, through the gloom of the darkened room, she watched Ty's fine lips curve up. "Yeah?"

"You know, it's completely unacceptable for you to be so happy that I won't be dating Brent."

"It is, yeah. I'm way out of line. But so what? It does make me happy. Really, really happy."

"You're worse than I thought."

"I am?" He had the nerve to look surprised.

"Way worse. You don't want me, but you don't want me going out with anyone else, either."

His eyes looked black in the darkness, intense. Full of dangerous emotions. "I never once said that I don't want you."

She hated that those words sent a hot shiver racing down the backs of her knees. "I don't even know where to start with you."

"You can jump all over my ass when I call you tomorrow night. Right now, though, you need to get back to the party, right? I'll wait here a few minutes."

No way that worked for her. She still needed to pee—and urgently now. He needed to get out there ahead of her. "Uh-uh. You first."

"Can I say *anything* that you don't argue with?"

"Doubtful. You first."

A moment later, he slipped out the door.

Nicole let her head fall on Sadie's shoulder. They sat on the sofa in front of the fire, the wreckage of the princess party strewn all around them. Sadie held a half-full glass of much-needed merlot. Nic had opted for lemon-scented tea.

The incessant giggling and squealing from upstairs in Em's room had stopped in the last twenty minutes or so. Apparently, the six partying princesses had finally dropped off to sleep in their pretty, pink-and-gold princess tent. As for Ty, Gavin and Drew, they'd left hours ago.

"Sade?" Nicole asked softly.

"Hmm?"

"You okay?"

"Yeah, of course. Why?"

Nic sipped her tea. "I don't know. You've just seemed a little sad the past week or so. Sad, and kind of far away."

Sadie met her best friend's eyes. This was probably the moment to tell Nic everything—what had happened in Vegas and about the past week during which Sadie and Ty had barely spoken, and also what had gone down in the craft room earlier that night.

But she didn't want to tell Nic all that. Especially not now, when it wasn't going to go anywhere between Sadie and Ty, anyway.

Better to simply leave the subject alone.

Except, well, Nic was her best friend in the world and had been for her whole life. They grew up always knowing they could count on each other, no matter what—and that Sadie wanted a certain man was exactly the kind of thing she would normally rush to tell Nic all about.

But a whole new level of awkward came into play here. There was just no way of knowing how Nicole would take the news that Sadie had a thing for Nic's ex.

Really, though, it wasn't as though Sadie and Ty had done anything wrong—they hadn't. Not in Vegas and not tonight.

After all, Ty and Nic were beyond over. Nicole had Gavin now and she loved him deeply. As a couple, Ty and Nic had completely moved on from each other.

But still. Nic might not take it well if she learned that her ex and her best friend had shared several smoking-hot kisses, that they would have ended up in bed together last Sunday morning in Vegas if Gavin hadn't poked his head out of Nicole's suite just in time.

No, Nic might not take it well. And why should she ever have to know, anyway? Nothing was going to come of what happened in Vegas.

Best to leave it alone.

However…

The kisses in Vegas had brought the past roaring back. It wasn't what happened in Vegas that made Sadie feel like a bad friend.

It was that kiss ten years ago.

That *had* been wrong. Yeah, Nic and Ty had been broken up for weeks when Sadie kissed him. But back then, Nic was a long way from closure when it came to Ty Bravo.

"So you're saying you're not sad?" Nicole asked.

Sadie sighed. "I'm okay. I really am."

It wasn't a lie, exactly. More of a deflection.

Nic took her hand. They twined their fingers together and squeezed at the same time. Nic whispered, "Sisters forever."

"And ever and ever…"

Nic leaned close. "I have to ask one more time."

Sadie had no idea what she meant by that. "Go for it."

"You sure you don't want to bring a plus-one to the wedding? Just say the word. You're allowed to change your mind. Bring someone you've gone out with—I know none of them are The One. But still. It's nice to have someone to hang out with."

"Nic. I am fine on my own."

"Well, if you change your mind…"

"You're the best. Thank you."

Nic picked up her tea and had another sip. "Guess what?" Suddenly, her voice vibrated with barely contained excitement.

Sadie met those sapphire-blue eyes. "You look so happy."

Nic giggled like a kid. "Because I am."

"Tell me."

"No one else can know."

Sadie held up her pinky the way they used to do when they were Emily's age. Nic hooked it with hers.

"I swear," Sadie whispered. "I will not tell a soul."

"Okay, then... Gavin and I are having a baby."

Sadie blinked. "Oh. My. Goodness... Come here!" She grabbed Nic close—and then pulled back to study her face. "I'm so happy for you."

Nic's smile bloomed wider. "My period was due Monday. I just took the test yesterday. I am...ecstatic. And Gavin's over the moon."

"Oh, I'll bet. Congratulations. I'm so happy for you guys." And she was.

She thought about Ty—lately, she always seemed to be thinking about Ty.

Ty, tempting her to go places she knew she shouldn't.

It was really hard to keep saying no to him. Sometimes, like right now, she couldn't help thinking that until the right man came along, why shouldn't she have great sex with the wrong one?

Nic elbowed her gently. "Whatever it is that's bothering you, you might as well tell me now. You know you will eventually..."

"Really, I'm okay," she lied. Right then, that seemed the wisest course.

Ty had to make himself wait until seven Sunday night to call Sadie. He felt hopelessly eager, and he knew it.

The kids were staying at Nicole's, so he stopped by Arlington's at five thirty for a steak at the bar. Back at his house, he poured himself two fingers of Maker's Mark, made himself comfortable on the big leather sectional in front of the fire and gave Sadie a call.

He grinned like a fool at the sound of her "Hello."

"What are you up to?" he asked.

"It's just me, Boo and Olive. We're trying to decide whether to read a juicy romance or watch *Yellowstone*."

"Damn. Your life is so exciting."

"Tell me about it. Nicole said you were helping out with cleanup at her house today."

"It took hours. There was frosting and glitter everywhere. But Em told me she had the best birthday ever."

Sadie chuckled. The sound seemed to curl around down inside him, warming him all over. "I'm glad she and her friends had a good time."

And a phone call wasn't enough. He wanted to see her. "Did you eat yet?"

"Yeah."

Well. So much for *I'll bring you dinner*. "How about if I come over? We can watch *Yellowstone* together."

She was silent.

"I'm completely striking out here, aren't I?"

"Oh, Ty…"

He did not like the sound of that. "You'd better just say it."

She made a reluctant little sound deep in her throat and then finally came out with it. "Last night, I seriously considered telling Nicole about Vegas."

"Wait. What? You're not serious."

"Didn't I just say that I *seriously* considered it?

But relax. I didn't say anything. I do feel bad about it, though, you know?"

That pissed him off. "Why? In case you've forgotten, Nicole and I have been divorced for three years—and she's marrying Gavin in three weeks."

"I know that."

"So admit it. There is no problem here. Think about it. We didn't even make it all the way to your bed at the Venetian." *Unfortunately.*

"I still feel like I've gone behind her back. She's my best friend. I tell her everything."

Now he really was getting annoyed. "We're not kids anymore. Some things just aren't her business. And I'm your friend, too."

"Yes, you are." She said it kind of tenderly.

And he felt marginally better. "Sadie, honestly. You know how she is. It's always all about her."

"That's not fair. She's so much better than she used to be."

"Not 'better' enough. If we tell her, there will be trouble. I think you know that."

"Still…"

"What?"

"Well, Ty. There's not only Vegas. There's that kiss ten years ago…"

"What?"

"Would you please stop saying *what*? You heard me."

"Sadie, no. Just no. Telling Nicole about that kiss now would only cause trouble. You have to see that. It was years ago. It was one kiss. She and I were broken up at the time."

"She was in love with you. She was pregnant with your baby."

"I had no idea she was pregnant when I kissed you. Are you saying that *you* knew?"

"Of course not. And even if we didn't know she was pregnant, it was still wrong."

"No. Uh-uh. That's not true. I'll say it again. She and I were broken up. I had the right to kiss anyone I wanted to kiss."

"Yeah, I guess you did."

He blew out a hard breath. "Finally, you're seeing reason."

"You just don't get it. Yes, *you* had the right to kiss *me*. But I was so wrong to kiss you. Ty, I knew very well that she wasn't over you and that made you completely off-limits to me."

"I don't get it. Look. I know she's your friend forever, that you two are like sisters. I get that. I respect that. But she also never fails to make it so she's the center of attention. It's always her life and her feelings that everyone has to be aware of. The rest of us—including you—are just bit players in her ongoing drama."

"That's not fair. You know that she needs—"

"I'll say it again. It was ten years ago. And it was one kiss—*before* we knew about Emily. After that, you and I barely spoke to each other for how long? A couple of years, at least. Deciding to come clean with Nic now is, well, you might as well just grab a hammer and hit yourself on the head with it. You'll only be causing pain to yourself and Nic and me, too—pain for no real reason."

She was silent again. He knocked back the rest of his whiskey and waited her out.

Finally, she said, "Okay. I do see your point."

Relief poured through him. "Thank you."

"And given that we're not taking what happened in

Vegas any further, I think we can table this discussion for right now."

Not exactly what he'd hoped to hear her say. He'd really hoped she might reconsider the two of them being more than friends. And as for tabling the discussion about that kiss ten years ago, well, that meant they weren't done with it. She could very well circle back to it in the future.

He decided to push a little harder on the issue of what *not* to say to Nic. "Okay, then," he said. "We're agreed. What happened at the Venetian is nobody's business but ours. And what happened ten years ago stays in the past where it belongs."

"Yeah. We're agreed."

With a sigh of relief, he turned the conversation to lighter subjects. When they said goodbye a half hour later, he felt reasonably certain that their friendship would survive.

Did he want more?

You bet he did. But even he had to admit that getting more with her presented challenges on just about every front.

In fact, getting more looked pretty close to impossible. Because his *more* and her *more* were two very different things.

Monday morning early, Ty arrived at Henry's.

Sadie heard the bell jingle over the door and her silly heart did something acrobatic inside her chest. She just knew it was him.

And it was. He'd brought Drew and Emily. They loved to come in for breakfast before school. She had plates up and down her arms and a table waiting to be served. But still, she stopped in midstep to send him a great, big smile and call out greetings to the kids.

The three of them took the lone empty booth by the back wall. Sadie served a table full of out-of-towners their breakfasts and then went to find out what Ty and the kids wanted.

She took their orders quickly, but then Emily had a thousand things to tell her—about her horse, Quincy, and the big Thanksgiving feast for thirty or so that would be happening out at the Rising Sun Ranch on Thursday.

All the branches of the Bravo family who lived in or near Medicine Creek would be there, along with Sadie, her dad and her mom. Nicole and Gavin, too.

"I get to help with the decorations!" announced Emily proudly. "It's going to be the biggest Thanksgiving ever! And, Sadie, there might be snow, a *lot* of snow. We might have to go out to the ranch early and stay late and maybe sleep in sleeping bags on the great room floor. It will be like camping out, only right there in the ranch house. So don't forget your sleeping bag."

Just about everyone Sadie knew had four-wheel drive and snow tires—and chains, too, for that matter. Most likely no one would be forced to stay over. But even if the snow got that bad, they wouldn't have to sleep on the floor.

Earlier that year, Zach had arranged to have the old bunkhouse out at the ranch renovated—on the reality show *Rebuilt by Bartley*, which starred Jobeth's husband, Hunter Bartley. But as it turned out, the ranch hands preferred to live in their own trailers. That left the new bunkhouse to serve as guest quarters. There were also extra rooms at Jobeth and Hunter's house, and upstairs in the main ranch house—and in the foreman's cottage where Edna Heller lived.

Drew said, "I can't wait to go camping in the ranch house."

Both kids looked so excited at the prospect of spending Thanksgiving night in sleeping bags that Sadie just went along with their plans. "Should be fun," she agreed.

Ty turned his cup over. She heard it clink against the saucer. Her gaze tracked to the sound and she found herself staring at his hand as he set the cup upright. A weird, hot thrill zipped through her, both forbidden and delicious.

Slowly, she raised her eyes to meet his. "I'll get the coffeepot."

"Thanks." A dangerous smile pulled at the corner of his fine mouth.

She gave him a quick scowl to let him know she did not approve of him giving her looks like that. Ever.

They were supposed to be keeping it friends, and friends *only*. And yet, that smile of his was chock-full of bad intentions. And the look in his eye made her breath get all snarled up in her throat.

"I would like to have orange juice with my pancakes, please," chirped Emily.

"Me, too!" Drew chimed in.

Sadie smiled fondly at his beautiful children and tried her best to put troublemaking Ty out of her mind. "Two glasses of OJ, coming right up."

Behind the counter, she cleared off empty plates, including those of both Lester and Bob.

"So, Sadie, how's your love life?" Bob winked at

her as she topped off his cup. He was obviously feeling frisky this cold November morning.

"Why, Bob Early. Are you asking me out?"

Lester snickered and Bob turned bright red. "I, er…" Then Bob chuckled, too. "Don't be tempting an old man, now, Sadie McBride. Like to give me a heart attack and wouldn't you feel bad then?"

"Well, now, Bob. I think you're tougher than you realize."

"Oh, you bet," Bob agreed, raising both skinny arms and flexing dramatically. "Pure power, that's me."

Sadie poured orange juice for the kids, put the glasses on a small tray and grabbed the coffeepot again. As she approached Ty's table, he was talking quietly to Drew. But then he glanced up.

The look he gave her caused her cheeks to heat and fluttery creatures to take flight in her belly. And then he made it worse. "There you are. Just the girl I was looking for." Every word dripped with sexual intent. "The one with the coffeepot," he added, as if mentioning coffee somehow made it okay for him to keep teasing her this way.

Lucky for him she was such a pro. Someone more easily rattled might have spilled scalding coffee in his lap.

"Here you go," she said evenly as she poured. Then she set the small tray on the end of the booth's table and passed the kids their juice.

"Thank you, Sadie," Drew and Emily sang out in unison.

"You are so welcome." She scooped up the tray and headed for the next booth over.

It was more of the same when she served them their

food. The kids were sweet and polite. Ty said he was starving and looked at her like she might be his sausage and eggs.

What is wrong with you? she longed to ask him right out loud. But she knew she would only make things worse if she called him on his unacceptable behavior.

At least he left the money in cash on the table the way he always did, so she wasn't forced to bring him change or a credit card receipt or make nice at the cash register.

The kids called goodbyes to her as they left.

"Bye, Sadie!"

"See you at the ranch!"

"Thank you," Ty said as they went out.

She waved at the kids and did not so much as glance his way.

The weather was bad that day. She had to go to Buffalo and then up to Sheridan through the driving snow both ways. A semitruck almost sideswiped her on the way home in the dark.

She'd never been so relieved to pull her Chevy Tahoe into her dry, safe garage. In the mudroom, her cats were waiting. She dropped her purse and coat on the bench just inside the door and gathered them up into her arms. With their silky fur against her cheek, one purring in either ear, she felt safe and comforted. And so glad to be home and out of the storm.

Once she'd greeted Boo and Olive, she changed her boots for fuzzy slippers and headed for the great room, where she dished up cat food, filled the water bowl, plugged in the electric kettle and felt relieved she wouldn't need to bother with dinner. She'd had a salad and Henry's excellent beef stew before she left the diner in Sheridan.

She'd just poured hot water over a tea bag, picked up the mug and carried it over to the sofa when her doorbell rang. Who would be out wandering the streets on a night like this? She set down her tea, turned on the gas fireplace and went to find out.

It was Ty.

She pulled open the door and there he stood, looking like every woman's dream of the perfect cowboy in dark-wash jeans and tooled boots. He was just too perfect, all long, powerful legs, broad shoulders and knowing blue eyes.

In reality, though, he was no cowboy. Yeah, he could rope and ride with the best of them. All the Bravos could. But he was a townie, just like her. Snow dusted the brim of his hat and the shoulders of his heavy jacket. It was really coming down now, covering the grass in her front yard, collecting on the roof of his Escalade, which he'd parked at the end of the walk.

"What's going on?" she demanded.

"It's cold out here." He stomped the snow off his boots, brushed it from his shoulders and then swept off his hat. "You going to let me in?"

With a disgruntled sigh, she stepped back and in he came. He made himself at home, hooking his hat and coat on the tree in the corner, even removing his fancy boots, revealing the heavy winter socks beneath.

Like he lived here or something, like he had every right to walk around her house in his stocking feet.

"Stay awhile, why don't you?"

He had the nerve to wink at her. "Thanks. I just might."

"You eat?"

"Yes, I did."

"Maker's Mark?" It was his favorite. The last few

years, since she and Ty had slowly become good friends, she always had a bottle in the cupboard just in case he happened to drop by. Because she wanted him to feel welcome at her place. And for as long as she'd been keeping his favorite whiskey in her cupboard, she'd never once felt there was anything wrong in that.

Until now.

"Maker's Mark would be great," he said. Halfway to the white quartz island that marked off her kitchen, she spun on her heel and faced him again. "Whoa." He put up both hands at her sudden about-face. "What'd I do now?"

"I'm just curious as to why, exactly, you're here?"

His big shoulders slumped. "I don't get it. Now, suddenly, you're suspicious if I stop by to see you?"

"Ty, please. Drop the innocent act. It's not convincing. Everything's changed. You know it. Don't try to pretend you have no idea what's up with me."

He just stared back at her, looking hurt.

"I'll get your drink," she muttered and headed for the kitchen again.

He was waiting on the sofa when she returned to the living area.

"Thank you." He took the drink from her, had a sip and set it down.

Her tea was right there on the coaster where she'd left it to answer the door. She picked it up. The warmth of the mug between her hands soothed her. Did she owe him an apology? Maybe.

"Okay," she said reluctantly. "I shouldn't have jumped all over you like that."

He studied her face for several seconds and then he said, "You're probably right to be suspicious."

She drew her legs up onto the sofa. He hiked a leg up, too. This really did feel too cozy, just the two of them, in front of the fire with the snow coming down outside. "What's going on?"

He picked up his drink and knocked back another sip. "Look. The truth is, I can't stop thinking about you. It's been way too long since I felt this way."

"What way is that, exactly?"

He scoffed. "Great idea. Play dumb."

"I'm not—"

"Yes, you are. And you know what? I don't really blame you. But let me ask you this. How many guys have you been out with in the past few years?" Before she could jump on him for razzing her about her search for a good man, he answered the question for her. "A lot. Let's just go with a lot. And now we've agreed on that, how many of those guys did you kiss the way you kissed me in Vegas?"

"Why are you doing this?"

He kept on pushing her. "Get honest. Look me square in the eye and tell me that even one of those bozos made you feel like you felt with me that night at the Venetian."

"Look, Ty. I just don't see what the point is here."

"Let me put it this way. After the divorce, I made up for lost time when it came to random women."

"You're not telling me anything I don't already know. Are you thinking that talking about other women will impress me? If so, you would be wrong."

"I'm not trying to impress you. I'm trying to make a point."

"Well, your point is escaping me."

"Lots of women, Sadie. Too many women."

"Ugh. Got it."

"And lots of sex."

"Didn't I just say I got it? You can stop."

"No, I don't think so."

"Yeah, really. Just stop."

"My point is, not one of those women I spent my weekends with could hold a candle to sharing a few kisses with you."

She drew a shaky breath and had no idea what to say right then. Because it was the same for her. She'd kissed a pretty large number of men in her search for the one to spend the rest of her life with. Ty's kiss left them all in the dust.

It was hard to get to sleep at night lately. She couldn't stop fantasizing about kissing him some more. When she finally did drop off into restless slumber, she dreamed of his mouth on hers, of their clothes just falling off, peeling away, leaving them naked, pressed close and warm together, her limbs wrapped around him, his big arms holding her so tight.

He braced an elbow on the sofa back and leaned even nearer. He smelled so good, of clean winter air and a hint of whiskey. It took all the willpower she had not to reach for him.

"You and me, Sadie," he said, low and rough. "We have this fire between us. This secret fire."

She blinked at him, dazed. The man was a born salesman, just like his dad. He could sell a drowning man a glass of water.

He went right on. "This fire between us, it's a fire of banked embers that smolder in secret, with nobody the wiser, never quite bursting into flame for a long, long time. Years. A full decade, that's for sure."

She'd had nothing but a few sips of tea. Still, she felt

drunk. Drunk on his nearness, on his dangerous words. "Ty, you're making zero sense."

"I'm making perfect sense and you know it, too. This tiny, dormant, invisible spark between you and me, it has burst into flame and there is no ignoring it. Not anymore, Sadie."

"Last night, we worked all this out. Last night, you agreed that we weren't going to go there."

"I was wrong to agree. I walked into the diner this morning and there you were, all round-cheeked and adorable, your hair up in that cute little topknot that bounces when you nod your head, looking at me in that way you have, that way that's just between the two of us. That way that says I'd better watch my step, or else. I looked at you and suddenly, it was all perfectly clear. I realized that this thing with us needs to be allowed to play itself out."

"Play itself—"

He didn't even let her finish. "Yeah."

She almost nodded, but she stopped herself just in time. "No. Uh-uh. Absolutely not. Next, you'll be saying we need to 'get it out of our systems.'"

His eyes were so steady, holding hers. Those eyes made promises—sexy ones, the kind that could be fulfilled in a weekend somewhere out of town. The kind of promises that would only leave her limp, satisfied and longing for more.

Not to mention eaten up with guilt for what she hadn't told her best friend.

"I just want you to think about it, Sadie."

"There is nothing to think about. It's a bad idea."

"It's not going to go away. It's going to eat at us until we give in."

"No. That's not true."

"Yeah, it is. So won't you just consider giving this fire the fuel to burn, letting it go wild until it burns itself out?"

She blew out a hard breath. "That is the worst idea in the history of bad ideas."

"Sadie, it's not. It's the best way to deal with a problem like ours."

"For you, maybe. Not for me."

"Nobody ever has to know."

"Sneaking around, that's what you're suggesting. That's all you've ever suggested.

He picked up his drink, swallowed the last of it and set the glass back down hard. "I should go."

No kidding. "Yeah. I guess you should."

"I really want to kiss you…"

"Don't."

A muscle twitched in his sculpted jaw. "Fair enough. Think about what I said."

No problem. She would have trouble thinking about anything else.

He rose. She got up, too, and followed him to the door, where he put his boots and jacket back on, and grabbed his hat. "Good night, Sadie." He looked suddenly so sad.

She wanted to reach out, wrap her arms around him, tell him again that she would always be his friend, but his plan was pure crap.

Too bad that if she put her arms around him, she might never let go. If she put her arms around him, he would kiss her and scoop her up and carry her to her bedroom.

And if she had her arms around him, she would let him do that. "Good night, Ty."

He tipped his hat as he went out the door.

Chapter Six

Ty woke the next morning to a foot of snow on the ground. He ate breakfast at home and then went to work with his snowblower. By ten, the snowplow had been by and most of the streets in town were clear.

He drove over to the office and worked until six, when Gavin showed up. Ty looked up from his desk into Gavin's dark eyes and thought how you never could predict with any certainty what might happen in life.

He and Gavin had met their sophomore year at A&M when Ty advertised for a roommate. Freshman year, Nic had come to College Station with him. They'd shared a small apartment in family housing—for a month.

But she'd wanted to have Emily in Montana, so she'd gone back to Wyoming at the end of October. She and the baby had returned after Christmas, but Nicole wasn't happy. She missed her life back home. The two of them argued constantly. That summer, they bought their first house in Medicine Creek and Nic and Em had stayed there permanently.

In Texas, Ty moved out of family housing and leased a two-bedroom apartment near campus. He met Gavin when he posted an ad for a roommate.

Right away he and Gavin were tight. Because who wouldn't be tight with Gavin? He was a good guy with a big heart, a man you could count on, a man who would be there when you needed him.

Ty had told Gavin a lot. Gavin had listened with no judgment, but still it was serious oversharing. Ty confessed he'd married Nicole because he'd felt it was the only right thing to do given the situation. He'd also admitted he was scared to death that he was a bad father. He'd missed Em's birth and he felt really guilty about that, about being in Texas so much of the time. At least, he was there the summer Drew was born.

But he and Nicole were always at odds. He refused to give up his education and Nic refused to live anywhere but Medicine Creek.

Gavin listened and said all the right things and reminded him that he went home every chance he got.

Ty and Gavin stayed roomies through senior year. Gavin dated widely and everyone liked him. He managed to remain friends with most of his exes. More than once during those years, Ty wished he *was* Gavin, free to get out and explore without the responsibility of a wife and kids waiting back home.

After graduation, Ty moved home for good. He partnered up with his dad. Gavin went on to law school. They probably would have drifted apart if Gavin hadn't made a point to keep in touch.

Finally, the year Ty and Nic divorced, Ty invited his college buddy to come on up to Medicine Creek for a visit. A Houston native, Gavin fell instantly and completely in love with small-town Wyoming. And then with Nicole. He hung out a shingle and began practicing family law.

As for Gavin's relationship with Nicole, he was all in from their first date. She felt the same about him.

Ty was happy for them, he really was. Just sometimes he wished…

Well, that his life could have been as smooth and satisfying as Gavin's always seemed to be.

Gavin asked, "What'd I do?"

About then, Ty realized his friend had been standing there, looking down at him, waiting for him to say something for a couple of minutes, at least. Ty blinked away the memories. "Just thinking that you're a damn good friend."

Gavin grinned. "I try."

"What's up?"

Gavin sat on the edge of Ty's desk and started fiddling with a salt dough paperweight Emily had made for Ty last Christmas. "Lately I see you everywhere I go, but we never get a chance to sit down for a little bro time."

"Hands off the paperweight—and you did not just say *bro time*."

"Yeah, bro. I did." Gavin finally let go of the paperweight. He was grinning. Ty couldn't help but grin back. "Let's get a drink," Gavin said, "and some food."

They went to the Stagecoach Grill. Twice, Gavin asked what was bothering him. Both times, Ty said, "Not a thing."

Gavin finally grumbled, "I give up. Whatever's going on with you, I'm happy to listen when you're ready to talk."

Ty almost let the truth out right then and there. *I kissed Sadie in Vegas. Repeatedly. Those kisses beat any sex I've ever had. But Sadie won't have sex with me. Because she wants a real relationship, and I don't—and because she's afraid that getting in bed with me would upset your fiancée.*

No. Bad idea to tell Gavin, who would listen and not judge and be the perfect friend he'd always been. And then, more than likely, tell Nicole.

Gavin couldn't help spilling his guts to Nic. The two of them told each other *everything.* Even if Gavin tried to keep a confidence, she would know he was hiding something, and she would keep at him until he told all.

Ty shook his head and signaled their server for two more drinks—and Gavin said in a near-whisper, "Nic's pregnant." He had a look of sheer joy on his handsome face.

Ty blinked in shock—but recovered quickly. "Wow. Congratulations."

"Thanks, man." Gavin looked around, clearly checking to see if anyone might have heard his hushed announcement. But it was a weeknight and only half the tables were taken. Gavin's secret was safe. "Don't say anything to anyone, okay?"

"Uh, sure."

"She's only a few weeks along and we agreed we wouldn't tell people for a while. I'd appreciate it if you didn't let on to Nic or anyone else that I told you."

"I understand. I won't say a word." Fat lot of good his keeping quiet would do. Nicole would take one look at Gavin and demand to know what her true love was hiding, then Gavin would crumble and confess that Ty knew about the baby.

But Ty had given his word and he would keep it.

"Thank you." Gavin wore a misty-eyed smile. "I hate to put you on the spot, but I had to tell you. Because you're my best friend and it's a little weird. I mean, I'm marrying your ex and she's having my baby."

"Not weird," Ty baldly lied. And then realized it wasn't a lie, after all. He honestly was happy for Gavin and Nic. "Not weird at all unless we make it that way—and we won't." The drinks came. Ty raised his glass. "To the newest member of the family."

"To the baby." Gavin beamed. They drank in unison. And Gavin said, "Whew. I'm glad you're okay with it. And I need you to know that I love Em and Drew like they're my own."

"I know you do."

"Do you think they'll be okay with a baby in the house?"

"Are you kidding? They're going to love having a little brother or sister."

"You really think so?"

"I know so."

Gavin sat back in his seat with a satisfied sigh. "Life is good."

Ty thought of Sadie again. What was she doing now? If he called her when he got home, would she pick up the phone?

"You sure you don't have something on your mind?" Gavin asked.

"I'm okay."

The server came by again. Ty asked for the check.

At home, he somehow managed to keep himself from calling or texting Sadie.

Wednesday morning, he drove to another café on the other side of town from Henry's. The food wasn't near as good, but he knew if he went to Henry's he would have a hell of a time leaving Sadie alone. His mouth had always gotten him in trouble when it came to her.

Now, he might be able to keep his trap shut, but keeping his eyes off her? He didn't think he could do that.

This was bad. He was out of control over Sadie Mc-Bride. How had this happened to him? Yeah, there'd been that kiss in high school. But as soon as Nicole told him she was pregnant, he'd put all romantic thoughts of Sadie from his mind—forever, he'd believed at the time.

Little did he know back then that ten years later, hot thoughts of Sadie would be back with a vengeance. He really, truly never saw it coming.

Thursday, he got up early and packed an overnight bag, just in case the predicted snowstorm kept him at the ranch overnight. Then he drove to the slate-shingled two-story house on North Street where he'd grown up.

It was just him, his mom and his dad for breakfast. His younger brother, Joshua, was in his senior year at UC Santa Barbara. Josh had a job down there in California and had to work during the four-day holiday.

After breakfast, Ty helped load his mother's contribution to dinner into his dad's fancy crew cab and then followed them out to the ranch, where the big main house smelled like all kinds of holiday heaven and the women bustled around mixing and pounding, chopping and stuffing and baking. The men sat by the fire in the great room drinking coffee, talking about beef prices, land deals and alfalfa crops, jumping up to help whenever one of the women called to them as they waited for the first of three back-to-back football games to start.

Ty had snagged himself a nice comfy leather chair not far from the big wood-burning fireplace where bright flames licked at a giant log. Jobeth and Hunter's toddler, Paisley, came trotting up dragging a stuffed purple sloth. "Hi!" She wore cute sweats printed with turkeys and sported a big orange bow in her dark, curly hair. "I Paiswee!"

"Hey, Paisley," he replied. And just in case she didn't remember him from the last big family event, he added, "I'm Ty. How you doing?"

"Humph," she said, and then climbed into his lap. "I sit."

And she did, plopping down on top of him. Hugging her sloth, she leaned back against him with a big sigh.

She was still sitting on him when Nicole and crew showed up. After greeting everyone in the great room, Nicole headed for the kitchen, Gavin right behind her, his arms laden with brown bags.

Drew and Emily made a beeline for Ty and Paisley in the big easy chair. Drew perched on one of the chair arms. Emily squeezed in on his lap next to Paisley, who'd been snoozing, but woke up long enough to say, "Hi!"

"Hi, Paisley." Emily leaned toward the toddler.

Ty looked down at their heads pressed close together, tight brown curls and straight blond locks shining in the light from the fire.

The doorbell rang again. Zach got up and answered. There were voices in the front hall as the newcomers shed their coats and hats and gloves. He heard Sadie say something and Zach's deep voice in reply.

And then Sadie and her folks trooped into the great room carrying grocery bags and covered bowls. Zach took up the rear.

Sadie looked so good, in a red wool dress that clung to her curves. She wore tall boots, and she'd pulled her thick, wavy hair back on one side with a big red clip. Her gaze found him.

She smiled, sweet and yet reluctant.

He felt a pinch inside his chest. Like an ache, but in a good way.

"You got all the kids," she said.

He nodded. "And a purple sloth, too."

Nicole called from the kitchen. "Sade! You make the cranberry sauce?"

"Oh, yes, I did!" Sadie called back.

A moment later, she vanished into the other room, her parents following in her wake. The big great room seemed emptier without her.

A few minutes later, her dad reappeared and found a seat on the sofa. Ty resisted the urge to ease out from under the three children sharing his chair with him and volunteer to help out with whatever Sadie was doing.

Emily said to Paisley, "I have to go. They need me to decorate the table."

The toddler sat up straight. "I go!"

Emily beamed. "Do you want to help?" Paisley's curls bounced with her nod. Emily slid to the floor. "Okay, then. Let's get to work."

Paisley handed Ty her sloth, climbed down off his lap and reached for Emily's hand. The two disappeared into the kitchen side by side.

Five minutes later, Ty's mom announced that she needed volunteers to move tables around in the formal dining room. Leaving Paisley's sloth in the big chair, Ty got up to pitch in.

They sat down for the big meal at three in the afternoon. Somehow, they'd managed to fit everyone into the dining room by connecting the tables in a rectangular configuration. As the host, it fell on Zach to say grace. He made the blessing quick and to the point, expressing thanks for the food, for family and for friends. A chorus of *amen*s went up. When Ty raised his head, his gaze locked right on the woman in the red wool dress seated almost directly across from him.

She looked like an angel, her head tipped down, thick eyelashes brushing her pretty pink cheeks. And then she opened her eyes and caught him staring. For a moment, they might have been the only two people in the room.

She looked away first. Edna passed her the green beans and Ty felt strangely bereft as she spooned a serving onto her plate and handed the bowl to Ty's cousin once removed, Nate, who sat to her left.

Outside the tall dining room windows, the world had turned pure white. The snow was coming down so thick and fast, you couldn't see the trunk of the bur oak ten feet from that side of the big, old house.

Henry said, "If you'll all excuse me, I should make a few calls, make sure tomorrow's shifts at the diners are covered."

"Of course," replied Tess.

Sadie spoke up. "Dad, I'll be glad to do it."

"I've got it." Henry pushed back his chair.

"What about Olive and Boo?" Ty asked Sadie.

She met his eyes across the table and a jolt of excitement shivered through him—one he tried his best to ignore. "I left them extra food and plenty of water. They should be fine until tomorrow."

Zach said, "I hope you all remembered to pack a bag just in case."

After the meal, there was more football and eventually coffee and dessert, including apple, pumpkin and pecan pie. By then, the talk centered on who would sleep where that night.

Emily got her wish. She and Drew would camp out in the great room by the fire. Nicole and Gavin would share a room upstairs. The extra rooms up there were assigned, followed by the available space at Hunter and Jobeth's house and the two spare bedrooms at Edna's place.

That left vacancies in the newly renovated bunkhouse, which had five private rooms and a shared living area. Ty's mom and dad took one of the bedrooms. Jason and Joseph, Nate's two sons, each got a room as well. Ty got one.

And so did Sadie.

Ty forced himself not to look at her when Tess confirmed their room assignments, though his pulse went haywire, and his face felt suddenly on fire.

Really, he needed to get a grip. You'd think he was fourteen with a first crush, the way anticipation roared through him at the thought of sleeping in the same building with Sadie. He should probably seek professional help. Because lately, his attraction to her verged on obsession.

Pointless obsession, he reminded himself. She'd made it painfully clear she would not end up in his bed. He needed to accept that.

So far, though, when it came to Sadie Jane, his libido overrode his brain at every turn.

"Tyler Ross?" asked a soft voice nearby.

He blinked and glanced up at Tess, who stood at his shoulder holding the coffeepot. "Refill?"

"Uh, great. Yeah. Thanks." She filled his cup. He gave her a big smile.

As Ty tried not to look at the object of his hopeless desire, his gaze snagged on his dad, who sat across the table next to her. Cash Bravo winked at him.

What the hell?

No. Uh-uh. Just no. There was no way his father could have caught on to his sudden fascination with Sadie. Ty might be a mess of frustrated yearning inside, but he had all that under control.

At the most, people might guess he was a little preoccupied. His dad was just messing with him.

Studiously ignoring both Sadie and his dad, he picked up his third cup of coffee and took a sip.

Hours later, in his cozy room in the bunkhouse, he stared up at the dark ceiling above the bed and mentally berated himself for drinking all that coffee. Sleep was not happening.

Maybe he should get up, wander out to the main living area, turn on the nice big screen Zach had provided for guests and watch something mindless while he waited to feel sleepy.

But he nixed that idea before he could throw back the covers. Sadie had the room directly across the hallway from his. If he went out there, he had a really bad feeling his stalkerish tendencies could easily get the best of him. He'd end up lurking there in the dark, his ear to her door, hoping for the slightest sound from within.

It was bad enough he couldn't stop thinking about her. He didn't have to turn into a creeper over her, too. Lacing his hands behind his head, he stared at the ceiling some more.

The faint tap on his door startled him.

Reminding himself that no way would that be Sadie, he turned on the lamp. Grabbing the sweatpants and long-sleeved Henley he'd tossed across the chair by the window, he yanked them on over his boxer briefs.

"Hey," Sadie whispered when he pulled open the door. He blinked at the sight of her, his fantasy made flesh, standing there in snowman pajamas and sheepskin ankle boots. "I'm sorry," she whispered. "I woke you up, didn't I?"

"Nope." Stepping back, he swept out an arm for her to enter.

Contrary to a fault, she hesitated there on the threshold, her full lower lip caught between her pretty white teeth. "Is this a bad idea?"

He considered reassuring her, but this was her move. If she'd decided to back out, he could at least be man enough not to try to stop her. "Probably."

With a slow nod, she stepped forward. He shut the door and followed her to the bed. When she sat on the end of it, he dropped down beside her.

Bracing her elbows on her thighs, she stared at the braided jute rug under their feet. "I couldn't sleep."

"Yeah, me neither."

She sat up—but only long enough to flop back against the bed. "I know a secret."

"Cool. I'm listening."

"I swore I wouldn't tell, so if I tell you, you can't tell anyone."

"You have my solemn word."

"Humph. I hope your word is worth more than mine…"

"Just tell me."

"Fine. Nicole's pregnant."

"I know." When she shot him a surprised glance, he explained, "Gavin told me."

"But it's supposed to be a secret."

"Yeah. Gavin told me that, too." He wanted to lie down beside her, but the blankets were all in a wad. "Get up—just for a minute. I'll straighten the covers."

She got up. As she toed off her house boots, he smoothed out the blankets and pulled the coverlet over them, plunking the pillows on top. Together, they climbed onto the bed and stretched out side by side, facing each other. He wondered why she was here as he watched her plump her pillow and then fiddle with her hair, guiding a tangled hank of it back behind her ear.

Was it possible she'd changed her mind about having sex with him?

Doubtful. Damn it. The look in her eyes said she wanted to talk.

She shivered a little.

He offered, "There's an extra quilt in the closet if you want a blanket."

"That'd be great."

He got up, took down the quilt and spread it over her before joining her under it. "Better?"

"Much." She cuddled her pillow and granted him a soft smile.

Feeling peaceful for the first time in days, Ty closed his eyes.

Sadie said, "Nicole is thrilled about the baby."

He looked at her again then, at her tangled hair and tempting lips. "Yeah, so's Gavin."

"I'm happy for them. I honestly am, Ty."

He dared to reach out, to guide a stray lock of hair off her cheek. Her skin felt like velvet. "You're happy, but…?"

She wrinkled her nose. "Well, the truth is, I envy her, too. I mean, I know it's petty, but Nic's found her perfect man—no offense."

"None taken. I was not in any way perfect for Nicole. Gavin *is*."

She touched him then, just a light brush of her fingers against his arm. Even through the thick waffle weave of his shirt, he felt that touch acutely. It sent warmth curling through him.

"I used to be angry at you all the time for never managing to give her the attention she needed," she said.

"Yeah. I remember."

A rueful smile curved her lips. "But I see things differently now. I know you tried your best to make it work with her, Ty."

"Sadie."

"Hmm?"

"You don't need to console me. I promise, I'm over it. Get back to your point."

"Right. My point is, Nic has her perfect guy and in eight and a half months or so, she'll have three kids. I've yet to have one. And as for my perfect man, he's failed to show up. I'm starting to get really irritated with him for that, which is pretty pitiful, really. I mean, how can I be pissed off at a man I don't even know yet?"

He stared into those green eyes of hers. Up close like this, in this light, he could see an amber ring around each of her pupils. That was the thing about green eyes. They changed colors slightly depending on the light.

"Ty?"

"Hmm?"

"Did you hear a word I just said?"

He nodded against his pillow. "You're pissed off at your perfect man because he hasn't shown up yet."

"*And* I feel bad for being envious of Nic."

"Right. That, too." He freed a hand from under the covers so he could skate a finger down her nose.

"What are you doing?" she demanded with a silly little snicker.

"Admiring your nose."

She groaned. "Sometimes you are just too weird, Tyler Ross."

"I like your eyes, too."

"Uh, thanks. I think."

"Next to red and violet, green is the rarest eye color. Less than two percent of people have green eyes."

"I'm aware," she replied in that tone he recognized from their school years, the tone that said she knew everything he knew—and then some. "Green eyes are actually caused by a genetic mutation resulting from a lack of melanin. I looked it up back in middle school science when we studied eye color genotypes."

"Ah." He'd looked it up, too. Recently. A week and a half ago, to be exact. After Vegas, when he couldn't stop thinking about her.

For a day or two there, he kept picturing her eyes, marveling that sometimes they were a pale, clear green and sometimes darker, sometimes more jewel-like. Before he could stop himself, he'd googled green eyes and read all about them. It was then that he began to realize he might be a little bit obsessed. At the time, he'd felt certain this strange sudden obsession with a woman he'd known all his life would quickly fade.

So far, that hadn't happened.

But he wasn't giving up hope. Maybe she would decide to have sex with him, after all. They could do what he suggested just last Monday—have some fun and get over each other.

And then finally go back to being close friends again as they should be, close friends without all the aggravating heat and pent-up hunger.

Not tonight, though. Not here, in Zach's fancy bunkhouse, with his mom and dad asleep down the hall.

Not tonight and probably not ever.

But hey. A man can have fantasies, can't he?

Sadie's amazing green eyes slowly drooped shut. He watched her for a while, thinking he should suggest that she sneak back across the hall to her own room. Carefully, he turned over to check the time.

After two.

Yeah, he should definitely remind her that she really ought to go. The last thing they needed was someone in the family discovering them asleep in his bed.

It didn't matter that sleeping was all they were doing. If his mom or dad found out, he would never hear the end of it. They both really liked Sadie. Sometimes he suspected that his folks had always believed that Sadie was the one for him.

They just didn't get it. One disastrous marriage had been one too many for him. He'd learned the lesson Nicole had drilled into him during every one of their never-ending arguments. He didn't have it in him to understand *or* truly love a woman. He was too selfish, always off doing what he wanted to do, leaving his poor wife on her own to take care of everything at home.

Uh-uh. True love and a happy marriage had never been for him. He'd accepted that fact long ago.

He focused on Sadie again and couldn't help smiling. She looked so cute, with her hands tucked under her cheek, like a sweet and well-behaved child. Her mouth was slightly parted, her face smooth, relaxed. Now and then, a soft little snore escaped her, and her caramel-colored hair was all over the place.

It felt…relaxing, to have her here beside him. She smelled so good, like vanilla and apples, both satisfying and wholesome.

What could it hurt to let her sleep for a little while? Carefully, so as not to wake her, he rolled over again and switched off the lamp.

Chapter Seven

"Ty?" There was a gentle tapping sound. "You awake?"

Sadie opened her eyes to daylight—and to Ty, sound asleep beside her. Caught in that hazy place between slumber and waking, she stared at him, bemused.

Tap, tap, tap. "Tyler?" Sadie recognized that voice. It was Ty's mom, Abby.

Was it possible this might be a bizarre dream? Stifling a groan, Sadie shut her eyes extra tight and hoped against hope that when she opened them again, she would be magically transported back to her own room across the hall.

But no. She was still lying right here in Ty's bed with Ty sound asleep beside her, his blond hair sticking out every which way and his lean cheeks dusted with morning beard scruff.

There was more tapping. Abby called, "Tyler!"

Right then, Ty's eyes popped open. They stared at each other. She must have looked every bit as freaked as she felt because he whipped a hand from under the quilt and put a finger to his lips.

She nodded in frantic agreement. Let him deal with Abby. She would lie here perfectly still and not make a sound. Because it would just be too weird to have his mom see them like this—sleeping together fully clothed.

Not that it would be any better if they were naked, just...

It wasn't that big of a deal.

And yet somehow, it felt that way. As though the two of them getting caught sleeping together with their clothes on somehow meant they had shared something more...personal than mere sex.

"Ty!" his mom called yet again.

"Just a second, Mom!" he called back in a tone of pure exasperation as he slipped out from under the covers and went to the door, which he opened just enough to stick his head out.

She heard his mom say, "There you are. I thought you'd never wake up."

He muttered something. Sadie had no idea what.

She heard Abby say, "It's after nine."

"Got it."

"Breakfast is..." There was more, but Sadie couldn't quite make it out.

Ty said, "Will do." His mom said something else, and he replied, "Got it. You guys go ahead."

Then, finally, he shut the door.

Sadie sat up and raked her hair back off her face. Faintly, she heard Abby's footsteps retreating down the hallway.

"Well?" she whispered.

"Breakfast is underway at the main house. Jason and Joseph are already there. My mom and dad are going over there now. We should get over there as soon as possible. My mom tapped on your door and got no answer. I said I would check on you."

"I can't believe I fell asleep—and why didn't you wake me?"

He rubbed at his scrambled hair and yawned. "I don't know. You looked so peaceful…"

Sadie pushed the quilt away and slid off the end of the bed. "I'm going to go pull myself together. Just go on over to the main house when you're ready and I'll be there soon."

"Sadie…" His voice trailed off.

She waited a count of three, but he didn't go on. "Just say it."

"You okay?"

"Of course."

He tipped his head sideways and looked at her for way too long. "You sure?"

"Positive." She pulled on her shearling boots and headed for the door. When she got there, she froze with her hand on the door handle. "What if somebody sees me?"

"Come on. It's really not that big of a deal."

"But it's weird, right? Like we had a grown-up sleepover or something. Like the two of us have something… intimate going on."

He held her gaze and said way too gently, "You're overthinking it."

"Am I?"

He gave her a firm nod. "Oh, yeah."

She blew out her cheeks with a hard breath. "Okay, then. You're right. I'm overreacting."

"I'll get dressed. We can walk over there together."

She just knew her face was red. Her skin felt way too hot. "No. I mean it, you go ahead. I'm going to take a quick shower." She was still standing there with her hand on the doorknob like a complete doofus. "Um. All right…" She opened the door—and stepped out into the empty hallway. A minute later, she was shutting the door to her room and engaging the privacy lock.

"Ty's right," she whispered to herself. "Don't over-think it." Straightening her shoulders, she headed for the en suite bathroom and a nice, hot shower.

It didn't take long to pull herself together. When she left her room, the door to Ty's room was open. She should just head for the front door.

But instead, she went over there and peeked in. He'd already left. The bed was made and his overnight case, apparently all packed, waited beside the bed.

In the bunkhouse's small front hall on the far side of the living room and kitchen area, she took her winter coat, mittens, gloves, snow boots and wool hat from the closet and put them on. Outside, another few inches of snow had fallen, bringing the blanket of white to what looked like about two feet deep. Overhead, the sky had cleared. The snow glittered under the bright winter sunlight. And someone had cleared the road between the houses.

At the ranch house, everybody teased her for being the last one up. She avoided eye contact with Ty and said she'd slept great. "Must be the country air."

"Help yourself to coffee," said Tess.

She poured herself a mugful and Edna served her

a yummy plate of ham, eggs and biscuits with butter and homemade jam.

Black Friday breakfast with the Bravos was lovely. She tried her best not to let her gaze collide with Ty's as she focused on the warmth of the big kitchen and the companionable chatter around the kitchen table.

Later, Tess produced a bunch of board games. For a few happy hours, they played Candy Land and then Clue. Everyone was laughing, the kids babbling away.

As for Sadie, she felt oddly wistful. So much lovely family togetherness, and yet all she could think about was last night with Ty. How good it had been, just lying there under that quilt with him. Nothing earth-shattering had been said and not a single kiss was shared.

But with him, she'd felt…understood, somehow. Like he really got her, in the deepest sense.

So strange.

To feel completely understood by Ty Bravo, of all people…

By early afternoon, a couple of the ranch hands had taken the snowblower and cleared the road to the highway. And the county snowplows had done their job on the road to town. It was safe to leave.

Nic, Gavin and the kids took off first. When Sadie's mom and dad left, she followed them.

At home, her cats were waiting just inside the mudroom door. She greeted them as she always did, crouching to gather them into her arms.

After she'd shed her winter gear, they followed her into the kitchen, where she performed the usual coming-home rituals of refilling food bowls and giving them fresh water. In her room, she unpacked her overnight suitcase and then got busy doing laundry and a few other mindless, necessary chores.

The knock came after she'd eaten a simple dinner of leftover chicken soup and a green salad.

Her heart might have skipped a beat, but her mind was a wall of grim determination when she pulled open the front door and found Ty standing there.

"Don't give me that look," he said. "You know we need to talk."

With a sigh of resignation, she let him in. "You want something to—"

"Nothing. Just to talk."

He took the green velvet easy chair, and she sat on the sofa. It got really awkward then. Neither of them seemed to know where to start.

Finally, she broke the aching silence. "Look. I know last night was, um, just between friends. I know that we didn't do anything but talk. And yet, I feel crappy about it. Partly because I started it. *I* knocked on *your* door. I just, well, you were right across the hall and I…"

He finished for her. "You couldn't stay away?"

She swallowed. Hard. And then answered honestly. "Yeah. I had this idea that we would hang out a little, talk for a while—"

"And that's exactly what we did."

"Yeah, right," she said with a heavy helping of sarcasm. "It was all so innocent and aboveboard. Except it wasn't, not really. There was a lot more going on between us than just hanging out. And that's why I feel that we're lying—to ourselves, to each other. To people we care about. But the lying isn't the worst of it."

"You're right. What we do in private is *our* business and no one else's."

"No, Ty. The real problem is that I need to stay away from you."

"No, you don't."

"Yes, I do. You don't want what I want and it can't go anywhere with us and, well, I'm just asking for trouble to keep seeking you out. Right now, we need to avoid each other for a *while*."

He scoffed. "Avoidance is not the answer."

"Oh, right. Because you have a better plan?"

"I do."

She knew then what he was up to. Did he ever quit? "Wait. Let me guess. It's the same old thing all over again. You want us to sneak around, to have some secret affair until you've had enough and you're over whatever this is between us. Then you actually imagine we'll be able to just go back to being Ty and Sadie, good buddies, like the hot, sexy part never happened at all." She shook her head. "I don't believe you sometimes. You're just too completely…predictable!" She didn't realize she was shouting until she stopped talking and the room suddenly echoed with silence.

He drew a slow, careful breath. "So, then. That's a no?"

"To being lovers for a while behind everybody's back? Absolutely. Hard no."

"Sadie, it's our business what we do in private."

"Yeah, you just go ahead and tell yourself that."

"You've got to see that this thing between us is not just going to go away all by itself."

"Well, then I don't know what to say to you about it. I'm not having a secret fling with you, I'm just not. I don't see sneaking around as the answer to anything."

"It's our business. It's not like we're cheating on anyone. We're both single and our private lives are our own."

"Translation. You don't want Nicole to know."

"God, no. That wouldn't be good for anyone."

"It doesn't matter how many times we go over this, we are not going to agree. We have to stop. We have to stay out of each other's way, at least for a while."

"No, we don't. We're friends. *Good* friends. Even if you don't want to take this where we both want it to go, we shouldn't have to give up our friendship. That's not right."

"Okay, I agree on that point. But what choice do we have? There's too much…heat now, between us. We just need to let things cool off a little, that's all."

The look on his face then? It just about undid her.

Because she knew how he felt. She felt it, too.

All of it.

The warmth in her chest whenever she thought of him. The little things that happened every day that she wanted to share with him. The thrill that zipped through her, electric and glorious, whenever she caught sight of him now.

She was at that point where she just wanted to tell Nicole that she and Ty were becoming more than friends. The point where she needed to get it all out in the open and deal with the consequences, so that whatever happened between her and Ty would have at least half a chance of not blowing up in their faces.

She went ahead and said it. "Even though I don't look forward to telling Nicole about us, I think we should."

He stared at her as though she'd just suggested they rob a bank. "You're not serious. You don't know how she can be."

"What do you mean, I don't know? I've known her all my life. Yes, she can be self-centered and overly dramatic, but she loves us both and she will eventually get past her own feelings and realize it isn't about her. And look at it this way. Really, you and I sharing a few hot kisses in Vegas shouldn't be an issue. We're both single. We did nothing wrong… I mean, Nic and Gavin are getting *married—your ex-wife and your good friend.* You don't seem to have an issue with that."

"Sadie, I don't know how to make this any clearer to you. None of us grew up with Gavin. He doesn't have all the baggage you, me and Nicole have to deal with. It's a completely different situation. Plus, Gavin doesn't make every little thing about him. Nicole, though. It's *always* about Nicole and you know it, too. So, no. Just no. Telling Nic is only asking for trouble, pure and simple."

"So we should sneak around like we're doing something shameful and wrong?"

"I didn't say that."

"Ty. It's what you meant. And sneaking around just doesn't work for me." She sank back against the sofa cushions. "What are we doing? This is going nowhere. You want some quick affair and I want an honest effort at a real relationship. It's not like I'm asking for a ring and a wedding and a baby. I only want a chance to see where this new thing between us could go."

He let out a low growl of pure frustration. "Come on, Sadie. Don't ask me for that. Don't ask me to lie to you."

"I'm not asking you to lie. Ever. I'm asking you to—"

"Change my mind about this? Uh-uh. That isn't going to happen. I want you. More than just about anything or anyone I've ever wanted. For right now. But I know myself and I'm honest about who I am. It's not going to last. I'm just not cut out for making it work long term."

"You have no faith in yourself."

"I'm realistic, that's all."

"Wrong. You're giving up without giving your heart a chance. I mean, I can live with trying and failing. What I can't live with is going into a love affair with you when you're dead certain that it's a losing battle. Beyond being honest with Nicole, I need at least a glimmer of hope for the future."

"Well, I don't want Nic to know, ever. And there is no future with me."

She should give up. How many times had they been over this? There really was nothing more to say.

And yet, she kept trying. "Ty, all I'm asking is why can't you be open to all the possibilities? Love is a beautiful thing. Yeah, maybe it won't work out for us. That happens. I get it. But we have a lot together, you and me. A real friendship. A solid foundation for more. And now, suddenly, we also have that magic thing, the heat. The desire. When I look at you, I don't know whether to grab you and drag you to my bedroom, or to ask you how your day went then tell you all about mine. I think we could have a lot together. I think we could have everything."

"No. Uh-uh. That's not going to happen. I'm sorry, Sadie. I can't be what you want. I can't—"

"Enough." She rose. Her legs felt kind of shaky, but she tried not to let him see that. "I understand. I do. And once again, we're right back where we started."

He sat with his elbows braced on his spread knees, staring up at her, his eyes full of hurt. "You want me to go."

"I do. And I want you to keep your distance from me, please."

"For how long?"

"Check back with me when you no longer want to get into my bed. If I'm over you by then, terrific. We can be friends again."

He accused, "You're just being vindictive."

"No. Like you, I'm being realistic."

He stood. "This isn't the answer."

She pressed her lips together and shook her head.

"All right," he muttered. "Have it your way. But, Sadie, I—"

"Please, Ty. Don't."

Either those words or the determined look on her face must have finally gotten through to him. A moment later, he was walking out the door. She locked it behind him. And then she wandered back to the great room, sank to the sofa and put her head in her hands.

Chapter Eight

The next day, Sadie, Nicole, Emily and the other three bridesmaids drove up to Sheridan for their final fittings.

The bridal shop owner served champagne to the grown-ups and offered sparkling cider for Emily. Nicole had cider, too, and they all tried on their dresses.

Nic was a vision in white lace. She'd gone traditional, with a fitted bodice, an illusion neckline and peekaboo lace sleeves. The skirt was a glorious confection of tulle and lace. They all applauded when she emerged from the dressing room.

The rest of them were wearing deep red velvet, each with a slightly different design. Sadie had chosen a sleeveless style with an open neckline, a shirred bodice and a flowing skirt with a thigh-high slit.

Emily glowed in her dress. It had an A-line circle skirt and fluttery sleeves. She giggled and twirled in front of the mirror, her pretty face a portrait of sheer delight.

"I look so grown-up!" she squealed, and then giggled some more. They all agreed that Em's dress was the prettiest of all—next to the bride's, of course.

After the fittings they went to Frackelton's right there on Main Street for lunch. The food was great and so was the lemon pomegranate sangria. Sadie had two of those. She laughed and chattered right along with everyone else and tried not to yearn for the man she couldn't have—and not to even think about how long it might be before she and Ty got their friendship back.

It could be never. Because right now it felt like she would never get over him. She'd end up dragging around, carrying a torch forever, a sad-sack singleton for the rest of her life.

Wouldn't that be funny in a depressing kind of way? Ty showing up at her door six months or a year from now, wearing a big, happy smile because he'd gotten over her and they could finally be friends again.

Except they couldn't. Because she still wanted him.

Yeah. Her friendship with Ty could be over already.

After lunch, she gave everyone a hug and waved them goodbye, then stopped in at Henry's in Sheridan to go over the ordering, approve the payroll and check the December schedule to make sure every shift was covered. She got home at six, climbed in bed at nine and barely slept a wink.

Nic called on Sunday afternoon. "Come on over. Have dinner with us."

She begged off. Somehow, seeing Nic made her all the more miserable. Nicole had it all. Sadie should be happy for her. And she was.

"One Minute" Survey

You get up to **FOUR books** <u>and</u> a Mystery Gift...

YOU pick your books – WE pay for everything.

You get up to FOUR new books and a Mystery Gift... absolutely FREE!

Total retail value: Over $20!

Dear Reader,

Your opinions are important to us. So if you'll participate in our fast and free "One Minute" Survey, YOU can pick up to four wonderful books that WE pay for when you try the Harlequin Reader Service!

As a leading publisher of women's fiction, we'd love to hear from you. That's why we promise to reward you for completing our survey.

IMPORTANT: Please complete the survey and return it. We'll send your Free Books and a Free Mystery Gift right away. And we pay for shipping and handling too! ← *We pay for EVERYTHING!*

Try **Harlequin® Special Edition** and get 2 books featuring comfort and strength in the support of loved ones and enjoying the journey no matter what life throws your way.

Try Harlequin® Heartwarming™ Larger-Print and get 2 books featuring uplifting stories where the bonds of friendship, family and community unite.

Or TRY BOTH!

Thank you again for participating in our "One Minute" Survey. It really takes just a minute (or less) to complete the survey... and your free books and gift will be well worth it!

If you continue with your subscription, you can look forward to curated monthly shipments of brand-new books from your selected series, always at a discount off the cover price! Plus you can cancel any time. So don't miss out, return your One Minute Survey today to get your Free books.

Pam Powers

"One Minute" Survey

GET YOUR FREE BOOKS AND A FREE GIFT!
✓ Complete this Survey ✓ Return this survey

1 Do you try to find time to read every day?
☐ YES ☐ NO

2 Do you prefer stories with happy endings?
☐ YES ☐ NO

3 Do you enjoy having books delivered to your home?
☐ YES ☐ NO

4 Do you share your favorite books with friends?
☐ YES ☐ NO

YES! I have completed the above "One Minute" Survey. Please send me my Free Books and a Free Mystery Gift (worth over $20 retail). I understand that I am under no obligation to buy anything, as explained on the back of this card.

☐ **Harlequin® Special Edition**
235/335 CTI G2AH

☐ **Harlequin Heartwarming® Larger-Print**
161/361 CTI G2AH

☐ **BOTH**
235/335 & 161/361
CTI G2AJ

FIRST NAME	LAST NAME

ADDRESS

APT.#	CITY

STATE/PROV.	ZIP/POSTAL CODE

EMAIL ☐ Please check this box if you would like to receive newsletters and promotional emails from Harlequin Enterprises ULC and its affiliates. You can unsubscribe anytime.

HSE/HW-1123-OM

❤ HARLEQUIN® Reader Service —Here's how it works:

Accepting your 2 free books and free gift (gift valued at approximately $10.00 retail) places you under no obligation to buy anything. You may keep the books and gift and return the shipping statement marked "cancel." If you do not cancel, approximately one month later we'll send you more books from the series you have chosen, and bill you at our low, subscribers-only discount price. Harlequin® Special Edition books consist of 6 books per month and cost $5.99 each in the U.S. or $6.74 each in Canada, a savings of at least 8% off the cover price. Harlequin® Heartwarming™ Larger-Print books consist of 4 books per month and cost just $6.74 each in the U.S. or $7.24 each in Canada, a savings of at least 16% off the cover price. It's quite a bargain! Shipping and handling is just 50¢ per book in the U.S. and $1.25 per book in Canada*. You may return any shipment at our expense and cancel at any time by contacting customer service — or you may continue to receive monthly shipments at our low, subscribers-only discount price plus shipping and handling.

▼ If offer card is missing write to: Harlequin Reader Service, P.O. Box 1341, Buffalo, NY 14240-8531 or visit www.ReaderService.com ▼

But she couldn't deny that she felt envious, too. Envious, and a little bit bitter that she couldn't even tell Nic what was bothering her because she'd promised Ty she wouldn't.

So yeah, she blew Nic off. Just for a little while, she promised herself. Right now, she needed space from both Ty and Nic.

She got through Monday and Tuesday without having to deal with either of them. Ty respected her wishes and skipped his usual breakfasts at Henry's. She was grateful to him for that—but at the same time, she couldn't help but glance toward the door every time the little bell there chimed. She didn't want to see him. But somehow, her hopeless heart had failed to get the memo on that.

Wednesday dragged by. She worked the breakfast shift in Medicine Creek as usual, split the rest of the day between Sheridan and Buffalo, and was back home by five. She'd just eaten half the giant meatball sub she'd brought from the Buffalo store when the doorbell rang.

It was Nic in her Realtor clothes—a slim wool skirt and blazer under a gorgeous red winter coat, with shiny black knee-high galoshes over her high heels. "Ty has the kids. I was on my way home and somehow my car just drove itself to your house."

So much for avoiding her best friend. Sadie put on a welcoming smile. "Tea? Or maybe some delicious sparkling cider."

"Cider, yes. I thought you'd never ask."

"I also have half a Henry's meatball sub."

"It's like you can read my mind."

Sadie ushered her in. Nicole removed the shiny boots and her shoes and took the slippers Sadie offered to keep her feet warm. They went straight to the kitchen, where Sadie heated up the other half of her sub and poured cider for Nic, wine for herself.

Nicole sat at the island and went right to work on the food. "So good, as always." She patted the stool beside her. "Sit. Tell me everything that's going on."

Sadie kept her cheerful expression in place as she hopped up beside her bestie. "Well, let's see." She fortified herself with a large gulp of wine. "I look amazing in my bridesmaid's dress."

"Oh, yes, you do. Best-looking maid of honor ever in the history of weddings."

They chatted about the final fitting and how great *all* the dresses looked. Nic said she'd closed a big real estate deal for Ty and his dad. "And I finally sold that gorgeous brick ranch-style house on Meadowlark Lane. The one with the daylight basement? It needs a lot of work, but it has good bones. The new owner loves it and plans to fix it up right, giving the living areas a more open look and renovating the big kitchen and all three baths."

Sadie congratulated her on both deals and reported that Henry's, Inc. would have the biggest-earning year so far. They toasted to their mutual success.

And then Nic asked, "So…you okay?"

"Oh, yeah. Fine. Why?"

"I don't know. You seemed kind of down when I called on Sunday."

Ty wants a fling with me, and he doesn't want you to know.

Just thinking the words made her cringe.

Maybe Ty was right that Nic never needed to know any of what had never really happened between her and

Ty. They'd kissed and they wanted each other and that was it. They weren't going there.

She admitted, "I get a little discouraged now and then."

"About the wonderful guy you haven't met yet?"

"Yeah. More or less."

Nicole ate a bite of her sub and dabbed at her lips with her napkin. "Ty tells me you're taking a break from dating."

Sadie sat up straighter on her stool. "He what?"

"I told Ty I'd met the perfect guy for you, and he said you'd told him that you were taking a break from meeting guys."

Okay, yeah. She had said that. And she *was* taking a break from men—or she had been.

But what gave Ty Bravo the right to speak for her on the subject of meeting guys?

Nic leaned close. "His name's Levi Hayes. *Dr.* Levi Hayes. He's in his midthirties, good-looking, about six-two, lean, but with broad shoulders. Dark hair and eyes. He's taking over Dr. Crandall's practice here in town."

Elroy Crandall had been a GP in Medicine Creek for as long as Sadie could remember. "Dr. Crandall's retiring?"

"That's right. And I just sold Dr. Levi Hayes the Meadowlark Lane house."

Sadie couldn't help but laugh. "So you're closing the house deal with him, and you suddenly just pipe up with, 'Now you've got your house, are you in the market for a special woman?'"

Nic gave her a playful slap on the arm. "I'm never that obvious. Give me some credit. Honestly, the way

I handled that conversation, it was just as natural as breathing. So beautifully smooth."

"Oh, was it?"

"Yes, it was." Nic poured herself another glass of cider. "Last week when I first showed him the house, the handsome and single Dr. Hayes asked about the best places in town to eat. Of course, I told him about Henry's and mentioned that my very best friend in the world, my sister in every way that matters, is one of the owners and also an entrepreneur who's opened two more Henry's in the past five years. I told him your name and said to say hi if he dropped in for breakfast Monday through Friday. Then this afternoon, when we found out that the offer we'd made on the house had been accepted, Dr. Hayes just casually mentioned that he'd been to Henry's yesterday and met you."

"What? I honestly don't remember him."

"He said that you wouldn't. It was busy. He said—his words—'I never got a chance to flirt with her.'"

Okay, she might be depressed over the situation with Ty, but Levi Hayes sounded interesting. "Oh, really?"

"Yeah. Really. He thinks you're 'very pretty' with 'a great sense of humor.' Those are direct quotes. He said he watched you joking around with your dad and the guys at the counter while the whole time you were filling coffee cups and clearing empty plates. It seems he's a big fan of the way you multitask."

Sadie sipped her wine and considered the idea of meeting Levi Hayes for coffee. Her heart said no, that only Ty would do. But she couldn't have Ty—except on his terms. And his terms simply weren't acceptable to her.

Nicole wasn't finished. "He's on Instagram. You can

see pictures." She whipped out her iPhone and brought up his profile. "Here."

Sadie took the phone and scrolled through Levi Hayes's feed. "He *is* good-looking. And he's got a great smile."

"Would I steer you wrong? He said he would love to call you—or to hear from you if that works better for you." Sadie handed Nic back her phone and Nic poked at it. "There." Sadie's phone buzzed from the end of the island where she'd left it when she got home. "I texted you his number. Call the guy."

"I'll think about it."

"A man like that isn't going to stay single for long. Not in this town."

"Nic. I said I would think about it."

"Time's a-wastin'."

Sadie groaned. "Enough."

Nicole heaved a dramatic sigh. "Well, I've done what I can. The rest is up to you."

Sadie neither saw nor heard from Ty on Thursday or Friday. Which was exactly what she wanted, she reminded herself. They needed to give each other a wide berth, at least for a while.

Maybe indefinitely.

She didn't call the new doctor in town. But on Friday, he came in for breakfast. She recognized him immediately from his Instagram feed. He had an air of authority, but he seemed somehow approachable, too.

When she poured his coffee, he said, "How are you, Sadie?" He could have simply read her name off her name tag. But after talking to Nic, she knew better.

"Doing well, Levi. How about you?"

He grinned then, a nice grin—playful and yet a little bit shy. "Your friend Nicole told you about me."

"Yes, she did. She gave me your number."

He winced. "You never called. I can't believe I struck out before you even really met me."

Okay, she liked him. His smile was even better in person. She appreciated a man who could be both self-assured and down-to-earth. And the man she longed for wasn't available. She needed to get on with her life. "Did I say I'd decided not to call?"

He held her gaze. "No. You didn't."

She pulled her phone from her pocket and texted him, one-handed, because she still had the coffeepot in her other hand. Call me.

His smartwatch chimed. He looked down at it. "I will," he said. "Tonight."

Levi did call that night. They talked a little. It was nice. Comfortable. The guy would do well as a GP in Medicine Creek. There was something so easy and open about him.

He asked her out. They settled on the Stagecoach Grill at seven.

When she got there right on time, Levi was already seated at a nice corner table. They ordered wine and appetizers. He was fun and easy to talk to. Things were going great.

Until their server appeared with the main course. "Here we go." The server set their meals in front of them. "Anything else I can get you right now?"

Levi sent her a questioning look.

"No, this is perfect." Sadie smiled up at the woman. "Thank you."

From that angle she had a clear view of the bar on

the far side of the dining room. The woman nodded. "Enjoy." She turned away.

Sadie should have shifted her focus to Levi—or maybe her dinner. But instead, she just sat there, staring at the bar. Because Ty was there with some older guy in a big black hat—no doubt schmoozing, in the process of working out some land or investment deal.

Black Hat was talking.

But Ty wasn't listening. He stared right at Sadie, a scowl on that beautiful mouth of his.

Her stomach had somehow tilted. The wine and the appetizer churned.

"You all right, Sadie?" Levi sounded worried.

That snapped her out of her trance, at least. She tore her gaze away from the man who only wanted her for a hot, sexy weekend—two, if she got extra lucky— and focused on the good guy across from her. "Sorry. I thought I saw someone I knew. I was wrong."

For the rest of the meal, she never once glanced toward the bar. Whatever Ty was doing over there, she didn't want to know. He could glower and seethe to his heart's content. She refused to care.

When the check came, she pounced on it. "You can get it next time," she promised.

Levi's smile seemed a bit forced now. Apparently, she was doing a lousy job of covering her true emotions, because she could see in Levi's eyes that he knew as well as she did there would be no next time.

Just the sight of Ty had done it. She was so far from over him. And using Levi to distract herself from her true feelings just felt wrong.

They said good-night on the sidewalk outside the Grill.

"Are you going to be all right?" he asked.

What could she say? "Of course."

"Call me," he said. "Anytime."

She looked up into his handsome face and thought that she would like to be his friend, at least. But it all felt too complicated right now, her mind and heart fully occupied with the man she couldn't have. "I will." It wasn't a lie. Not exactly. Maybe she would call him, but not anytime soon.

A light snow was falling. She watched him walk away. When he turned the next corner, she blinked and looked around, feeling oddly lost, completely alone.

There was a brightly lit tree just inside the front window of the Grill, all festive and bright. The lampposts up and down the street were decked out for the holidays with green garland, red bows and twinkle lights. It was only five blocks to her house, and she'd left her Tahoe at home. Pulling up the hood of her warm winter coat, she started walking.

When she turned the corner onto her street, she spotted Ty's big black Escalade parked under the streetlight beside her front walk and a thunderbolt of pure fury shot through her. She walked faster, stomping through the thin layer of new snow, reaching her place in less than a minute. Ty sat on the porch in one of the two wooden rockers she'd found at a yard sale and refinished herself.

Throwing back her hood, she marched up the steps and straight to him. He rose to face her, his eyes as bleak as the set of his perfect mouth. "Where's your date?"

She stopped two feet away from the toes of his fancy boots. "You leave my date out of this."

But he didn't leave Levi out of it. "I heard he's bought

out Dr. Crandall's practice and everybody likes him. Nic sold him a house."

"Oh, you've been busy, haven't you, asking around about Levi? Find out anything shocking?"

He tipped his head down. Now the porch light fell on the brim of his hat, casting the sculpted planes of his face into shadow. "Look. I was just…checking the guy out, making sure he's okay. What's wrong with that?"

"What is going on with you? What are you doing here?"

He pushed back the sides of his heavy shearling coat and stuck his hands in his pockets. "Hell if I know."

"This is not cool."

"Okay, look." He swiped off his hat. "I'm sorry. You're right. I shouldn't have come. I've got no business being here."

"At least we agree on that much. You need to go. Now."

He was fiddling with the brim of his hat. "I just hate this," he muttered. "I miss you, damn it."

Her heart did the melty thing—which was totally unacceptable. "You haven't said a single word that changes anything. I understand that the only long-term relationship you've ever had was a mess, full of Nic's confusion and drama and your bitterness that you felt you had to get married when you weren't even old enough to legally buy beer. I get that you're afraid to try again. You have every right *not* to try again. But that means you need to leave me alone. Please."

"Just tell me. When will this be over? When can we be what we used to be?"

Never. We know too much now. "I don't know how to answer that," she lied.

"My life without you, I don't like it. You're my best friend. There is no other you."

Then take a flier, give us a chance.

She longed to say it. She could taste the words on her tongue, a little bitter yet somehow full of hope.

But a girl can only put herself out there so many times and be rejected before she finally learns that sometimes it's just better to keep her mouth shut.

"Good night, Ty."

At least he didn't try to follow when she let herself in the front door and locked it behind her.

Her two favorite furballs were waiting, sitting side by side four feet from the door, their tails curled around their front paws, mirroring each other. She went to them and gathered them close as she heard Ty's Cadillac start up and drive away.

The next day was the first Saturday in December. In her family, they always called it Decoration Day. They let their employees run the restaurants and together they decorated her house and the house where she'd grown up.

On Sunday before dawn, they went to work on the diners, putting up small trees by the POS and cash registers, hanging garland and shiny ornaments in the windows. They draped strings of lights along the windowsills and from the ceiling, too.

And they always saved the hometown store for last. Nic, Gavin and the kids joined them there at eleven thirty. Sadie and her mom put out finger food for them in one of the booths. They snacked on chicken nuggets and fries as they put up an eight-foot tree near the door. It was fun, a family tradition Sadie had been part of for as long as she could remember. And this year, it helped her keep her mind off the man she couldn't have.

Nic seemed wound up pretty tightly that day. There were so many last-minute details to pull together for the wedding next weekend. She kept calling the wedding planner in Breckinridge, which was a little extreme. It was Sunday, after all. Shouldn't the poor woman be enjoying a day off?

When Nic let the wedding planner off the phone for the fourth time that afternoon, Sadie grabbed her hand.

Nic scowled at her. "What now?"

"Come with me." Sadie pulled her through the swinging doors into the kitchen.

"Sade. Where are you taking me?"

"This way." She moved on into the storeroom, where floor-to-ceiling shelves were stocked with everything from canned goods to paper products and cleaning supplies. The light popped on automatically when they entered.

"Oh, wonderful," Nic sneered. "The storage room. I love it here."

"This way." Sadie shut the door and led Nic on to the second row of open shelving. "Okay."

Nic pulled her hand free of Sadie's grip. "Okay, what?"

"I can see that you're stressed. Let me help. Whatever you need me to do, just say it. I'll get it done. Stop torturing the poor wedding planner. It's Sunday, you know? She deserves a day off."

"First of all," Nic said briskly, "I'm no more stressed than usual. And for your information, the wedding planner is working this Sunday. She happens to be in her office today at the resort." Nic sighed then. "You really don't have to worry."

"But I do worry."

"Come here." She pulled Sadie in for a hug, then took her by the shoulders and announced, "I promise, we're good. I've got it all under control."

"You're sure?"

"You know me, I want everything perfect. But I've had enough therapy to understand that perfection is not the goal. I might look frazzled, but I'm okay."

"I still want to take some of the burden off your shoulders."

"I know you do. And if it gets so bad that I can't handle it, I promise to take advantage of you."

"You'd better."

Nic glanced up at the floor-to-ceiling shelves on either side of them. "And now we're back here with only canned peaches and take-out containers to eavesdrop on what we say, how's it going with Dr. Hayes? Rumor has it the two of you were spotted looking cozy at the Stagecoach Grill Friday night…"

As Sadie tried to decide how much to say about what had happened with Levi, Nicole groaned. "I know that look. And I don't get it. He's hot and sweet with a great sense of humor. And he's a doctor for crying out loud. What went wrong?"

"You're right. He's a terrific guy. I really like him."

"So…?"

"It's just, well, the timing is bad." It was the truth. As far as it went.

"The timing…?"

"Yes. Before you gave me his number, I'd already decided to take a break from all that, anyway."

Now Nic braced her fists on her hips and scoffed. "All what?"

"You know, the apps, getting set up by all the nice ladies in town, going out with strangers. I'm tired, Nic. I really am. For a while at least, I want a break."

Nicole shook her head. "You realize you won't find the guy for you by taking a break from guys."

"I know. Believe me. And give me some credit. It's not like I'm a slacker on the find-a-man front."

Nic didn't even try to argue that point. "I know you're not."

Sadie had been looking for years. In high school, she'd hung out, had dates. And then kind of settled down with Kevin Purdy. When that was over, there was Paul.

"Remember Paul?" Sadie asked.

"Of course. You were crazy about Paul."

"Yeah." Paul was her first. She and Kevin had never gotten quite that far.

Nic frowned. "Paul moved to Seattle, right?"

"Right." Sadie had met Paul Mendoza at community college up in Sheridan. They'd dated for a couple of years. For the first six months of that time, she'd *known* Paul was the one. During the holidays of their freshman year, they'd become lovers. She was over the moon for him.

It had taken another year and a half for her to finally face the fact that she and Paul were not a lifetime match. In the spring of her second and final year at Sheridan College, she'd turned down Paul's marriage proposal. He moved to Washington State and Sadie went to work building her chain of diners.

Nic said, "And Reggie Carver. He was a ball of fire."

"Yes, he was." Sadie had met Reggie three years after it ended with Paul. Reggie owned an ATV and motorcycle dealership down in Buffalo. Reggie liked sports—all sports. They went ATVing. They rode dirt bikes and snowmobiles. They watched every Cowboys game and drove out of state more than once to cheer the team on from the stands. Reggie loved hockey, too. Didn't matter which teams were playing. They watched the games live whenever possible, and they had a ball.

But…

After a year with Reggie, she'd started to wish that they could maybe cuddle up by the fire and watch a movie now and then. Or go out to dinner and then walk home in the twilight, holding hands.

And she really wanted a man she could talk to, not an overgrown kid who couldn't wait to get out in the woods with a three-wheeler between his legs.

By then, she and Ty had gotten close—just as friends, of course. She realized she was spending a lot more time talking with Ty than she ever had with Reggie. Or Paul, for that matter.

When Reggie said he wanted his freedom, she felt nothing but relief. They'd ended it and she'd gotten serious in her hunt for that special man.

How many guys had she met for dinner at Arlington's or drinks at the Grill? A bunch. But she'd yet to meet a single man she wanted to spend more than a few evenings with—other than Ty.

Sadie loved hanging out with him. Talking. Laughing. Razzing each other, advising each other on work, on life in general.

Whenever she had a problem, she couldn't wait to share it with Ty, to get his take on it.

Now she wanted to do more than talk and laugh and work out life's problems with him. She wanted to hold hands, to cuddle. To sleep with him—fully clothed or otherwise.

Life was so unfair. She had it bad for Ty and he seemed to feel the same about her. Yet he refused to give in and love her. And since those sad moments on her front porch Friday night, she couldn't stop second-guessing her choice not to go ahead and say yes to that fling he wanted to share with her.

Because what if Ty was *it* for her?

What if he truly was her "one"—the only one for her?

If so, she had this awful, sinking feeling that she was never going to get the life she dreamed of. Not with some guy she hadn't even met yet.

And not with Ty, either. Because Ty couldn't get past all the leftover crap in his head from his unhappy marriage.

"What's so fascinating about that particular can of tomatoes?" Nic asked wryly.

Sadie realized that she was, indeed, staring blindly at a ninety-ounce can of whole, peeled plum tomatoes. "I was just, um, taking a stroll down memory lane, re-calling the, er, high points of my long and uninspired dating history."

"Oh, Sade. You only have to keep trying. Your guy will come along."

"Maybe." She put her arm around her lifelong friend. "But right now, please don't set me up with anyone else. I honestly am taking a break from men—and we need to get back on the job. All that garland isn't going to hang itself."

"You're right," Nicole agreed. "And Ty should be here any minute to pick up the kids."

"Oh, really?" Sadie felt like a complete faker as she tried to sound casual.

"Yeah. He's taking them out to the ranch to visit Em's horse. And then they'll stay at his place tonight—and maybe for the rest of the week. He's been great, offering to take them if I need a break, what with the wedding coming up so fast."

"Well, that's good."

Nic looked at her sharply. "Are you okay?"

"Uh, yeah. I just…oh, I don't know." She was babbling. She needed to stop. "I just didn't realize he was coming, that's all."

"What's wrong?"

Sadie put on her most innocent expression. "Wrong? Nothing. Nothing at all…"

Nicole didn't look the least convinced. "You sure?"

"Absolutely."

With a shrug, Nicole whirled on her heel and pushed through the swinging doors out to the front of the diner. Sadie was two steps behind her. On the other side of the doors, Ty stood on a ladder tacking a giant, sparkly swag of pre-lit garland over the service window.

Miranda, the server, scooted around him to get out on the floor. "Sorry," she said way too breathlessly, looking up at Ty as though she wouldn't mind at all if he fell on her.

Sadie had always liked Miranda, who worked flexible hours and got along with just about everyone. As of now, though, she was having second thoughts about the easygoing, good-natured server. Did she have to be so obvious, the way she fawned over Ty?

"That looks great, Ty," Miranda said with over-the-top enthusiasm.

Sadie reminded herself not to think bitchy thoughts about one of Henry's most likable and dependable employees. Miranda had done nothing wrong. And who could blame her for appreciating the sight of Ty up on a ladder tacking up garland, looking like you could count on him for any little job that might need doing around the place.

As he glanced over his shoulder to return Miranda's smile, he caught sight of Sadie gaping at him from just outside the swinging doors and the grin dropped right off his face.

Without so much as a nod of acknowledgment, he returned to the job at hand.

Ty didn't even want to see Sadie.

The sight of her got him all knotted up inside. She wouldn't let him show her a good time so they could get this sex thing between them out of the way and restore their friendship. And then she got pissed at him when he stopped by her house to check on her after her dinner date with the doctor.

What the hell were friends for if not to look out for each other? Yeah, it had bugged him to no end to see her having such a good time at the Grill with a man she'd just met—after she'd told him right to his face that she was taking a break from dating random guys.

Not that it was any of his concern who she dated. Or if she dated at all.

Not anymore, anyway. Especially not after Friday night and her announcement that they needed to stay away from each other for some lengthy but unspecified period of time.

He'd lain awake until dawn that night stewing about

that, about how, after all these years, after the way they'd come to count on each other to work out a problem, to be there when one of them needed to talk, to always offer the other a helping hand, to cheer the other up when things weren't going so well...

Just like that, she was willing to throw their friendship out the window.

He shouldn't be here. After Friday night, he'd planned to steer clear of Henry's indefinitely.

Instead, when Nic suggested he drop on by the diner to pick up the kids, he'd jumped at the suggestion. Why?

Because he couldn't get Sadie off his mind. He couldn't stop hoping that she'd either decide to have a secret fling with him and give them both a break from all this sexual frustration—or figure out a way that they could somehow skip right on past the sex thing and go back to being just friends again.

Either would work fine for him.

But her idea of turning their backs on each other only made him want to bust up the place.

Was he being unfair and unreasonable about their situation?

Damn straight.

He didn't know what to do about it and that aggravated him even more.

But he was here. Might as well make himself useful.

He helped out for a while hanging stuff on the walls and stringing twinkle lights. The whole time he managed to avoid making eye contact with Sadie again.

Finally, he told the kids they had to go. They bundled up in their coats and mittens and headed for the ranch.

Back at his house that night with Drew and Emily

tucked in bed, he got out his phone and scrolled through his contacts. In five days, he would board a plane to Colorado for Nic and Gavin's wedding. He could steer clear of Sadie until then, but next weekend was going to be his definition of hell. She would be unavoidable— the maid of honor to his best man.

He needed a distraction, something to take his mind off the woman he couldn't have.

Maybe he should call someone friendly and sexy and fun. He'd told Nic he'd take the kids all week, but she and Gavin would be heading for their tropical honeymoon straight from Colorado. They wouldn't get back home until Christmas Eve. Nic would want time with Drew and Em before the honeymoon. He felt reasonably certain that he would have at least a day or two for himself this week.

Bringing up his contacts, he started scrolling the names and numbers of women he'd spent time with—in LA, in San Francisco. In Dallas or Seattle. They were all fun and easy on the eyes. He could just start reaching out, find a nice woman who wanted to join him for a little getaway.

A day or two with someone sweet and willing should help him move past his obsession with Sadie, right?

At the very least, it would take the edge off all this… wanting. This feeling that something important was missing. That everything was empty. Joyless. Wrong.

He reached the last name in his contacts. And then he started at the top and scrolled through again.

But he never once tried to call anyone. The more he thought about doing that, the more his stomach churned.

He didn't want just any nice, pretty woman.

He wanted the one with the green eyes and the smart mouth. The one he couldn't stop thinking about lately.

The one who'd asked him to please keep his distance from her.

Chapter Nine

The nonstop Friday morning flight from Sheridan to Denver took an hour and a half. Like everyone in the wedding party, Sadie had booked her flight months ago. They all flew out on the same plane.

Including the man Sadie was currently avoiding.

She'd just stuck her carry-on in the compartment overhead and settled into her seat when he appeared at the top of the aisle looking impossibly handsome in a blue wool shirt and his usual heavy shearling coat. Of course, she was staring right at him when he spotted her. There was a long, heated moment. Her breath caught in her chest as her heart lifted—and then sank.

They both looked away at the same time. He stopped three rows in front of her, in first class, of course. Astrid Chen, who had the seat beside her, leaned close and whispered, "What is it about Ty Bravo? Every time I set eyes on him, I think about breaking my celibacy streak. I swear to you, Sadie. If he wasn't Nicole's ex…" Astrid flopped back in her own seat with a drawn-out sigh. "I mean, we all know that Nicole is so over Ty. But still, that could get messy, right?"

"Right," Sadie replied grimly, hoping Astrid would leave it at that. Her wish came true. Astrid said no more on the subject of Ty and his celibacy-shattering sexual magnetism.

Vans and rental cars waited at the Denver airport to take them to the rustic, charming Arrowleaf Lodge overlooking the town of Breckenridge and its famous ski resort. Nic and Gavin had booked a limo with driver. Emily and Drew were riding along with them. Sadie's dad, who would give the bride away, had rented an SUV for him and her mom, and Sadie, too. After stopping off at a Denver liquor store, they reached the Lodge two and a half hours later. It was gorgeous, with panoramic views of the ski resort's five peaks and of the pretty town of Breckenridge below.

By then it was after two. Sadie checked into her room and put the champagne and sparkling cider she'd bought in the minifridge to chill. She ordered a snack tray to be delivered to her room that evening, and then headed for the rehearsal, where she tried not to make eye contact with the best man as the wedding planner put them through their paces.

At the rehearsal dinner, Nic introduced her to Gavin's family—his mom and dad, his sister and her husband, and his grandmother, Edith. They were very much like Gavin, low-key and laidback. Gavin, Sr. gave a great little speech about how if his only son just *had* to leave

Texas, at least he'd found himself a beautiful bride up there in the wilds of Wyoming.

"And we've been waiting too long for a grandson and granddaughter." Gavin's dad winked at Drew and then at Emily. "I'm thinking these two will do just fine."

Next, Gavin got up to thank the best man and the ring bearer. He gave Drew a ring-bearer security badge with his name on it, a cool pair of black-framed sunglasses, a Ring Security briefcase and hat. As for Ty, Gavin presented him with a gorgeous pair of monogrammed cuff links and tie clip to match.

It was after nine when the dinner broke up. Sadie's dad and mom took over with Drew and Emily for the night. Gavin had his family to visit with. Maybe Ty would hang out with them, too.

Not that it was any of Sadie's concern where or how Ty spent the night before the wedding.

Nicole gathered up the gift bags she'd stashed under the table and caught Sadie's eye. "Your suite?"

She nodded. "Let's go."

Off they went—Nic and Sadie, Erin, Astrid and Cindy, too.

Once they were all in Sadie's suite, she broke out the champagne, the bottle of sparkling cider and the plastic champagne glasses she'd packed in her suitcase. She called down to the kitchen to have the snack tray sent up.

The three other bridesmaids got in a huddle. When they broke apart, they excused themselves. "We'll be right back!" Astrid promised.

When the door closed behind them, Nic let out a screech and grabbed Sadie in a hug. "I can't believe it's finally happening."

Sadie held her away to look at her beautiful face. "You are positively glowing."

Nic laughed. "I'm so happy, Sade—did you like Gavin's family? They're nice, huh?"

"Very—and how's Emily doing?"

"Well, she started in on me to let her come with the rest of the bridesmaids tonight, but Moma was ready for that." *Mōma*, a combination of Mona and Momma, was Nic's special name for Sadie's mom, who'd been a mother to her since they lost Brenda all those years ago. "Moma promised they would watch *The Black Stallion*, which both Em and Drew were happy about. So I gave Em her bridesmaid's gift, and she went off to eat too much junk food and watch a horse movie with her brother and the grandparents."

"Perfect." Sadie's grin melted away as she noticed that Nic's eyes were suddenly misty. "Hey…" Sadie gathered her into another hug. "You okay?"

Nic nodded. "Sometimes I want to pinch myself. All those years with Ty, things not really working out between us, you know?"

Sadie swallowed down the lump in her throat. "I remember."

"I thought so much had passed me by. But here I am, with the man of my dreams, two beautiful, healthy, happy children and the best friend ever in the whole wide world."

"I try." Sadie hugged her again. She was happy for Nic, she truly was.

They heard giggling out in the hallway. Sadie let in the three bridesmaids, who had a big bag of extra snacks to go with the snack tray Sadie had ordered. As the three eager women piled in the door, the room service guy appeared. Sadie tipped him and took the tray.

They sat in the suite's living area, drinking champagne and cider, munching an endless array of snacks as Nic gave sweet speeches thanking them for being her attendants.

The bridesmaids' goody bags were perfect, packed full with aromatherapy shower steamers, Christmas-themed long johns and heavy red socks. And there was more—a customized silk sleep mask, a box of Sleepyhead Tea and a white noise machine.

"I tried to think of everything," Nic said. "Including a way to block out any noisy people out in the hallway. I want you all fresh and rested for tomorrow." They piled on to hug her and remind her how wonderful she was.

Seeing her so happy made Sadie happy, too. Those envious feelings she felt guilty about lately just melted away. Nic had made it through a difficult childhood and an unhappy marriage to finally claim a life she loved. About time she had everything she'd always dreamed of.

The bridesmaids' party broke up around ten thirty. After extra hugs and more laughter, they headed off to their own rooms.

Sadie washed her face, brushed her teeth and put on her new Christmas long johns, which were printed with sprigs of holly and Christmas bells. She'd just climbed into bed, turned on the white noise machine and donned her monogrammed sleep mask when the tap came at the door.

Ty. She just knew it would be him, breaking their agreement all over again, showing up at her door to tempt her.

But still, her silly heart pounded faster as she pushed the sleep mask up onto her forehead and marched over there. A glance through the peephole confirmed her suspicion.

Resting her head against the door, she ordered her heart to slow the heck down.

Ty's voice, pitched low, reached her from the other side of the door. "Come on, Sadie. Let me in…"

Nicole was on another floor. But Sadie's parents and the kids were just down the hall. For all Sadie knew, the other bridesmaids could be on this floor, too. The last thing she needed was for one of them to spot Ty at her door in the middle of the night—okay, fine. It was only 10:45. But still…

"Sadie…"

She slapped back the security bar and yanked the door wide. "What?"

Those blue eyes made a slow pass from her head to her stocking feet and back again. "Let me in."

"Fine." She grabbed his wrist and pulled him into the suite, pushing the door shut as soon as he cleared the threshold. Turning to face him in the small entry-way, she folded her arms across her middle. "And you're here because…?"

"I miss you." He looked her up and down again, caus-ing all manner of havoc inside her.

She'd missed him, too. A lot.

Not that missing him changed anything. She needed to firmly remind him that he'd agreed to stay away from her. And then she needed to send him on his way.

But she didn't.

As the seconds ticked by and they stood there, star-ing at each other, the thousand and one reasons she should deny her desire for him seemed suddenly flimsy and without substance. He annihilated her resistance by simply standing in front of her looking like everything she longed for but couldn't have.

She glared at him harder in a doomed attempt to resist him.

He said, "Cute pj's."

"Thank you."

He took the sleep mask off her forehead. "This even has your name on it."

She took it from him and hooked it on the dead bolt lock above the door handle. "Bridesmaid's gifts—and anyone could've seen you at my door."

"So what? We're both single and past the age of consent. Not to mention we're friends, remember? Or at least, we used to be." His gaze ran over her, exciting her. "But now you just want me to leave you alone."

"Don't look at me like I've hurt you, Ty."

"But you have."

"I'm just trying to make the right choices, do the right thing for me, you know?"

He moved a fraction closer, crowding her in the limited space. "I know. And I don't blame you. I don't like your damn choices, but I do understand them. I know how you are, and I know what you want. I also know I'm not the one for you." His voice was almost a whisper. It curled around her like smoke as his wonderful, clean scent taunted her, tempting her to go where she shouldn't.

"You have to…" *Go*, she reminded herself. *The last word in that sentence is* go.

But she didn't say it. She *couldn't* say it. Not right now, not when she wanted him so much, not when he was standing in front of her in that blue shirt that made his eyes look like the wide Wyoming sky in high summer.

She was tempted.

So tempted.

To take what he offered, to have at least a little of what she yearned for—the two of them, together, just one time. Or two.

Their friendship was blown all to hell anyway at this point. Ruined by this impossible firestorm of wanting.

As for her duty to Nic, well, the more she considered that duty, the more she wondered why, exactly, Nic ever had to know? Okay, to sleep with Ty and not tell Nic reeked of dishonesty—dishonesty to her lifelong best friend, the true sister of her heart. But Ty wasn't Nic's anymore and Nic really was over him.

When she looked at the situation that way, she had no trouble with the concept of keeping a fling with Ty to herself.

Because why shouldn't she at least have what he was willing to give her? Why shouldn't she have him right now, when he was free and she was, too, when neither of them owed explanations to anyone else.

Yeah, she would suffer for it later, no doubt about that.

But she was suffering now, feeling achy and bitter, resentful and so sad. Why push away what she *could* have with him? Even if it would be settling, to take less than what her heart demanded.

Settling for being with him now seemed a whole lot better than staying strong and having nothing. Plus, if she sent him away now, where would she put all this pent-up longing?

She'd been waiting years for her man to come along. And not just waiting, but actively seeking him in every way possible. How many friends and acquaintances had she asked to set her up?

Who knew? She didn't.

How many boring coffee dates had she accepted, where she knew the guy wasn't the one, but she went out later with him, anyway. How many dinners out had she ended up sitting through, though she'd realized in the first ten minutes that she and the stranger across from her were just wasting their time?

She was like some old romantic song played on repeat, but somehow never getting to the part where the right man showed up and loved her.

"Don't kick me out, Sadie. I keep thinking about Thanksgiving night, about you and me in the bunkhouse, just hanging out, in bed with all our clothes on. I could get behind that tonight, I really could." Ty dared to move even closer. Now she had her back to the wall, and he was right there, her breasts brushing his chest, her eyes locked on his.

He bent his head—but not to kiss her. His forehead touched hers. It felt good. It felt right, their heads together, his breath warm on her cheek as he whispered, "I don't know what this is. I keep trying to get past it. To put it behind me so we can have what we used to have."

Well, now that was bull. "You do know what this is."

"No."

"Yeah, you do. But let's not argue about it."

His hands, warm and firm and surprisingly soothing, briefly closed around her upper arms. A moment later, he let go, but only to brush his palms slowly up to her shoulders—and then back down again.

Through the soft fabric of her pajama top, the light touch felt like heaven, like he surrounded her, all heat and strength. She loved that, just the feel of him, right up against her, barely touching her, but so completely *here*.

Her breath came in shallow, hungry little bursts.

It was so good, just her and Ty, alone together behind a shut door with no one waiting for them on the other side.

She rested a hand on his chest. His heart pounded deep and hard, like it wanted to get out, get closer to her.

The thought made her smile. She slid her palm upward to his rocklike shoulder. Keeping her eyes locked with his, she wrapped her hand around the back of his neck. "I've never had a fling, Ty. Never had an affair I knew would end. Never had a one-night stand. I've only been with two guys."

"Paul and Reggie," he said gruffly, like just the thought of them annoyed him to no end. "I remember."

"I went into those relationships believing they would last—or at least, hoping that they would."

He closed his eyes and breathed in carefully through his nose, letting the air out the same way. But he didn't say a word.

Smart man.

She laid out her terms. "So, then, here's the deal. Nobody will know. It will be our secret, yours and mine, for tonight, and then tomorrow night, that's all."

His big body tensed. "No. Hold on just a—"

"Shh." She tightened her grip around his neck. Lifting on tiptoe, she pressed her lips lightly to his. They felt so good, his lips, hot, fleshy. She wanted to bite them. "Two nights." She kissed the words onto those bitable lips. "We cut it clean when we go back home."

"But what if that's not enough? What if we find out we want more?"

A thrill zipped through her, sharp and sweet. That he doubted two nights with her would do it for him.

Good. Let him miss her again when they got back home.

She would certainly miss him. "That's what I'm offering. Two nights. Or not. Stay here in this room with me tonight. Or go."

He lifted a hand and pressed it to the side of her face. The roughness of his big palm against her cheek felt so good, so exactly right. "Tonight, *and* tomorrow night," he clarified.

"That's what I said."

"But when we get back home, I want us to be friends again."

"Haven't you had enough flings to know that you're not supposed to be thinking of what happens after? Even I know that, and this is my first. All you need to decide right now is yes or no to tonight and tomorrow night."

His eyes burned her in the most arousing way. "Yes." He bent close again. His mouth touched hers—and opened.

A sound escaped her. Gleeful. Hungry.

"Sadie…" He said her name against her lips in a lovely, rough growl.

She wrapped both arms around his neck and yanked him tight against her as those big hands of his glided downward to clasp the twin curves of her bottom. Grabbing hold and lifting her, he guided her legs around his waist.

It felt so good to have him, hard and ready, right there where she longed for him.

"Bed," she said, between hot, endless kisses. He hoisted her higher and started walking. She laughed a little into the kiss.

"What's funny?" he demanded, pulling away enough to frown at her.

She tightened her arms around his neck and beamed up at him. "I just can't believe we're actually doing this."

He walked faster, skirting the couch and an end table, headed for the open bedroom door. "Please don't even think about calling a halt."

"No worries." She sighed as she pressed her lips to the chiseled edge of his jaw. "I'm in. I won't back out on you."

"That's what I needed to hear." He took her mouth again. She lost herself in his kiss.

When he got to the bed, he turned and sat down on it. Now she was in his lap, arms and legs still twined around him, kissing him for all she was worth as he went to work getting her out of her long johns.

"You are really good at this," she observed, as he whipped her pajama top off over her head.

"Not wasting a moment," he muttered against her skin as he caught her bare nipple between his teeth.

Tingles shot through her, arrowing out from the point of contact, zipping downward to loosen her core. She shivered in pleasure, melting inside.

As she moaned in delight, he moved to her other breast and toyed with it, too. Cradling his golden head close, she marveled at how good it felt, how completely natural—the two of them on this big bed, about to do things she'd only recently even let herself imagine she might ever do with him.

Still holding his head against her breast with one hand, she eased the other between them and managed to undo two of his shirt buttons. He got the message and helped her, getting hold of the fabric on either side, tugging to untuck it from his belt. He left her breast to claim her lips again. She sank into another beautiful, endless kiss.

And then he was grabbing her bare shoulders, holding her away, his eyes blazing into hers. "Stand up."

She blinked at him. "Huh?" He took hold of her waist and lifted her until she scrambled upright and stood above him on the bed, one stocking foot on either side of his lean hips as he hooked his fingers under the elastic of her pajama bottoms and dragged them down. With her legs spread wide, they didn't get far.

Laughing, she let her knees buckle.

He caught her. Pushing her gently down to lie on the bed, he dispensed with her pajama pants and red socks.

Then he sat back on his knees and looked at her, stretched out in front of him, naked as the day she was born. "So pretty…" How could two little words hold so much tenderness? He trailed a finger down the center of her, stirring shivers as he went.

A soft moan escaped her, but then she knocked his hand away.

He gave her a manly pout. "Be nice, Sadie."

She gazed up at him looming above her. He still had on all his clothes, and she suddenly felt way too naked. "Take off your shirt."

Swiftly, he undid the rest of the buttons, including the ones at his cuffs. She watched as he shrugged the shirt off his shoulders and dropped it over the far side of the bed. He looked so good, his body hard and nicely cut. A light dusting of bronze-colored hair formed a T across his broad chest and down over his six-pack, disappearing beneath his silver belt buckle.

"Take everything off," she said, her voice calm and even, though butterflies danced in her belly and her heart knocked hard and fast against the cage of her chest.

He slid off the bed and reached into a pocket of his dress jeans, coming out with a handful of little foil packets, which he set on the night table at the head of the bed.

She sat up. "You came to my door planning to have sex with me?"

He didn't look the least repentant. "A man can't live without hope, Sadie."

She eyed the pile. "That's a lot of hope. How many of those things did you bring?"

"Enough." He dropped to the edge of the bed, pulled off one of his fancy tooled boots and the sock beneath it. "At least, I *hope* I brought enough..." He had the nerve to wink at her as he yanked off his other boot. Barefoot now, he stood and took off his pants. Stark naked, he climbed back on the bed.

Of course, he looked amazing without a stitch on— all broad and strong and muscular. He was a big guy.

Everywhere.

Nervous all over again, she drew in a shaky breath.

Sex. Sometimes it seemed way too nerve-racking to be worth the effort.

"Uh-uh," said Ty. "No, you don't."

She watched, wide-eyed, as he crawled up beside her and pulled her close. Those big arms went around her and suddenly she was engulfed in all that heat and hardness, with her nose pressed against his throat.

When she dared to tip her head back and meet those blue, blue eyes, he kissed the space between her eyebrows. His lips were so soft. "Don't get freaky," he whispered. "Stay with me now."

She buried her head under his chin again. "I have no idea what you're talking about."

He chuckled. And then he tipped up her chin and kissed her, a gentle, coaxing kind of kiss. Completely unhurried.

Like he had forever and nothing to prove. Like he wouldn't mind if the two of them ended up lying here all night, sharing leisurely kisses and maybe a few tender touches. And nothing more.

The sweet, slow kiss ended. He braced an elbow on his pillow and rested his head on his fist. She did the same. They shared a smile as he trailed his fingers in a slow caress up the outside of her thigh, over the swell of her hip and down into the curve of her waist, stirring up all manner of arousing sensations as he went.

She inched closer and wrapped a leg over him. His erection pressed against her. With a shaky little breath, she touched her lips to his.

He opened to her. His tongue met hers, sliding. Twining.

Her insecurities melted away like frost on a window in the warm light of the sun. She rolled, pulling him with her.

Now she was under him, his big body pressing her down. She wrapped both legs around him. Her heart beat an eager rhythm under her ribs.

He took her face between his hands and held her there, his eyes open, looking into hers. "Did you ever think…?"

She whispered, "You and me, you mean?"

"Yeah."

"Like this, you mean?"

"Yeah."

"Oh, Ty. I didn't dare."

"Me neither." He pressed his forehead to hers again, as he had back there at the door. "Not until lately, anyway."

"Until Vegas."

"Yeah, since Vegas, you're *all* I think about." He caught her mouth again, kissing her deeply now, taking charge.

She wrapped herself around him. He rolled her to the top position, and she braced her knees to either side of him. When he palmed a breast with one hand, she moaned and lifted into his touch. His other hand slid down over her belly to explore all the secrets between her spread knees.

The world blew away. There was just Ty and those knowing hands of his, playing her, hitting every note just right, creating his own special symphony until she was panting and begging and crying out his name.

He rolled them again and she was beneath him, her head on the pillow. Slowly, he kissed his way down the center of her body. She speared her hands into his hair and begged him some more as he settled her thighs over his shoulders and did things with that mouth of his that she'd never known were possible.

She came, the release rocketing through her. He kept on stroking her with his tongue and those clever fingers of his. Just when the hot, pulsing shimmer of pleasure faded down enough that she thought it might be over, he used his fingers some more in a certain, swirly way and did something impossible with his tongue...

And off she went to paradise all over again.

When she finally opened her eyes, he was grinning up at her from between her open legs.

"You are such a bad man," she whispered. "But in such a very good way..."

He crawled up her boneless body and reached for one of the little foil pouches.

She groaned, feeling completely relaxed, limp, done for. "Somehow, I feel like I'm not holding up my end of this deal."

"Oh, yeah, you are." He sounded lazy and happy and very sure of himself—and of her. She watched, mesmerized, as he tore the top off the pouch and expertly rolled the condom down over himself.

When he reached for her, she reached back, wrapping her arms around him, gathering him to her. He came into her slowly. She stared up into his eyes, hardly believing this could really be happening.

With Ty.

After all these years...

He buried his head in the crook of her neck and whispered her name, "Sadie..." Like he found this moment as hard to believe as she did, that the two of them were here, together, in this raw and intimate way.

Joined with her, he rolled to his back. She blinked and looked down at him.

"Ride me," he coaxed.

And she did, tucking her folded legs against him, sitting up, rolling her body in a slow, rocking rhythm until she felt herself approaching the edge again.

"Go for it," he said, his big hands on her hips now, his body lifting up into her, sending her flying as she moaned his name. "That's it." He groaned. "Oh, yeah..."

And he followed right after her. She stared down at him, dazed with wonder as she felt him pulsing deep inside.

A few minutes later, he got up to deal with the condom. She glanced over at the hotel clock. It was past midnight.

He came out of the bathroom. She rose and went in.

When she finished in there, he was back in her bed, leaning up against the headboard, looking like every woman's dream of the perfect, sexy lover. He held out his hand.

She hesitated. "It's getting kind of late..."

"Get over here. Come on."

Her heart felt light as a moonbeam as she went to him and climbed in beside him. He wrapped an arm around her and pulled her in close to him.

She thought of tomorrow, of brunch with the other bridesmaids. Of all the wedding-day activities that stretched through the nighttime and into Sunday morning.

Ty pulled her closer. His lips brushed her temple. "We've only got two nights. We need to make the most of them."

She leaned her head on his big shoulder. "You realize we've got a full day and night of wedding activities tomorrow—and we *are* here for the wedding, after all. I mean, this thing that's going on with us is secondary."

He leaned closer. "For you, maybe." Her breath caught at those words. "Look at it this way. We can handle a couple of late nights. It's not going to kill us."

She laughed. "You sound so determined."

He stroked a slow hand down her tangled hair. "I am." Gently, he guided a lock of hair behind her ear. "Don't make me go yet."

She leaned close and kissed him, whispering, "You're right," against his lips. "It's only two nights. We should make the most of them."

"Now you're talking." He pulled her close against him. And when he kissed her, he made it slow and deep.

That kiss melted into another one.

And another one after that.

Sadie woke to winter sunlight peeking between the bedroom curtains. She was lying on her side with a warm, heavy arm resting in the curve of her waist— Ty's arm.

She blinked at the bright slice of sunlight. "Ty…"

His arm tightened around her. "Huh?" He nuzzled the back of her neck.

She rolled to her back. More asleep than awake, Ty adjusted his body to accommodate the change in her position. Pulling her even closer, he stuck his nose in the side of her neck and covered her breast with his hand.

The truth was, she wanted to shut her eyes and drift right back to sleep with him all wrapped around her.

But then she looked at the blue numerals on the face of the bedside clock: 11:30. Brunch was in half an hour with the bride and all the bridesmaids, Emily included. From there, they moved on to the hotel spa for hours of pampering.

"Ty, I have to get up…" She tried to gently push him off her.

He thwarted her with very little effort. "No." He cuddled her closer. "Come on, relax."

"I have to meet Nic and the rest of them in the restaurant at noon. It's eleven thirty. Do the math."

He mumbled more objections. She grabbed one big shoulder and shook it until he finally opened his eyes. "Ty, I have to get moving. Now."

"I heard you. Brunch," he said on a growl. "And then the spa. Didn't you do all that in Vegas?"

She threw back the covers, jumped from the bed and braced her hands on her hips. "You have to get out of here—and please make sure no one sees you."

He yawned. And then he grinned. "You're so cute when you're naked."

She grabbed her pillow and bopped him on the chest with it. "Up. Now."

Grumbling under his breath, he pushed the covers back and rolled from the bed, rising to his feet on the far side, where he stretched and yawned some more. Really, he was one magnificent specimen of a man.

But right now, she had no time to waste admiring his broad shoulders and hard, narrow waist. Bending, she picked up his shirt and threw it at him. He caught it neatly.

"Get dressed. Now, Ty."

He just stood there, holding the wadded shirt against that beautiful chest of his, smirking. "Last night was fantastic."

Her bones went to butter at that look on his face. "Yes, it was."

"Can't wait for tonight."

"Neither can I. But first, we've got a wedding to get

through." She pulled on her pajama top and bent to grab the pants. "Get dressed."

Finally, he shook out the shirt and stuck his arms in the sleeves.

Two minutes later, she was pushing him toward the door.

But when he reached for the doorknob, she caught his arm. "Let me check the hallway first."

He grabbed her around the back of the neck and dragged her up close. "Kiss me."

"We are wasting..." Before she could finish her sentence, his mouth covered hers.

Oh, the man could kiss. She surrendered to the play of his lips on hers—but only momentarily. "I mean it." She pushed him away. "You *have* to go—now stay right there while I check to make sure the hallway is empty."

With a shrug, he stepped back. She opened the door and checked both ways. Nobody.

"Okay. Go. Now." She pulled the door wide enough for him to get out.

"Tonight," he said low as he edged past her.

"Go."

He went. She shut the door and headed for the bathroom and the world's shortest-ever shower.

Ty's suite was on the floor above Sadie's. He let himself in and headed straight for the bedroom, where he quickly shed his clothes again and climbed into the bed.

He expected to drop right back to sleep, but instead he ended up just lying there with his hands laced behind his head, staring up at the rustic light fixture suspended from the beamed ceiling, thinking about what a great night he'd just had.

The only thing wrong with what had finally happened between Sadie and him was that she'd kicked him out way before he was ready to go.

At least he had tonight to look forward to. He couldn't wait to take full advantage of every minute with her before they had to call it quits.

And about that…

He scowled at the light fixture.

Calling it quits so fast was a bad, bad idea. The thing about a love affair—short or otherwise—was to make sure to let it run its natural course.

If you called it quits too soon, way too much time could be wasted hopelessly wanting the other person when you could have so easily just kept the good times rolling until a natural ending presented itself.

He would have to get his arguments in order and then discuss that with Sadie tonight when he finally had her to himself. One way or another, he intended to convince her that they needed to spend more nights together.

Two just wasn't enough.

A half an hour or so later, he gave up on trying to sleep. It wasn't happening, so he showered and got dressed. Today, Gavin would be hanging with his family, so Ty had no wedding-related duties until he had to put on his tux in the late afternoon. By now, Emily would be having a ball with Nic and Sadie and the other bridesmaids. No need to check on her.

He called Mona to find out how Drew was doing. Turned out the three of them—Mona, Henry and Drew—had ridden the gondola down into town. They were playing in the snow at High Line Railroad Park.

Ty rode down there to join them. They went for lunch and then it was time to head back up to Arrowleaf

Lodge, where his own parents were due any minute. They would attend the wedding and then take the kids overnight.

And while his folks watched Drew and Em, he and Sadie would get some much-needed alone time. The wedding and reception couldn't be over with fast enough as far as he was concerned.

Despite her lack of sleep last night, Sadie felt great.

The day passed too slowly, though. Sadie smiled through it, knowing that tonight was coming, that she would have Ty all to herself as soon as they could get away.

After brunch and the spa, the bride and bridesmaids took a break. Sadie went back to her room where she wondered what Ty was doing and felt too excited to enjoy a nap.

Eventually, she got up, put on her makeup and went down to join the others off the wedding chapel in the bride's room, which had separate vanities and lighted mirrors for Nic and all her bridesmaids. A couple of stylists from the spa helped with their hair and the wedding planner dropped in more than once to see how things were going.

Twenty minutes before Nic's walk down the aisle, they were ready, Nicole in her glorious white gown and full-length lace veil of tulle edged with lace, the rest of them in deep red velvet.

Suddenly, it was time. Bouquets in hand, they left the bride's room and followed the wedding planner down a hallway that opened into a vestibule at the back of the chapel.

As they waited for the wedding march to start, Sadie turned to her best friend. "You are beyond stunning."

"Love you, Sade," Nic whispered.

As tradition demanded, Sadie smoothed Nic's white gown and arranged her veil just so. "Perfect," she whispered.

Nic gave her a radiant smile and a slow nod.

"Take your place," the wedding planner whispered in Sadie's ear. She got in line behind the other bridesmaids.

It was almost barnlike, that chapel, and it hadn't seemed all that impressive during the rehearsal yesterday. But now, it was a vision of rustic beauty.

Pretty wooden chairs with white satin cushions had been arranged in rows for the pews. The gorgeous round medieval-looking chandeliers overhead glittered with golden lights. Yesterday, unlit, Sadie had hardly noticed them up there in the shadows of the peaked ceiling. But tonight, they blazed brightly.

Thick spruce trees heavily decked with lights framed the ceiling-high windows up in front where the bride and groom would say their vows. Twinkle lights were everywhere, crisscrossing the windows, spilling down the rough walls. On a wide ledge midway up both side walls, pillar candles burned, creating a soft, golden glow.

The music changed and the processional began. The woman who would perform the ceremony appeared from a side door and stood at the beautiful podium carved with vines and trumpet-shaped flowers.

Gavin and Ty came out next and stood to the right. Ushers escorted Cindy, Astrid, Erin and Emily down the aisle, each to her designated spot on the left.

"Now," prompted the wedding planner softly in Sadie's ear. She proceeded up the aisle alone and took her place with the other bridesmaids. When she glanced to the groom's side, there was Ty, unbearably handsome in his tux.

He winked at her. She thought of last night and the night to come. She just knew she was blushing.

Drew, with his ring-bearer briefcase, looking quite official and adorably serious, marched to the altar followed by Astrid's little niece, Poppy, who carried a white basket full of red rose petals, which she scattered as she went.

And then at last Nicole appeared on the arm of Sadie's dad. She looked absolutely stunning in her white dress. Carrying a giant bouquet of winter blooms and greenery that trailed almost to the floor, her glowing smile was visible even through her veil. Sadie's dad whispered something to her, and she gave him a tender smile. Then he turned her over to Gavin and took his seat in the front row beside Sadie's mom.

The officiant emerged from behind the podium. Sadie took Nic's bouquet. Nic turned to Gavin. Slowly, he lifted her veil.

As they exchanged their vows, Sadie tried to keep her focus where it belonged—on Nic and Gavin and this special moment.

But somehow, she couldn't stop herself from glancing at Ty. As though he felt her gaze on him, he turned his golden head a fraction to meet her eyes. A frown crinkled his brow. She could almost hear him asking, *What's wrong?*

And that was when it happened. As Ty gave her that worried look and Nic promised to love and cherish

Gavin for the rest of their lives, Sadie came face-to-face with a terrible truth.

All these years she'd been putting herself out there, looking so hard for her own great love and never once admitting to herself that he'd been right here with her all along—with her, but never hers.

It was Ty. She loved Ty.

Worse than that, she always had.

Chapter Ten

If Ty never attended another wedding, it would be way too soon.

Maybe it wouldn't have been so grueling if there wasn't something off with Sadie. But ever since that moment in the chapel, when she'd looked at him so strangely, she'd been knocking herself out avoiding him. Every time he got near her, she pasted on a fake smile and wandered away.

By midnight, most of it was over, at least. They'd made it through the ceremony, the pictures, the cocktail hour in the Lodge's separate reception hall. He'd survived the dinner, the speeches, the toasts, the first dance and the family dances that followed—including the one where he danced with the maid of honor.

She'd come into his arms downright reluctantly. He wanted to kiss her so badly. She smelled so sweet, and she looked so good in that red velvet dress that clung to her soft curves and had a tempting slit up to one smooth thigh. He couldn't wait to peel it off her, to take her thick bronze hair down and wrap it around his fist.

He had her in his arms, but she managed to hold herself away from him as they danced.

He pulled her close and whispered, "What's going on?"

She looked up at him, pasted on a fake smile and baldly lied, "Not a thing."

He knew then that he would have to wait until they were alone to find out the truth. That made the rest of the evening interminable.

When Nic threw her bouquet, Sadie caught it. She didn't really have a choice. Nic lobbed the gigantic thing straight at her. She grabbed it with both hands to keep it from smacking her in the face.

Everybody applauded wildly.

Nic ran to her and hugged her. Sadie laughed and hugged her back. But Sadie's laughter was forced. Ty knew her heart wasn't in it.

About then, he really started to worry. He had to exert real effort to keep from making a fool of himself because he wanted to trail after her, begging her to talk to him, until she gave in and told him what was wrong.

The later it got, the more he considered grabbing her, dragging her into a hallway or a random closet and demanding to know what had happened with her. But he had a bad feeling that if he put pressure on her, she would only say it was nothing—and then lean close enough to whisper that she didn't really feel up to seeing him later tonight.

By the time Nic and Gavin finally cut the five-tiered vanilla cake, Ty was all tied in knots as he watched the bride and groom mug it up for the photographer, feeding each other giant bites of fluffy cake, buttercream frosting and huckleberry filling.

After the cake, Ty's parents were ready to take the kids up to bed. He hugged them good-night and said he would see them in the morning. They would all meet for breakfast at nine.

After another hour of watching everyone party and trying to keep track of Sadie, who continued to actively avoid him, the bride and groom finally made their exit in the least complicated ritual of the evening. They were staying right there at the lodge, so Gavin simply swept Nic up into his arms and carried her out of the reception while the remaining guests hollered, whistled and applauded.

As the best man, Ty played host for the rest of the evening. He made certain any gifts brought directly to the wedding were gathered up and handed over to the Lodge concierge. They would pack them and mail them home. He checked on Gavin's parents, his grandmother, his sister and her husband, sitting with them for a while, chatting about nothing, making sure they didn't feel left out.

At some point during that time, Sadie slipped away. When the evening finally came to an end at a little after two and the last few guests headed up to their rooms, she was already gone.

Not that it mattered. He knew where to find her.

He was the last guest to leave the reception hall and rode the elevator up to her floor alone. The doors slid open on an empty lobby area. The hallway that led to her suite was equally deserted. At her door, he tapped three times.

Nothing. He waited, glancing from side to side, feeling like an intruder in a deserted building—furtive. Up to no good.

He knocked again, louder.

Just when he was about to say to hell with being discreet and make some real noise, she opened the door.

Relief poured through him at the sight of her in the same pajama bottoms as last night, wearing a hoodie with *Sheridan Bruins* printed across the front. Her face was scrubbed clean of makeup, and she'd put her hair in one thick braid, the silky tip curling over the *S* in *Bruins*.

He wanted to throw her over his shoulder and carry her straight to bed. "Are you going to let me in?" His voice sounded strange to his own ears—ragged, like he'd had to scrape the sound off the bottom of his throat.

She stepped back. He crossed the threshold fast, before she could even think about changing her mind, and then shut and locked the door behind him.

Sadie turned and started walking.

He followed her into the sitting area, where she dropped to the sofa and offered glumly, "Have a seat."

This was not the greeting he'd been hoping for.

But maybe she planned to tell him what the hell was going on. That would be good because he had absolutely no idea.

He remained on his feet as he realized he might have to adjust his expectations. Pushing her for more nights looked less and less likely. The way she stared up at him now, those chameleon-green eyes full of shadows, her soft lips turned down at the corners, he very much doubted he would even get tonight.

"Look, Sadie. At least get honest, okay? You want me to go?"

She flipped her braid back over her shoulder and shook her head no.

Inside, he was nothing but questions followed by demands. *What is it? Talk to me. What went wrong?*

Somehow, he kept his mouth shut as he sat down beside her. She surprised him and leaned her head on his shoulder.

With slow care he raised his arm and wrapped it around her. She lifted her gaze to meet his.

He just wanted to kiss her.

To hold her. To promise her that, whatever had turned her so lost and sad at the wedding, he would do what he could to make it all better.

As he tried to find the words that would fix whatever had gone wrong, she lifted her mouth to him. "Kiss me."

They should talk first.

But that sweet mouth was right there. So pretty. So tempting. Plus, kissing her was so much easier than trying to coax her into telling him what the problem was—easier and also a hell of a lot more enjoyable. He brought his mouth down to hers and wrapped his arms around her.

"Ty." She opened to him, tasting so good, of toothpaste and desire. As the kiss deepened, he stroked the satiny skin of her cheek and then ran his fingers down the thick length of her braid. Getting hold of the elastic at the end, he gave a little tug, and it slid off in his hand.

"Give me that." She took the elastic from him and dropped it in the art glass dish on the coffee table. And then she snuggled closer. "What now?"

"Bed."

"Okay," she replied, but didn't move. So he rose, pulled her to her feet and scooped her high into his arms.

She made the cutest sound, a little hum low in her throat. And then she lifted her lips to him again. He kissed her some more, his tongue tangling with hers as he carried her into the other room.

The bed looked like a tornado had hit it, the covers thrown back, the sheets wrinkled, like she'd been tossing and turning for hours.

She stirred in his grip. "Let me down."

He lowered her feet to the rug, and she climbed onto the bed. Going up on her knees, she reached for him. "Here, let me help you."

He stared down at her, bemused, as she unpinned his boutonniere and dropped it on the nightstand. She took his jacket by the satin lapels and eased it off his shoulders. He caught it before it fell and tossed it on the nearby chair.

She didn't stop there. She untied his bow tie and dispensed with the onyx studs down the front of his shirt, dropping them next to his bow tie on the night table. Next, she took his wrists and removed his cuff links, her touch so steady.

So sure.

Of what, he didn't know.

But he wanted her. So much.

Enough that he could hardly wait to have his arms around her again. He went to work, shrugging out of his suspenders and then his shirt, throwing the shirt toward the chair, toeing off his dress shoes, getting rid of his socks. Down went his tux pants, his boxer briefs along with them. He tossed them away in a wad as she watched him, wide-eyed.

And then he reached for her.

She laughed then. The sweet sound reassured him—that everything was all right, that she wanted this as much as he did.

"Come here." He hauled her close. They fell together across the bed.

"All day," he whispered gruffly as he wrapped her hair around his hand, pulling her head back so he could see her eyes. "And all night, too. All I could think of was this. And you…"

They kissed, long and slow and deeply. That kiss faded into the next one. And the one after that.

He stroked his hand downward, slipped his fingers up under her hoodie and then eased them down beneath the front of those pajama pants. Her soft belly tightened beneath his palm.

She let out the sweetest little cry when he found the hot, wet core of her. He kissed that cry right off her beautiful mouth. She grabbed him close as he stroked her, opening for him, urging him on.

When she came, she cried out. And when she went limp with a long, sweet sigh, he held her close for the longest time, thinking of everything he couldn't give her, of how to get through this, how to get over her.

She stirred, clasping his shoulder, stroking his chest. "Ty…"

"Come here." He kissed her. And then he got hold of her hoodie and whipped it off over her head. Her bare breasts tempted him. He wrapped his hand around one and sucked her dusky nipple into his mouth as she wiggled out of her long john bottoms.

"Ty…"

He looked up with a questioning sound. She lifted her head enough to capture his mouth.

They kissed some more, teasing kisses that slowly turned deep. She tasted so good. He ached for her, for more of this. He wished tonight could last forever.

He'd never had a friend for a lover before. It was a revelation—that sex could be equal parts thrilling and comfortable, fun and sizzling hot. He couldn't get enough of her. Before he left her this time, he needed to convince her that this was too good to walk away from. They needed time to get over each other, time to…

What?

He almost laughed out loud.

At himself. At his own arrogance.

She didn't want what he wanted. He knew that. She still had dreams of love. Of…more.

Whatever the hell *more* was.

He had no right to try to coax her into giving him pieces of her. She wanted a man to give everything to, a good guy who wouldn't hesitate to give everything right back. If he wasn't ready at least to try for that, he needed to stop scheming, stop figuring out ways to convince her that they should make this two-night fling a full-blown secret affair.

"Ty?" She cradled his face between her hands and looked at him, a look both patient and tender—and intimate, too. She knew him so well, knew that he had something on his mind.

She was right.

He should be a better man. But he wasn't.

He really hadn't had enough of her.

And he doubted that all the good intentions in the

world would be enough to keep him away from her—not until he'd gotten over this need he had for her.

When they were home, he would go to her. Talk to her.

Make her see that more time together would be a good thing. He would remind her that they'd tried to call it quits before it even really started—last month, after Vegas.

And look how much good that had done.

Some things you couldn't just walk away from. Some things you had to surrender to, let them happen. Some things, you couldn't turn your back on too soon.

"Where *are* you?" she asked.

He kissed her, quick and hard. "I'm right here."

"You sure about that?"

"Yeah. Right here. With you."

She gave him another smile then, a wry smile that told him she didn't believe him, but she was willing to let it go. "Whatever you say." And then she sighed. "I'm sorry that I was...distant, earlier."

He bent close and brushed her lips with his. "It's okay."

"I'm glad you're here now," she said. "I really am. And life's too short. Let's not waste a minute."

"Good idea." He dropped a line of kisses across her collarbone and up the satiny flesh of her throat. When he reached the smooth line of her jaw, he bit her lightly and then ran his tongue over the place where his teeth had been.

"After all," she reasoned in a breathless whisper, "it's our last time..."

He didn't argue the point. No reason to ruin tonight with talk of the future. Later for that.

He ached for her. Covering her mouth with his, he

eased his arm around her and pulled her soft naked body good and tight against him.

She moaned in response. He bit her lip. At her pleasured moan, he swept his hand down her thigh and guided it up to wrap over his hip. He pressed his aching erection against her belly. A low, hungry sound escaped her parted lips.

It wasn't long before he was reaching for the nightstand drawer, fumbling around until his fingers closed on one of the foil pouches he'd left there last night. As soon as he'd ripped the pouch open with his teeth, she took it from him and did the honors, rising above him to claim control.

He stared up at her as she rocked on top of him. So beautiful—Sadie, riding him. Never in a million years would he have guessed that this might happen.

But it had. And no way could he lose her.

Not yet…

Chapter Eleven

At 5 a.m., Sadie made herself say, "You really have to go now, Ty."

He tried to stall. "Just a little while longer. I'll go at six, I promise you, I will…"

She held firm. "No, really. You have to go now." Sliding from his hold, she jumped from the bed.

"Get back here." He grabbed for her.

"Uh-uh." She stepped out of reach and pulled on her pajama pants and hoodie. "Come on, Ty. It's time. Get up."

He shook his head and made a sad face. Had any man ever looked so effortlessly hot, sitting there against the headboard buck naked, his hair sticking out every which way? Really, he was a danger to the hearts of women everywhere.

But she stayed strong. Grabbing his clothes off the chair, she stepped close and shoved them against his broad bare chest. "*Now*, please."

His shoulders slumped. "Fine." He threw back the covers and shook out the wrinkled tux and shirt, then took his sweet time getting into them. When he'd finally tied his shoes and stuffed his bow tie and cuff links into a pocket, she grabbed his hand and pulled him to his feet again.

At the door, he took her in his arms one last time. When he kissed her, she kissed him back, going all in with it, pressing her body tightly to his, wrapping her arms around his neck, wishing with all her heart that she didn't have to let go.

But she did. She'd stolen two nights of heaven with him. And that would have to be enough. Every moment in his arms only made her want him more. She needed to let him go now while she could still do it without begging him to stay.

Pulling back, she put on a smile. "Good night."

His hair was still scrambled, his cuffs rolled instead of fastened properly and he'd lost one of the studs for his shirt. He had that look, like he would sweep her up in those big arms again and carry her straight back to bed.

"Don't," she said firmly.

His beautiful mouth had a mutinous curve, but all he said was, "Breakfast. Nine o'clock in the restaurant."

"I'll be there—let me check the hallway…"

He scoffed. "Right." But he did step aside. She peeked out. Not a soul.

A moment later, he was gone.

She locked up and went back to bed, where Ty had left his boutonniere on the nightstand next to an empty condom wrapper. Shaking her head, she dropped the wilted rose and the foil pouch in the wastebasket.

Sitting there, staring down at the discarded boutonniere, she thought of the bouquet Nic had made sure she caught. Like many brides, Nic had wanted it back. After all, the bouquet meant good luck for her marriage. Sadie had turned it over to the wedding planner, who would arrange to have it shipped home.

"Oh, why not?" she asked the empty room as she rescued the rose from the trash. Maybe it would bring good luck for...?

What? She had no idea. But she wanted it anyway, as a memento of her two beautiful nights with Ty. She wrapped it in tissue and tucked it into her cosmetic bag before climbing back into bed.

She didn't really expect to be able to sleep—and she was right.

After an hour of restless tossing and turning, she got up, showered and got dressed. She packed. When all that was done, she still had over an hour before breakfast. So she made coffee in the room and channel-surfed the Sunday morning talk shows until it was time to go downstairs.

Breakfast wasn't so bad. Nic and Gavin were there, to be with the family—both his and hers—one last time before heading to Denver for the first leg of their trip to a gorgeous resort on St. Thomas Island.

Nic glowed with happiness and chattered nonstop, so there was rarely a lull. And whenever Nic fell silent to eat a bite of her breakfast, Emily picked right up where her mother left off, treating the table to her own plans for the holidays, which included the Christmas assembly at school, where she would be playing Mrs. Claus.

"I get a gray wig and those glasses with wire frames *and* a long red dress with white fur on the sleeves. And

I've been practicing being old. You have to move slowly and act like your back hurts."

Ty teased her, "I don't know, Em. Mrs. Claus has a lot to do up there at the North Pole. I'm guessing she's still in pretty good shape."

Emily frowned. She loved to perform and took the job seriously. "I'm going to see what Mr. Warbly says about that." Mr. Warbly taught fifth grade at Medicine Creek Elementary. A drama buff, he organized and directed all the school productions.

Ty's dad was grinning. "I've been old for a while now, Emmy. You need any pointers, you come to me."

"Oh, Grandpa..." Em rolled her eyes.

And then Nic turned to her in-laws to ask about their Christmas plans and to promise that next year, they would find a way to get together during the holiday season.

Mostly, Sadie only had to smile and nod and laugh in the right places—and take extra care not to let her gaze stray in Ty's direction. Twice, she glanced up and found herself looking right at him. Both times, Ty caught her doing it and gave her a secret smile. That smile made her chest ache.

Breathe, she silently reminded herself. *Look away.*

Finally, breakfast came to an end. Nic, Gavin and Gavin's family, headed for the airport in Denver.

As a treat, Ty and his dad had chartered a jet to take the rest of them back home to Wyoming. They climbed into chauffeured SUVs for the hour-long drive to Eagle/Vail airport.

The McBrides rode in one car with most of the luggage piled in the back. Ty, his parents, and Emily and Drew were in the other.

Sadie appreciated the hour on the road, a quiet time to stare out at the mountains and the snow piled high on either side of the highway. It was a relief to be free of the possibility she might accidentally make eye contact with her weekend lover.

The chartered jet was pretty much what she'd expected. Like a flying living room in which everyone got a big, reclining leather seat and a nice little table to set food and beverages on. Em and Drew were in heaven. They had sodas and snacks and looked out the windows at the gorgeous, snow-covered scenery below. Sadie simply felt grateful that Ty was up in front, and she was near the back. Whenever he got up, she had plenty of time to make sure she didn't accidentally end up sharing so much as a glance with him.

Her parents had left their big Jeep at the airport in Sheridan. Sadie rode home with them. She carried her stuff in, turned up the heat and called Marilee Lewis, who owned a pet grooming business that she ran out of her charming Victorian house. Marilee also boarded pets on occasion. She'd taken Boo and Olive for the weekend.

"Welcome home!" Marilee greeted her gleefully. "Come on down. Boo and Olive are right here waiting for you."

Sadie jumped in her Tahoe and brought the cats home. They were sweet, as always, happy to have her fuss over them, but not the least upset that she'd been gone.

After all, they had each other to love and count on.

Ty knew he should wait at least a few days to reach out to Sadie. He should give her some time to miss him, to face the fact that she was no more over him than he was done with her.

But then again, Sadie was so damn pigheaded. Even if she wanted him as bad as he wanted her, she could so easily dig in her heels, decide that he was bad for her, and she needed to steer clear of him at all costs.

No. That wouldn't do. No way.

By the time he got home that night, he couldn't wait to get over to her place. But he had the kids while Nic was on her honeymoon. So instead of getting right on the Sadie situation, he spent the evening being a dad, making sure school assignments were on track and Drew and Em had everything ready to go for the next day.

Then in the morning, he considered taking them to Henry's for breakfast. But no way he could get Sadie alone while she was working. She'd be racing around taking orders and pouring coffee. He would be left trying not to stare at her like some lovesick fool.

And that wouldn't do. Bob and Lester were too observant. They might pick up that he'd developed something of an obsession for his ex-wife's BFF.

After he got the kids to school, he had work to catch up on. That night, his mom took the kids for dinner. That would have been a great time to track Sadie down—except for the dinner meeting in Sheridan he couldn't back out of. It was him and his dad schmoozing a motel tycoon. The man had properties all up and down the state. He was looking for land so that he could build more.

It was almost ten when they finished the meeting. Ty called his mom. He wasn't surprised that she'd already put Em and Drew to bed in the pj's she kept at her house for nights just like this one.

"Maybe let them sleep?" she coaxed. "You can pick them up in the morning, or I'll take them to school."

"Thanks, Mom. You're the best."

"You're welcome. Your dad there with you?"

"He's on his way home. Call me in the morning. I'll bring over everything they need." He thanked her again and said goodbye.

It was snowing. He drove back to Medicine Creek with the wipers on high, the fat flakes coming at the windshield out of the dark, the clouds overhead blotting out the stars. He planned to go straight home.

But he ended up at Sadie's house.

He pulled in next to the curb at the end of her front walk and then just sat there with the lights on and the engine running, reminding himself that she had to work at five tomorrow morning and he shouldn't be here right now.

The light was on in her bedroom, which was off the foyer at the front of the house. As he stared at it, he saw the curtain move.

He turned off the headlights but left the engine running until she came out wearing a puffer coat over red-and-green-plaid pajamas. She looked so cute, with her hair in that fat braid just like the other night, her arms folded across her chest and a frown on her face.

He turned off the engine, got out of the vehicle and marched up the walk to join her on the porch.

"What do you want?" She frowned even harder. It was not a good beginning to this delicate conversation he intended to have with her.

Too bad. He'd come this far. No way he was leaving until he'd said what he came to say. "Just to talk."

"Haven't we already said it all?"

"Not as far as I'm concerned, no."

With a resigned sigh, she led the way inside. "You want anything?" she asked as she hung up her coat.

You. I want you. "No, I'm fine." He hung up his jacket and hat next to her coat, toed off his wet boots and followed her into the great room on stocking feet.

She gestured for him to sit on the sofa and pointedly positioned herself in the green chair across the coffee table from him, making it achingly clear he would have little hope of getting his hands on her. "How many ways can I say this? I really don't think there's anything more to talk about."

He leaned in, braced his elbows on his thighs and looked her square in the eye. "Yeah, there is. This thing with us, it's not just going to go away. We need to—"

"Stop. If you're going to say what you said the last time you showed up here out of nowhere at night, please don't."

"Sadie…" He let her name trail off as he accepted the fact that she was right. He had nothing new to say. He should have thought this through before showing up here. Should have figured out ahead of time how to make her admit that they couldn't stop now.

But he hadn't. Because when it came right down to it, he couldn't give her what she wanted. And she was through settling for less.

"Please, Ty. You should go. You should go now."

"But we need more time together. All I can think of is you. And I know damn well that you feel the same.

It's not over. I can see it in your eyes. You want to be with me, too. You think I don't know that?"

"Not in secret. Uh-uh. No, I do not."

"Are you going to try to tell me you're over me? That lie won't fly. This is me you're talking to. I know you. I've known you since we were—what?—three years old and you hit me with that toy shovel in the sand box at Patriot Park."

"I kind of wish I had that shovel right now," she muttered. "I'd hit you with it again, maybe get lucky and knock some sense into that thick skull of yours."

"That's not funny."

"No, I guess it's not. But how many ways can I tell you that I'm not up for more of the same? I want a real relationship. I *deserve* a real relationship—however far it goes. I want both of us going into it honestly and openly, with the intention of making it work."

He put up both hands. "You know I'm not the guy for that."

"Yes. I do know—or at least, I know that you believe you're not. And that's just as bad as if you really were the good-time, no-commitment guy you're always making yourself out to be."

"Okay, wait—just hold on a minute here."

"Hold on for what?"

He wanted her. He wanted her so bad. But he didn't want her lying to herself about him. "Sadie. I'm never going to be the guy you're hoping for."

She made a low sound of pure frustration. "Please. You already are exactly the guy I'm hoping for."

"No."

She shut her eyes, tipped her head back and drew in a slow, careful breath. "Look. I love Nic. You know I do.

She's a sister to me. But that doesn't mean I can't be objective about how she used to be—how she still is in a lot of ways. When you two were together, I was team Nicole all the way. I blamed you the same as she blamed you for everything that wasn't right between the two of you."

"I know you did. And I will take that blame. I resented the hell out of her, Sadie."

"You were young, and she was so demanding. And let's be honest, before you found out she was pregnant with Em, you were over her."

"Still, I could have done better with her. I wasn't the husband I should have been."

"So? You messed things up. Don't we all? Look, I was young, too, then. I saw her suffering and I needed a bad guy to be the cause of her pain. You were it. But it's been years since I put the blame on you. I see things differently now. I see that you did what you could to make it work with her. And when it didn't, you made sure she had everything she needed to create a good life, a life she could be proud of. I see that you're an amazing dad and your kids adore you. You and Nic both, you did the best you could. But you were hardly more than kids yourselves and you didn't have a clue then how to make it work."

How was he supposed to unpack all that? He couldn't. He didn't even want to. "Sadie, I didn't come here to talk about the past."

"Of course, you didn't. But as long as you let the past define who you are, we *need* to talk about it."

"Wrong."

A sound of pure frustration escaped her. "You are not to blame because Nic never had a dad, and her mom was a pill-popping drunk who died too soon and left her to wonder what was wrong with her that her parents didn't stick around for her."

When was she going to shut up about all this? "Can you stop about Nic? She's got nothing to do with you and me."

"That's not true and you know it."

He wanted to get up and leave, but he couldn't stop hoping that somehow, he would get to hold her again. "You're just… You're making no sense."

"Maybe not." She straightened up tall and flipped her braid back over her shoulder. "One more thing about you. You're a good friend, the best—I mean, yeah, things are rocky between us now, but I hope we can be friends again, later. When we're finally really over each other."

He couldn't help sneering at that. "And when do you think that's going to be?"

"I wish I knew. But your reasoning sucks. You will never convince me that because you're not willing to hold up your end of a loving relationship, we need more secret nights together. That's just not true, not for me—I mean, I admit, I loved those nights we had. They were beautiful."

"So why stop now?"

"Because secret nights only go so far. I want more. And unless you're ready to give me more, we've got nothing else to say to each other."

He should have a comeback ready. But he didn't. He'd blown this visit all to hell, no doubt about that.

And now, he had nothing more to add, no decent rebuttals to her way-too-valid arguments. All he could do was sit there, wanting her, finally starting to accept that what he'd had with her so far was all he was ever going to get.

"How many ways can I say it, Ty? If you and I are going to be together again, it's going to be up front and out in the open. If you want to be with me, everyone in town—including Nic—is going to know about it. If you want me, you need to look me in the eye and tell me that you're in it for real, no sneaking around."

Two minutes later, Ty had his boots, jacket and hat back on and he was out the door.

Sadie didn't exactly know what to do with herself right then, so she trailed after him to the porch. She ended up standing on the Welcome mat, shivering, with her arms wrapped around herself and her poor heart in tatters as he climbed into his Escalade and drove away.

It hurt so bad to let him go. But what else could she do? They were going nowhere together, and she refused to be a going-nowhere girl.

Back inside, she wandered over to the sofa and sat down. She cried a little, for herself. For Ty, too. He really was so much better than he gave himself credit for.

The cats jumped up, Olive on one side, Boo on the other. She petted them and listened to them purr. They were showing her the love, offering her comfort.

When she went to bed, they trotted along right behind her, jumping up to join her, cuddling up close. She turned off the light and hoped that the soft sound of their purring would lull her to sleep.

Ty went home to an empty house and his big bed that had never had anyone but him in it—and one or the other of his children when they needed him to chase the nightmares away.

He spent a sleepless night alternately thinking of all the things he should have said to Sadie, and then reminding himself that it was better this way. He couldn't give her what she demanded. He'd chased her for weeks now. It was time to leave her alone, take the hint and move on.

At least in the morning, there was more to do than time to do it in. His mom called at six with a list of what the kids needed to get ready for school. He packed their lunches, ran around collecting all the stuff they had to have, then drove over there.

His mom made them all breakfast. After the meal, he managed the chaos as Em and Drew got dressed in the clothes he'd brought for them and organized their packs. Then he took them to school and went on to Cash Enterprises from there.

The kids rode the bus home. Somehow, he made it back to the house ten minutes before they arrived. They had a Skype call with Nicole as he put dinner together. There was schoolwork to sort out and laundry to deal with.

Once he got Em and Drew to bed, he had presents to wrap. He spent three hours in the spare room getting that done. At least the tree he and the kids had put up last week looked a little less lonely with packages piled beneath it.

Wednesday wasn't quite as frantic. He had his housekeeper there to help out. She cooked and cleaned and finished the laundry he hadn't gotten around to. And she stayed until five, so he didn't have to rush home to be there when Drew and Em got off the bus.

Yeah, he felt like a hamster on a wheel, barely staying on top of everything that needed doing, but what else was new? On the bright side, full-time fatherhood and the demands of his business kept him from dreaming up new excuses to go see Sadie again. He missed her. It was bad. But he didn't have a spare minute to do anything stupid.

Nights were the worst. He kept stewing over the things she'd said on Monday. That he needed to stop blaming himself for the million and one ways he'd messed up his marriage, that he was a good father and a good friend, too. That she'd loved every minute of their too-short secret affair.

He hadn't been to the diner since before the wedding. He missed Henry's cooking and the smart-ass remarks of the guys at the counter. And he missed Sadie, bringing the coffee before anyone even asked for it, taking care of everyone and doing it with style and a great sense of humor.

Thursday was the school's Christmas Craft Fair followed by the Christmas Pageant. He drove over at three and met up with his mom and dad.

They took the kids around the fair. He sprang for a few handmade gifts and ornaments. The fair offered fast food. They loaded up trays with steamed hot dogs, mediocre burgers and greasy french fries. Not the healthiest dinner ever served, but the kids loved it, and he didn't have to cook.

Sadie and her folks came for the show. Ty's mom had saved seats for them. Sadie ended up sitting to his left. She gave him a careful smile and said, "Hello, Ty."

He said hello back. And that was it. The sum total of their conversation that evening.

He tried to concentrate on what was happening on-stage, but she was right there, so close. All he had to do was lean her way a fraction and he could smell apples and vanilla. She'd put her hair up in a loose knot with sweet, shiny bits escaping to curl at her nape. He wanted to tug on those wispy curls, to put his arm around her, to lean in close and breathe in the scent of apples. He wanted to whisper how cute Em was all done up as Mrs. Claus, and what a great elf Drew made in his pointy hat and those funny red shoes with the turned-up toes.

But no. None of that could happen. Because those things he imagined started with him wrapping an arm around her and leaning close, as a man does when he's in a relationship with a woman—or at least when he's casually dating her. Ty Bravo didn't do relationships. And the only kind of dates he had were with women who didn't live in town.

Later, he had trouble sleeping, same as last night and the night before. Tonight, though, he didn't think much about how he needed to keep himself from trying one more time to get Sadie to see things his way.

Tonight, he started seeing the situation in a different light entirely. For the first time, he wondered if maybe he was making things a lot harder than they needed to be. All he had to do to be the guy with his arm around Sadie at the Medicine Creek Elementary School Christmas Pageant, was to go to her and tell her he was ready to be in a relationship with her.

Somehow, when he thought of it that way, it didn't seem so completely impossible. Yeah, he'd always told himself that he was never going to the relationship place again. But that was before he'd let himself imagine having a relationship with Sadie.

True, there could be hell to pay when Nic got home and found out that he and Sadie were a couple.

But maybe not. Nic had changed a lot in the past few years. She didn't fly off the handle hardly at all anymore. And she had Gavin, who was everything she'd ever dreamed of in a man. No reason to assume she would freak out and make everyone suffer because her ex-husband had it so bad for her best friend that he was willing to try being half of a couple again just to get close to her.

In the morning, he was up extra early. He made the kids' lunches and then he woke them with the news that they were going to the diner for breakfast. They loved the diner as much as he did and got ready to go in record time.

When they got there, the place was packed. Most of the booths were occupied and there wasn't a single free seat at the long counter. He pushed open the door and the kids went in ahead of him, stopping just past the full-size Christmas tree they'd helped decorate Sunday before last.

Sadie, in her usual jeans, T-shirt and green apron, had her arms full of plates as she emerged from behind the counter. She glanced over and spotted him. Was that a scowl she gave him?

If so, she hid it quickly behind a big smile for Emily, who shouted way louder than she needed to, "Sadie! We're here!"

"Finally!" added Drew.

Bob Early spoke up from his seat at the counter. "Ty Bravo. Where the hell you been? We thought you died."

From the service window into the kitchen, Henry called, "Hey, kids!"

Ty gave him a wave as Drew shouted, "Hi, Grandpa Henry! I want pancakes!"

"Done!" replied Henry.

Sadie lifted her chin at a table full of dirty dishes. "We'll get that booth cleared for you." And then she turned away to serve the food she'd just picked up at the window.

A moment later, the dishwasher, Zeb, pushed through the swinging doors to the kitchen with a gray bus tub and a wet towel. He cleared off the dirty table and wiped it clean.

Ty and the kids sat down, and Mona came bustling over to set their places and give them tall plastic glasses of water. The kids chattered nonstop, sharing more than anyone ever needed to know about how today was their last day of school for two whole weeks.

"All right, then," Mona said. "What'll you have?"

As the kids asked for short stacks, scrambled eggs and orange juice, Ty dealt with his disappointment that Sadie hadn't been the one to take their order.

He asked for his usual. Mona nodded. "Sadie will be right over with the coffeepot."

And she was. The gray winter day suddenly seemed so much brighter as she filled his cup, even though she barely spared him more than a glance before moving on to fill cups at the next booth over.

A few minutes later, Mona appeared with their breakfast. She was the one who refilled his coffee. Sadie seemed to have completely disappeared.

When they got up to go, Zeb was already filling his gray tub with their dirty dishes.

Ty asked him, "Where'd Sadie get off to?"

"She left for the Buffalo store, I think." Zeb stuck their glasses in the tub and gathered up the flatware.

"Daddy, we have to get going." Em pulled on his hand.

"Yeah, Dad." Drew took his other hand. "Let's go."

The kids led him out to the car. He dropped them off at school and then went on to the office. All day, he kept wondering if Sadie had left for Buffalo earlier than usual to keep from having to deal with him.

He had no right to be pissed off about that.

But he was. He was kind of a nervous wreck anyway, trying to figure out what he would say to her, how he would convince her to give him a chance at the relationship thing. The least she could do was stand still long enough for him to ask if they could talk later.

It took him till one in the afternoon to drum up the nerve to pick up the damn phone. He considered sending a text. But for some reason, he had a feeling she would find it harder to dismiss a call.

She didn't find it hard at all.

The call went straight to voice mail, and he stumbled through his message. "Hi, Sadie. It's Ty. Listen. I, uh, really need to talk to you. I was thinking I could come over, maybe? My mom's taking the kids tonight, so I'm free. And if you would just call me back and tell me when you've got a few minutes to talk to me, I'll be there. And I, uh…" *Uh*, what? He had no idea. "Anyway, talk to you soon."

He hung up before he could make a bigger fool of himself than he just had—if that was even possible. But then, as soon as he ended the call, he realized he'd never even hinted at what he needed to talk to her about.

She would end up assuming it was more of the same—him pushing her to continue hooking up in secret, disrespecting her boundaries when she'd asked him to stay away.

An hour limped past. And then another. He went home to meet the kids when they got off the bus.

Sadie still had not returned his call. And he almost forgot the kids had a Skype call with Nic at four. They sat on the sofa with his laptop talking to their mother and Gavin for half an hour. Ty stuck his head in once just to say hi. The newlyweds looked happy in their beach clothes and straw hats. The kids talked over each other, anxious to fill their mother in on each and every little thing that had happened since their last call on Tuesday.

At five, he drove the kids to his folks' house. His mom and dad would take them out to the ranch tomorrow to hang around the horses with Jobeth. Tess had invited them to stay for dinner at the main house. He was invited, too.

His mom patted his cheek like he was five again. "You know they would love to have you, but if you want another evening for yourself, go for it. The kids can spend the night with us, and you can pick them up Sunday morning."

"That'd be great, Mom." If things went well, he might get two nights with Sadie.

But to claim those two nights, he needed to find a way to get her to talk to him.

As a rule, on a weeknight, she got home from the Sheridan store at least by six or so. He waited until six thirty, thinking maybe she'd get home, check her voice mail and call him back.

Didn't happen. He drove over there. When he pulled up in front, the lights were on inside.

No doubt about it. He'd been put on *ignore*. No time like the present to say what needed saying. He jumped out of the Escalade, ran up the front steps and rang the bell before he could lose his nerve.

She did not come running.

After a reasonable period of time that only seemed like a century, he rang the bell again.

His phone went off in his pocket.

He pulled it out and took the call. "Let me in, Sadie."

"Ty, I don't want to do this again. I really don't."

Words tumbled over themselves in his head. Most of the time, he was a pretty good talker, but right now, he barely remembered his own name. "I'm not here for that."

Silence. Had she hung up on him?

But then finally, she spoke. "Then why *are* you here?"

"Because I heard you the other night. I get it. And I am hoping that you and me, well, what I mean is, I would like to try…" He hesitated, like some green kid who had no clue how to tell a girl that he cared.

"Try what?"

"Damn it, Sadie, yes! I want to be with you. I want to take a chance with you. I just hope you will still consider taking a chance with me."

The door swung wide.

She stood there in snug jeans, a Henry's T-shirt and stocking feet, with her phone in her hand. "Taking a chance, how?"

His brain blanked. He blinked and tried to find the right words. "A chance to be together, you and me, out in the open, no sneaking around."

She frowned, still wary. "What made you change your mind?"

"You. Everything. How much I miss you…" He swept off his hat and pressed it over his heart. "I don't know what I'm doing, I really don't. But, Sadie, for you, I'm willing to try."

Her eyes changed. Now they were seafoam green and shining bright. "Well, then. I guess you'd better come in." She took hold of his hand and pulled him over the threshold.

Chapter Twelve

Could this be real?

Sadie's poor heart felt like it might just beat its way out of her chest. She needed to get away for a minute, pull herself together, try to get her mind around what he seemed to be offering her.

As she shut and locked the door, she said, "Take off your coat and come on in the great room." And then she turned and left him there. Because if she kept on looking at him, she wouldn't be able to hold herself back from grabbing his hand again and dragging him straight to her bed.

In the great room, she took the chair. She was guarding herself, protecting herself.

From what?

She knew him. If he said he was ready to be with her in a real and honest way, he meant it. Ty didn't tell sweet lies. He didn't say things he wasn't willing to back up with action.

When he emerged from her little square of entry hall, she pointed at the sofa.

He edged in behind the coffee table and sat. "Now what?"

She sandwiched her hands between her knees and answered sheepishly, "Back there at the door you said you didn't know what you were doing."

"Well, I don't."

"Yeah, I get that. Because neither do I, really."

"Aw, Sadie…" He started to rise—but then caught himself and sank back to the cushions.

Her eyes brimmed. If she didn't watch herself, she'd start bawling like a baby. "I didn't expect this. I really didn't."

"Join the club." His voice was gruff. "And please tell me the truth, Sadie Jane. What's going on here? Have you changed your mind, is that it?"

"Changed my mind…?"

"About you and me."

She gasped. "No! Not a chance."

He drew a slow, shaky breath. "Then why am I still stuck here on the sofa all by myself?"

She swallowed. Hard. "I don't know. I wasn't thinking, I guess. I mean, I wasn't expecting you to, um, offer me everything I asked you for."

He stood and came around to her. When he held down his hand, she put hers in it.

And when he pulled her up, she threw her arms around him and looked up into his beautiful eyes. "I guess we're doing this, huh?"

"Oh, yeah. You bet we are."

She lifted up and his mouth descended. For a while,

they just stood there by the green chair, kissing endlessly, wrapped up in each other.

And then he took her hand again. He turned for her bedroom.

She followed him happily, thinking how strange life could be. All those years of relentlessly hunting for the right guy—from Kevin in high school, to Paul and then Reggie. Through all those coffee dates and boring restaurant dinners.

When all along, it was Ty. Without even knowing it, she'd been waiting for Ty.

And now, at last, he was here. *Really* here. With her.

In her room, he turned on the lamp by the bed and took her face between his two big hands. "You and me, Sadie Jane."

"Yeah. You and me, Tyler Ross. We've got so much to talk about."

He put a finger against her lips. "Yes, we do. Soon." He stuck his hand in his pocket and pulled out a wad of little foil pouches.

She tried really hard not to roll her eyes. "Just like in Breckenridge. Pretty sure of yourself, aren't you?"

"Not really. But I like to be ready if things go my way." He dropped the condoms on the nightstand and reached for her again.

When he kissed her, she opened to him, forgetting all the things that would have to be worked out, surrendering to the pure joy of that moment—of her and Ty, together at last.

They undressed quickly and fell across the bed, kissing, laughing, kissing some more. His hands were magic.

He touched her in the sweetest, most arousing ways. With her mouth locked to his, she reached down between them.

Before she could curl her fingers around his hard length, he caught her wrist. Groaning, she broke their kiss to meet his eyes.

"Together," he said on a rough husk of breath. "Now…" And then he was reaching for a condom. She helped him, taking the pouch, getting it open, carefully rolling it over him.

"Come here." He took her shoulders, guided her onto her back and came down on top of her.

"Ty…" She whispered his name as he filled her.

His eyes burned into hers. "So good, Sadie. You and me…"

"Yes. Exactly. You and me…"

He pressed in even deeper. It felt so good. So right, to be wrapped all around him, holding him tight. They moved slow and sweet, together.

And then faster, harder. She clung to him, lost in those eyes of his, as he rocked within her, taking her higher, all the way to the top of the world, and then over into free fall.

Her climax bloomed all through her, hollowing her out, then tightening into a long, sweet pulse of sheer, perfect pleasure.

When she went limp, he rocked into her even deeper than before. She could feel him hitting the edge, going over. And then his big body went still. A groan rose up from deep inside him as he came.

She held him close and tight, believing in him, in what they might have together, happy in a way she'd never been before.

* * *

After midnight, they got up. Ty put his pants and shirt back on. Sadie pulled on her pajamas and led the way to the kitchen. He took a seat at the central island as she heated up stew for him.

"Are the kids at your mom's?" she asked when she set the bowl in front of him.

"Yeah. She'll keep them till Sunday morning—and this is great. Thanks."

"You're welcome. My dad's special recipe." She was beautiful, all rumpled and satisfied-looking in those flannel pajamas.

He ate more stew. "You have the weekend off?"

"Yes, I do."

"Spend it with me?"

"Yes," she replied with no hesitation. "I would love to spend the weekend with you."

"I'm glad." He patted the stool beside him.

She took it. "I've been thinking."

"Uh-oh."

For that, she bopped him on the arm with the back of her hand. "We do have to talk this through, and you know it."

Damn, she had attitude. He'd always liked that about her. Sadie laid it right out there. She never played coy, never dropped clues or batted her eyelashes in hopes he would fall at her feet.

"I know we have to talk about it," he said. "Naturally, I would prefer to spend every moment rolling around in bed with you, but I get that's not how it's going to be."

She wrapped her hand around his upper arm, leaned in and kissed him. "I like being in bed with you, too."

He smirked. "I know."

She groaned. "The ego on you."

"Get used to it. I'm going to be around a lot."

Her expression softened. "I'm glad." But then she glanced away. He waited for her to come out with it. A few seconds later, she did. "All right. Look, I know I'm the one who insisted we were going to stop sneaking around, but I think we need to make sure the kids have no idea that we're more than good buddies until Nic gets back from her honeymoon."

He froze with a big bite of stew halfway to his mouth. "Why?"

"I just think it's better if we tell Nic we're together before the kids find out. Otherwise, they might say something to her before we've had a chance to catch her up on what's going on. She would be blindsided and that could really freak her out."

He set the full spoon back in the bowl. "You know her as well as I do. Chances are, she'll be freaked out no matter how we handle it. Freaking out is her specialty."

"That's not fair."

"Maybe not. But it's usually true. And I've got to ask. Why does every damn thing have to be about Nicole?"

"You're exaggerating."

"No, I'm not. It's always about Nicole. She's a diva and a drama queen."

"Not so much anymore."

"Okay, not as much as she used to be. But she still has a real tendency to make everything about her."

"It's a special situation. She's my best friend and *your* ex-wife."

"*Ex*, Sadie. You just said it. She's my ex. Which means that, except when it comes to Em and Drew, she's got no claim on my personal life."

"That's true. It's me she could be angry with."

He shook his head. "Nah. We're both getting blamed, believe me."

Sadie had no comeback for that. "Maybe she'll surprise us…"

"Hey," he said, realizing they should at least try to look on the bright side. "Maybe she will."

Sadie let out a soft, worried little sound.

"C'mere." He wrapped an arm around her.

She leaned her head on his shoulder. "The least we can do is make sure she's the first to know that you and I are together." She looked up at him so hopefully.

He gave in. "Fine. What time is it in the Virgin Islands?"

"Three in the morning or so. Why?"

"When it's nine or ten there, we'll call her together, a video chat, and tell her the big news."

"What? No. Not while she's on her honeymoon. That wouldn't be right. Come on, it's not that long to wait. She'll be back a week from Sunday, on Christmas Eve. We'll talk to her then."

He scoffed. "How is Christmas Eve a good choice? They're taking a red-eye to Denver and then a nonstop flight to Casper. It's a two-and-a-half-hour drive from there. They won't get here till five or so on Christmas Eve. The kids will be bouncing off the walls with excitement over her return and the holiday. There's not going to be a good time that night to talk to Nicole about you and me. And then the next day is Christmas. That's no good, either. The truth is, no time is the right time."

"Then we'll tell her on the day after Christmas, I promise you, Ty. One way or another, we'll talk to her then. But no matter what we do, how we handle it, it's possible she'll be hurt."

"Right. Because everything is always about her," he said, aware of his own bitterness on the subject, knowing he should dial it back.

She was shaking her head. "It's a trust thing. A *truth* thing. It's O's before bros."

"O's...?"

"Yeah, ovaries. And timing does matter. You can't seriously think it will be better if we tell her on video chat during her honeymoon?"

"Look. We have to face the facts. No matter what we do or how we handle it, she's likely to go full-out drama queen on our asses."

Sadie groaned. "And here I thought you and Nic were in a good place about each other now."

"Mostly we are, yeah. But she still gets to me now and then. She's a lot of work, that woman. And I'm not even married to her anymore."

The two cats appeared from the short hallway to Sadie's room. Side by side, they trotted over and stretched out at the base of her chair. With her stocking foot, she petted the calico one. Her face was tipped down to them, but he could see she was biting her lower lip.

"Go ahead, Sadie, just say it."

She looked up at him. "Say what?"

"That you don't want to tell *anyone* about us until after we've talked to Nicole."

Her mouth dropped open. "How did you know that?"

"It tracks. The kids are the most likely to say something to her, but anyone could, really. I get that. Damn. That woman is so lucky to have you for a friend."

"You think? Right now, I'm not so sure. Plus, I just

feel like a hypocrite. I mean, Monday I told you I would never sneak around—and now look at me, asking you to sneak around until the day after Christmas."

"Hey." He stroked a finger down her velvety cheek to her throat, eased his fingers under her hair and then wrapped them around her nape. "Roll with it." He pulled her closer. "Sneaking around has its own special charm."

The corner of her mouth twitched as she tried not to grin. "You're a bad influence. And you know what? I actually like that about you."

He nuzzled her ear. She smelled like heaven—his own personal paradise. "Welcome to the dark side."

A soft sigh escaped her. "You're just trying to distract me from my disappointment in myself."

He nibbled her cheek. "Is it working?"

"Yeah. Please. Don't stop now…"

A few minutes later, he took her back to bed. They used two more condoms before dropping off to sleep.

He woke the next morning with his arms wrapped around her and her hair in his face. Gently, he smoothed the tangled strands aside to kiss her neck, followed by every other part of her he could get his mouth on.

It was great.

When they finally crawled out of bed, they ate breakfast and then showered together.

That took quite a while.

In the afternoon, they went to his house. He packed a bag and they returned to her place, where they hung around the rest of that day and all night, just the two of them, doing nothing, often minus their clothes.

Doing nothing with Sadie was the best time he'd ever had.

They talked about the future in a generalized way.

She said she was too hands-on to open another Henry's at this point. "I can't do much more than I'm already doing *and* have a life."

"You'd have to learn to delegate."

"As I said, I'm bad at that."

"Just because you haven't done it yet doesn't mean you can't learn—and you *have* done it up to a point. You have managers who run each of the stores when you and your folks aren't there. The question is, do you really want to expand any more than you already have?"

"At this point, no. I'm happy with the quality and service we provide. Each store is like a home away from home. I don't want a whole bunch of corporate-style diners. That was never the dream. Plus, I have other things I want to do, important things."

"Like?"

She didn't answer right away. They were in the kitchen. He was mixing up the topping for garlic bread as she sautéed chicken on the cooktop. Staring down at the browning chicken, she drew a slow breath and said, "I'm going to want more kids."

He wasn't the least surprised. "What? You've got kids I didn't know about?"

She slanted him a sharp glance. "Very funny. I was thinking about Drew and Emily."

He deserted the garlic bread to go to her and wrap his arms around her from behind. "Chicken smells good."

She pushed the browning thighs around in the pan with a pair of tongs and refused to glance his way. "You know what I mean, right?"

He eased her hair away from her ear so he could whisper in it. "I wouldn't mind another girl."

She fiddled with the chicken some more. "I might want a boy, too."

"So, two more?"

She turned the fire down under the pan, set down the tongs and turned to face him. "Boys. Girls. One of each, doesn't matter. But two more would be so nice. I mean, if possible…"

He realized two was just fine with him. "Yeah. Two more sounds good."

"It's all just, you know, hypothetical."

"But it's what you want."

"It is, yeah."

"Okay, then. As I said, two more is fine with me." He put a finger under her chin and kissed that sweet mouth. "How long until you would be ready to start working on that?"

"Hmm. I figure it's good to have a little time to be a couple first."

He kissed her again. "That makes sense."

"A year, two at the most. Then we throw out the contraception and get to work making babies happen."

"Good plan."

She looked at him sideways. "I'm surprised you're so agreeable. I mean, I know this is all just talk, but you do seem willing."

"It's not just talk, Sadie." He looked at her steadily so she would know he meant what he said. "I am willing."

"But you were a teenager when you became a dad. If you had more kids in the next few years, you'd be well into your fifties before your kids would be out on their own."

"So what? My dad's almost seventy. You ask him,

he'll tell you that being a dad never ends—not until a man stops breathing, anyway."

"But Cash was older when you were born. He had years without the responsibility of raising children. You didn't."

Ty couldn't help but smile. "It's true that when Nic had Emily; I wasn't ready, not in the least. And Drew was a surprise, too. I wasn't much good as a father there at the beginning. I was going to school more than a thousand miles away and also bitter about the whole situation.

"But then I grew up a little. I got over myself. I started to understand that my kids needed me—and I needed them, too. I started paying more attention, *being* there for them. Turns out I love being a dad. So yeah, I would do it again. As long as it was with the right woman this time." His mouth curled in a hint of a grin. "And by the right woman, I mean you."

She leaned up for another kiss. "All, um, hypothetically speaking, of course."

He winked at her. "Hell, yeah."

"I probably should tell you that I also want to get married. Eventually."

He pretended to look shocked. "You're kidding me. I never would have guessed."

"Well." She looked down and said too softly, "Ever since it ended with you and Nic, you've been all about being free. So, the fact that I do want to get married needs to be addressed."

"Hey." He tipped up her chin again. "I didn't realize until very recently that it's all about finding the right person. The right person makes getting married downright desirable."

Her eyes got bigger. "You mean that?"

"Yeah, Sadie. I do. And the right person for me… is you."

"Well. I'm really glad to hear that. Because I feel the same about you." She threaded her fingers into his hair and surged up to press her lips to his. He returned that kiss eagerly, cradling her close. Just as he was about to scoop her up in his arms and carry her off to her bedroom, she shoved at his chest. "I know that look. And I love it. But right now, I need to get back to my chicken."

They finished preparing the dinner. She opened a bottle of white wine and they sat at the table to eat. The food was great.

And he had Sadie for dessert.

That night went by way too fast.

Before he knew it, he was back in his Escalade Sunday morning, headed for his mom's house to pick up the kids. He didn't see Sadie the rest of that day. It was awful.

Now that he'd admitted to himself that he was ready for a relationship as long as it was with her, he wanted her with him every day, and all through the night. But until the big talk with Nic, he had to pretend they were just friends whenever anybody else was around.

He called her as soon as he got the kids to bed.

"I don't like being apart," he said in response to her hello.

"I don't, either, but it won't be for that long."

A week was way too long. "Tomorrow? Can you get away?"

"Tomorrow is a full day of work for me. Ty, it's only a week."

"It's not right. We just got things worked out and now we're in a holding pattern."

"I'll tell you what. I can get home by five or so. Bring the kids over here to my house for dinner tomorrow night."

He almost felt like he could breathe again. "We'll be there."

"Remember. No PDAs."

"I remember—and I still don't like it."

"Ty…"

"What?"

"You're repeating yourself."

He was and he knew it. "Okay, Sadie Jane. I will behave."

"I don't like it, either," she confessed. "But I really don't want Nic to hear it from one of the kids—or someone else. Not from anyone except you and me."

What could he say? "I understand."

Dinner Monday night was great—as far as it went. He and Sadie pretended to be just friends and the kids seemed oblivious to how much had changed. He didn't get to throw her over his shoulder and carry her off to bed the way he longed to do. But seeing her, hearing her voice, hanging out with her and his kids, that was good. Really good.

Tuesday, he didn't see her. They talked a little on the phone that evening, but it wasn't enough. He hated being apart from her more each day.

Was he ridiculous?

Too bad. He finally knew what he wanted. And he had to pretend that nothing had changed until they talked to Nicole. He figured he had a right to be a whiny fool about it.

Wednesday morning, he took the kids out to the ranch. Tess and Jobeth had volunteered to look after them for the day so he could catch up at work.

He'd barely said hi to Ramona, ducked into his office and opened his laptop when there was a tap on the door. "It's open!"

His mother stuck her head in. "Got a minute?" Without waiting for a reply, she slipped in and shut the door behind her.

He was checking email, frowning at the realization that he had a couple of meetings he couldn't put off much longer. "What's up?"

She took the big cowhide chair across the desk from him. "I'm just going to go ahead and say it."

"Uh, sure. Something wrong?"

"Nope. Far from it." She sat back, crossed her legs, propped her elbow on the chair arm and started fiddling with a curl of her chin-length blond hair. Something was definitely going on with her.

He closed his laptop. "Okay. What is it you're just going to go ahead and say?"

"Did you have a nice weekend?"

"Mom. Come out with it, why don't you?"

She did some weird throat clearing. "Well, then. All right. Rumor has it that your Cadillac was spotted out in front of Sadie's house very early Saturday morning. It was still there Saturday night—and Sunday morning, too."

His immediate response was a feeling of satisfaction. Because he wanted to be with Sadie, and he wanted the world to know. But Sadie didn't want anyone to know—at least not until they'd had that talk with Nicole. "Somebody needs to mind their own damn business."

His mom had a look—a guilty look. And then she said flatly, "Okay, there's no rumor."

"Uh, what?"

"It was me."

"It was you, what?"

"I just had a hunch, you know? About you and Sadie. Your dad and I have always felt she was perfect for you."

"Wait. What? You have?"

"Of course. Sadie is smart and snappy."

"Snappy?"

"Yeah. Quick. On the ball. She's fun and she's completely down-to-earth. She's all about taking care of the people she loves. Someone like her, that's what you need in your life. A woman who says it like it is and doesn't put up with your crap."

"Mom, seriously? My *crap*?"

She waved a dismissing hand. "Sorry, poor word choice. But you know how you can be."

"Not really. Though I'm sure you're going to tell me."

"What I mean is, you need someone straightforward. Someone who lays it all right on the line."

"Okay…"

"Look. I swear to you, I never would've said a thing, but you two have become such good friends the past few years. And then, at the wedding, I sensed a certain—I don't know, energy, between you. I just knew you two were getting even closer. So, over this past weekend, I just might have left the kids with your dad and casually driven by your place and then her place. I might have done that more than once. And wouldn't you know? Every time I drove by Sadie's, your car was there. We are talking at eleven at night on Friday, four thirty in the morning Saturday. And then Sunday morning at right around four."

Where to even begin with all this? "Mom. I never pegged you for a stalker."

"Well, that's because, as a rule, I'm not. And I do feel guilty enough to come clean about it here and now. I'm sorry. You're a grown man and your mother should not be out tracking your whereabouts in the middle of the night."

"You got that right. Don't do it again."

"I won't. But I just had to know. And I need to say that my unacceptable behavior was driven by the best of intentions and all the love in the world."

"It's fine, Mom—I mean, please don't make a habit of it."

"I promise you I won't."

"Good. And you're right. I'm all in on Sadie."

She leaned back in the chair and sighed at the ceiling. "I knew it!"

"You need to keep it between you and Dad for now, though. Sadie wants to break the news to Nicole that we're together before anyone else finds out."

"Of course, absolutely. Until you give us the go-ahead, your dad and I will not say a word."

"Thank you."

"But I've been thinking..."

Now he was the one sighing. "Say it."

"You need more time with Sadie, just the two of you."

"I agree. But with the kids and work—mine *and* hers—and having to pretend we're just friends around people in general, there *is* no time for the two of us, not until we tell Nicole we're together, which isn't happening till the day after Christmas."

"Because…?"

"Trust me. There are reasons."

"When do the newlyweds get back, exactly?"

"Around five on Sunday."

"All right, then. How about this…?"

He looked at her sideways because who knew what she might say next? "How about what?"

"Why don't you bring Drew and Emily to us on Friday afternoon? We'll take them to the ranch. You know how they love it there. They can hang out with the horses and we'll all four sleep in the bunkhouse, where they can camp out in the common room if they're in the mood. I'll bring them back to you by noon Sunday."

"Aw, Mom…" He got up, circled his desk and pulled her out of her chair for a hug. "You're the best."

She patted his shoulder as she stared up into his eyes. "You look tired. But you also look happier than I've seen you in years. And I'm happy *for* you. Friday, then?"

"Yeah. Thank you."

With a final, fond pat—on the cheek this time—she left him alone.

He waited till that night after the kids were in bed to text Sadie. Can you talk?

She called a few seconds later. The first words out of her mouth were, "Everything okay?"

"It's better now that I hear your voice. I miss you."

"Miss you, too. What's up?"

He wanted to hold her. And come Friday night, he would. "My mom's volunteered to take the kids to the ranch for the weekend. I'll drop them off at three on Friday…"

"Pack an overnight bag," she commanded. "Come stay with me while they're gone."

"I was hoping you'd say that…" He tried to decide whether or not to tell her that his mom and dad knew they were together. It would only worry her. And why did she even need to know?

"Ty?"

"What?"

"Is something going on?"

How did she do that? Sometimes she read him like a large-print book. "What do you mean?"

"Stop with the evasions. Just tell me."

He gave it up. "My mom and dad know we're together."

She hitched in a sharp breath. "Oh, Ty. You told them?"

"No."

"Then how…?"

"My mother guessed." He recapped the conversation he'd had with her that morning, adding, "Please don't worry. She's thrilled about you and me. And I told her you wanted to talk to Nicole before anyone else can know. She gets that and she won't say anything to anyone. My dad won't, either."

"But someone could drive by my house and see your car, just like she did…"

"So what? Not everyone is my mother with a special interest in me and the meaningful relationship she's been hoping I'd find. Most people won't be paying the least bit of attention. And if they did happen to notice, there are any number of reasons my car could be parked at your house. Everyone in town knows we're friends. And anyway, we're both single, so nobody's cheating. Honestly, what is there to spread stories about?"

She thought that over for way too long before admitting, "I suppose you're right."

"Because I *am* right—and you've got to stop worrying about Nic. No one's going to chase her down and tell her that we're together before we tell her ourselves. It's not shocking to anyone, except maybe Nicole."

"I get that, I do. And maybe I'm a little overprotective when it comes to her."

"A *little*?" He gentled his tone. "Everything is going to work out. You need to stop worrying about it."

"I'm trying—and back to your mom. You said she's happy about you and me..."

"I did—and she is."

"Oh, Ty. I'm glad. Really glad. I've always liked Abby. She's so strong. Smart, too."

"That's pretty much what she said about you."

"Well. That's nice to know."

"And can we talk about something more interesting now?"

"What's more interesting than your mother?"

"Is that a trick question?"

"Hmm." She was grinning. He could hear it in her voice. "Maybe."

He was grinning, too. "I need you to tell me how much you miss me."

"So, so much."

"Good. Because I miss you, too—and I have an idea. On Friday, why don't you come to my house for a change? Not even the nosiest busybody in town will know you're there all night because I'll pick you up. Bring Olive and Boo if you don't want to leave them at home."

"Nah. They like home best. I'll run back over here Saturday to feed them."

"Okay, then. That's settled. Now, about those important things we really need to talk about…" He lowered his voice to a teasing growl. "What are you wearing?"

She snickered. "I'll never tell."

"Let me guess. Those hot plaid pajamas."

"You think my plaid pajamas are hot?"

"Everything you wear is hot. And as for those pajamas, I want you to take them off right now. Take them off very slowly…"

They stayed on the phone for another two hours. He went to bed late with a big smile on his face.

Sadie got home Friday evening to find Ty waiting outside in his car. She pulled to a stop alongside him and leaned across the seat as she rolled down the passenger-side window. "I have to feed the cats. Come on in." She took her foot off the brake and turned into her driveway.

He was waiting at the front door when she pulled it wide. A moment later, he was over the threshold and taking her into his arms.

One kiss became two—and then three.

Reluctantly, she pushed him away. "We'll never get to your house at this rate."

"Who cares?" He reached for her again.

She danced out of his reach. "Let me put out fresh food and water for the cats, grab my overnight bag and we're out of here."

At his house, she dropped her bag on the floor in the front hall and set her purse on the narrow table there. She'd just hooked her coat on one of the pegs by the door when Ty caught her hand. "Come here."

She let out a happy cry as he swung her up into his arms and carried her off to his bed.

Later, they raided his fridge and cooked dinner together. They were loading the dishwasher after the meal when he started kissing her again. That led right back to bed.

It was past midnight when he collected her overnight bag from the front hall for her. They showered together. Eventually, standing side by side at the twin sinks, they brushed their teeth.

"I could get used to this," he said around a mouthful of toothpaste foam.

She rinsed before replying, "Oh, me, too..."

They went back to bed, but not to sleep. Instead, they whispered to each other in the dark, sharing secrets, making plans. She had no idea what time it was when they finally drifted off into dreamland.

Bells were ringing. It took Ty a moment to realize he was hearing the doorbell.

He fumbled on the nightstand for his phone, which lit up in his hand. It was 10:34 in the morning—and he had two texts from Nicole, one at nine thirty: Just off the plane from Denver. Long story. Will be @ your house @ 10:30.

And another at ten fifteen: Are you home? I hope so. We're coming straight to your house. Missing the kids. Can't wait to hug them.

The doorbell chimed again.

Beside him, a sleepy-eyed Sadie swiped her hair back off her forehead and said, "Someone's at the door."

"I know." He grabbed her around the back of the neck and planted a hard kiss on her sweet mouth before breaking the news. "It's Nic and Gavin home a day early. She sent me a couple of texts that they were on their way from Sheridan—too bad I didn't wake up and read the damn things before the doorbell rang."

Her eyes popped wide-open then. "Oh, no!"

"Yep." He rolled out of bed and grabbed for his jeans. "Stay here. I'll deal with them."

"But, Ty…"

The doorbell rang yet again as he tugged on a wrinkled black T-shirt and raked his fingers through his rumpled hair. "Stay here. Don't worry."

"But…"

He silenced her with another hard kiss and headed for the door.

By the time he got there, Nic had rung the bell another time and started knocking.

"All right, hold your horses!" He pulled the door open and tried not to glare at his ex-wife, who stood on the doormat with Gavin right behind her. "Nic, you have to give a guy a moment to put on his pants, you know?"

"You were still in bed?" she scoffed.

"Nic…" Gavin spoke to her chidingly. "It's Saturday, people sleep in."

"You're right!" She sent her groom an adoring glance over her shoulder and then blasted an aggressive smile at Ty. "I'm sorry. We left a day early, so we got to Denver last night and then took this morning's flight to Sheridan." She tried to see around him. "Where are my babies? I've missed them so much!"

"They're at the ranch with my folks."

"What?" She was kind of bouncing up and down. "No…"

"Sorry."

She blew out a hard breath. "Okay, well, we'll have to surprise them there…"

"Good idea. Welcome home, you two." He started to shut the door.

Nic stopped him. "Uh, Ty…"

"Yeah?"

She was bouncing from foot to foot now. "Mind if I use the powder room? I really do have to pee."

He remembered then. With both Em and Drew, she was constantly running to the bathroom. "Sure." Way too aware of poor Sadie, waiting in his bedroom wondering what was going on, he stepped back and ushered them in.

"You're a lifesaver." Nic brushed right past him, vanishing as she turned the corner at the end of the front hall. The half bath was right there, off the kitchen. He heard the door shut.

Gavin hunched into his winter coat, his hands in the pockets. "She's never been away from them this long before," he offered sheepishly.

"I get it." He considered leading Gavin into the great room, but that would only encourage them to stick around. "How was the trip?"

Gavin's eyes lit up. "Amazing. Nothing like two weeks on a tropical island with my best girl."

"You look great. Tan and happy."

"I feel great. We took a catamaran to Little Buck Island and snorkeled with the green sea turtles. I almost hated to come home…"

They made small talk for a couple more minutes, until Nic finally reappeared at the end of the hall. Pulling on her coat as she went, she came marching toward them. "What a relief! I…" She stopped in midstep. "Is Sadie here?"

Ty tried to stay cool. *How could she know?*

"Come on, Ty." Nic flung out a hand toward the narrow hall table. "That's her favorite cross-body saddle purse right there." Next, she pointed at the coat rack. "And that's her jacket."

He fumbled for a good lie. "She, um, she came by yesterday and, uh—"

"Ran off without her coat and purse? It's freezing out there. What's going on? She's here, right? I can't wait to see her. Sadie!" she shouted. And then she laughed, like it was all a big joke. "Come out, come out, wherever you are!"

Apparently, Gavin had put two and two together. He looked as freaked as Ty felt as he tried to step in. "Nicole, come on. We should…" The sentence died an untimely death.

Because Sadie appeared at the end of the hallway, fully dressed, with her hair neatly combed. "Hey."

Nicole blinked and slid a glance at Ty in his wrinkled shirt, bed-scrambled hair and bare feet. "Wait a minute. What's going on? I don't…" Everyone just stood there, witnesses at a train wreck, as Nic figured it out. "Oh. My. God…"

Ty had eyes only for Sadie. She must have felt the force of his stare because she looked at him then. He watched her beautiful face as she accepted the fact that there was no way now to keep up the charade until the day after Christmas.

"It's okay, Ty," she said softly, her eyes steady on his. And then she faced Nicole again. "I spent the night here. Ty and me, we're together."

Nicole blinked. "What? *What?*" She had that look. Shocked. Completely disbelieving. Then came the fury. "How long has this been going on?" She glared at Sadie. "We're best friends." And then she swung her anger to Ty, "You're my ex-husband. And I didn't *know*? Neither of you had the decency to tell me what you were up to?"

Who the hell did she think she was? "What are you talking about, Nicole? Everything is not always about you. You and I have been divorced for three years. You've got no say when it comes to who I'm with."

"Don't give me that. You've got no right to mess with Sadie."

"I'm not *messing* with Sadie. She and I—"

"Oh, please. Everyone knows how you are."

"Nic!" Sadie said sharply. "Stop."

"Nicole, come on, now." Gavin caught her arm. "Baby, you need to stop this. Let's just go."

She yanked free of his grip and turned her fury on Sadie. "How could you? How could you ever? I mean, I always suspected there was something going on between you two, but I told myself it was just me, being insecure, having the usual trust issues. I guess I got that wrong, didn't I? So right now, this minute, you need to just tell me the truth, Sadie. Were you two going behind my back while I was married to him?"

"What the ever-loving hell, Nicole?" Ty had heard about enough. "There's been nothing between Sadie and me. Never while you and I were together. Never until just recently. You've got it all wrong. But that's how you roll, isn't it? You never could pass up a chance to exercise all your over-the-top emotions."

"Ty." Sadie touched his arm. "Please."

He shut his eyes and drew a slow, steadying breath. "Fine. You deal with her."

She turned to Nicole. "Let's go into the other room. We'll sit down. We'll talk. Calmly, okay?"

Nicole threw up both hands. "There is nothing you can say to me right now! Not after this. Nothing. Ever. Again." She spun on her heel and marched to the door. Yanking it wide, she went through. Gavin caught it before it banged against the hall table. With a last apologetic backward glance, he closed it quietly behind them.

Chapter Thirteen

Ty and Sadie were left standing in the front hall, staring at each other like two bedraggled survivors of some natural disaster. He didn't know what to feel.

Would he lose Sadie over this? He'd damn well better not. And what about the kids? Would they end up with their parents at each other's throats again?

What an ugly mess. "I'm sorry, Sadie."

"Oh, Ty…"

He held out his arms and felt a rush of sweet relief when she came right into them. The knot in his gut loosened a fraction as he held her tight and pressed a kiss into her silky hair. "This is on her. Really, who the hell does she think she is?"

Sadie looked up at him. Her eyes were so sad—sad, and way too determined. "I have to go talk to her."

He held her tighter. "Why?"

"Because I love her. She's my sister, Ty, she really is.

She needs to be reminded of that. She needs to know that I would never betray her, and neither would you. She needs to understand that I'm never giving up on her. That none of us are. Not ever."

He tipped up her chin and kissed her. "She's in the wrong."

"That's not the issue here."

"Sadie, you don't know how she gets."

"Please. How many times do I need to remind you that I know exactly how she gets?"

She was right, as usual. Sadie and Nic had always been inseparable, two peas in a cozy little pod. "You're right. You know her best. But I really think you should let her cool off, at least."

"No. I need to go to her now."

"She's probably on her way to the ranch to get the kids."

"I don't think so. She lost it and she knows it. And she's worked so hard to overcome her, uh…personal demons. She has coping strategies. I think she'll go home and take some time to cool down before picking up the kids. I also think she'll be hoping that I'll come and work it out with her."

"She's got a lot of nerve, always did."

"Maybe so, but I should have told her about us sooner."

He probably ought to keep his mouth shut. But he didn't. "I wanted to call her a week ago. You said no. You said we had to wait till after Christmas."

"I remember. And in hindsight, I get that you were right. In hindsight, I should have told her how I was feeling about you on the night of Emily's birthday party."

"Wait a minute. That was more than a month ago."

"Yeah. It was also after what happened in Las Vegas, and I was thinking about you all the time. She knew something was bothering me that night. When she asked me what was wrong, I blew her off. I lied and said there was nothing. But you were on my mind."

"Still, we weren't together then."

"Correct me if I'm wrong but wasn't that the night you dragged me into Nic's craft room to try to talk me into a hot Christmas fling?"

He felt ashamed. "I was an ass."

"Maybe a little bit. As for Nic, if I'd told her I was catching feelings for you that night, if I'd explained about Vegas then, she would have had more time to start accepting the idea of you and me together."

"Uh-uh. If you'd told her that night, she would have lost it, just like she did today."

Her shoulders lifted in a small, resigned shrug. "Maybe—but, Ty, I need to go talk to her now."

"I still don't like it."

"I know." She rubbed his arm, soothing him with her touch.

He warned, "She's going to say bad stuff about me."

Undeterred, she lifted up and pressed her sweet mouth to his. "It will be all right, I promise you."

"I'll drive you."

"It's just around the block and it's not snowing. I'll walk."

What else could he say? She intended to do this and there was no way he could stop her. "I'll be here. Waiting. Don't believe a damn word she says."

She went on tiptoe again and whispered, "Stop," against his lips.

"That's what you said to *her*," he grumbled.

"Yeah. So take the high road on this. Just because Nic's flinging dirt around doesn't mean *you* have to." She kissed him again.

He kissed her back, hard. "You're such a good person. Just don't let her walk all over you, that's all I'm saying."

"It will be fine."

He was far from convinced. "Not only a good person, but way too damn optimistic." He gave it one more shot. "I'd better go with you."

"No. She's my best friend and my sister and you are going to let me deal with her. Stay right here." She kissed him once more and then waved her phone at him. "I promise to call if I need you."

"I'll come running."

"I have no doubt."

Outside, it was cold and clear.

Not nearly as confident that this was the right move as she'd tried to make Ty believe, Sadie zipped up her heavy jacket, stuck her hands in her pockets and set out for Nic's house.

When she turned the corner onto Nic's street and saw Gavin's Range Rover out in front, she walked faster. She'd barely turned onto the stone walk leading up the porch when the front door flew open, and Nicole burst out.

They met at the foot of the steps and threw their arms around each other. "You came for me." Nic was crying.

"Of course." Sadie sniffed back her own tears and hugged her friend closer. And then she took a neatly folded tissue from her pocket. "Here."

Nic wiped her eyes and then her nose. "Come in. I'll send Gavin to Ty's. We can call them when we're done."

Five minutes later, Gavin was gone. It was just the two of them, sitting by the fire in Nic's still-chilly house not far from the beautifully decorated tree.

"I'm so sorry," Nic said. "Somehow, to hear you say that you and Ty are together, it was just... I couldn't deal. All of a sudden, I was eighteen again, eighteen and pregnant and nobody wanted me. I did what I used to do. I lashed out."

"Hey." Sadie put her arm around Nicole and pulled her closer. "It's okay."

"No. It's not. You and Ty have every right to be together. And I need to be better than all the insecure crap inside my head."

"You *are* better. And you are wanted. By Gavin because you're the love of his life. By me, your best friend no matter what. By your kids who adore you. By Mom and Dad. By Ty, really—as the mother of his children. You're a great team, you and Ty, the way you work together to raise your kids. You're doing an amazing job with that, both of you. You are loved, Nic. You are wanted. Truly, you are."

Nic gulped. "I have to tell you something."

"Anything. What?"

She had her hands in her lap and she was twisting them. "Now and then, when Ty and I were married, I really did wonder if there was something between you two."

"There wasn't," Sadie said. And it was true as far as it went. She and Ty had always been careful to keep their distance from each other while he and Nic were together. It had worked, too. Sadie went on with her life—broke up with Kevin, got together with Paul and later with Reggie. For years, she had put all romantic thoughts of Ty completely aside.

Nic said, "I have a confession. That night back in high school when I told you I was pregnant?"

Sadie felt a prickle of unease. "I remember."

"That day there'd been a student council meeting…"

The prickle turned to a full-out shiver. "Yeah. I remember that meeting." As if she could ever forget it.

Nic took her hand again and wove their fingers together. "We were broken up then, Ty and me…"

Sadie nodded. "Yeah, I remember."

"I was there, when the meeting ended—there, outside the classroom. I was waiting in the hallway, thinking I would catch Ty on the way out of the meeting, that I would talk to him, work up the nerve to tell him I was having his baby, admit to him that I was so scared and didn't know what to do. But he didn't come out and neither did you."

"Nic…" Sadie tried to find the words.

But then Nic squeezed her hand again. "It's okay. Let me finish?"

"Uh. Yeah. I'm listening."

"I remember the door to the classroom was open. I peeked in and saw you and Ty. You were standing close together, talking. I couldn't hear the words you said, but it looked intense."

"Oh, dear God…"

"Sade, let me just say the rest."

Sadie wrapped her other hand around their joined ones. "Please. Go ahead."

"And then you grabbed his arm and dragged him into the supply closet. I almost went into the classroom then. I wanted to put my ear to that closet door, to hear what you were saying in there. But I didn't quite have the nerve. When you came barging back out by yourself, I turned and ran off down the hall."

Sadie drew a ragged breath. "I can't believe it. I mean, all these years, you never said a word. I never had a clue you were out there."

A tear trickled down Nic's cheek. "I didn't want to know what happened in that closet. I used to think you would tell me. I was *afraid* you would tell me and then I would have to deal with it. But you never did."

"I've wanted to tell you. I honestly have. But I had fears, too. I was afraid the truth would make you hate me. That you would never trust me again. That I would lose you forever."

Nic looked down at her hands. The fire cast a golden glow on the side of her face. The track of that one tear glittered in the light. "He kissed you in the closet, didn't he?"

Sadie sucked in a hard breath—and answered honestly. "Yeah."

"Did you…kiss him back?"

"I did, yeah. But then I pushed him away…"

"Sade, I think I'm ready now, you know? Will you tell me what happened in that closet, tell me all of it?"

Sadie let a moment of silence elapse, in case Nic changed her mind. But Nic only waited. So Sadie said, "It was like this…"

And she told Nic what had happened that day exactly as she remembered it—the argument, the kiss that never should have happened. What she'd said. And what Ty had said.

When she finished, she added, "That's it. That's all of it."

"I knew it," said Nic. "He was already through with me then. And, Sadie, I was through with him, too. I told myself I was still in love with him, but it wasn't true. If not for Emily, Ty and I would have been over and done."

"Maybe so. But what happened is that he asked you to marry him, and you said yes. And from then on, I was on *your* side, period. You were both young and unprepared to be married, let alone to be parents. But you did your best. And then, when it was over between you two, Ty and I became friends. That's all we were, good friends. Nothing changed after that until Vegas."

"You were with him in Vegas?"

"I kissed him in Vegas—more than once. That night, you went off to be with Gavin, then the other brides-maids got drunk and wandered away together. It was just me and Ty. We gambled and had a great time and ended up kissing. It would have gone further, but we got to my room—and Gavin stuck his head out of yours. That stopped us. Ty went back to his own suite."

"But now you're together—you and Ty? I mean *really* together?"

"We are, yeah."

"I'm going to want the whole story later. You're going to have to tell me everything. But right now, I just need to know that it's good between you?"

"It's so good. Nic, I'm just going to say it, to get it right out there. Ty's the one for me."

Nic stared at her wide-eyed. Slowly, she nodded. "So you're telling me that you're in love with him?"

"Yes, I am."

"Well…" Nic sniffed. And then she sighed. "I get

it. I do." For a little while, they just sat there, holding hands by the fire. Finally, Nic laid her head on Sadie's shoulder. "If he hurts you, he's going to have to answer to me."

"It won't be a problem because he's not going to hurt me." Sadie said that with confidence. Because she believed in Ty. She really did. A thrill went through her, that she trusted him completely.

No, they hadn't said the words yet, she and Ty. But she knew he loved her just as she loved him.

"Now, come on." Sadie stood and held down her hand. Nic took it and Sadie said, "I love you, Nic."

"Sade." They grabbed each other close. Nic whispered, "Love *you*. So much."

Sadie took her by the shoulders. "We okay, now?"

"We are. Yeah."

"Good. Let's head on back to Ty's."

As they put their coats on, Nic grumbled, "I suppose I'll have to apologize to him."

"I think that would be an excellent idea."

"It went really well, all things considered," Ty said.

"It did," Sadie agreed.

She and Ty were finally alone again. He and Nic had said sorry to each other and shared a hug to prove it. And a few minutes ago, Nic and Gavin had headed for the ranch to pick up the kids and take them home to her place.

Sadie shifted on the sofa beside him. Stretching out, she put her head in his lap and smiled up at him.

He bent close to brush a kiss across her lips. "What happened at Nic's house?"

"When I got halfway up her front walk, she ran out

to meet me. We stood there at the foot of the steps, hugging it out. Then we sent Gavin over here and she apologized to me for losing it."

"Simple as that, huh?"

"More or less." Sadie turned her head and stared at the Christmas tree by the glass door that led out to the back porch. Like the tree at Nic's house, it was all lit up, shining bright. "She told me she saw us, you and me, back in high school, that day I pulled you into the supply closet and you kissed me."

He sucked in a sharp breath. "Sadie."

"Hmm?"

"Look at me."

She turned her head and gazed up at him again thinking how fine he was, how much she loved him, feeling the joy bubble up inside her that they'd found their way to each other at last. Life truly was full of miracles.

"Start at the beginning," he said. "Tell me all of it, what you said, what she said…"

And she did—all of it, including the hard parts.

When she finished, he said gruffly, "You're amazing."

"Thank you."

"And I should give Nic more credit."

"Yes, you should. She's come a long way."

"It's all going to work out, isn't it?" There was wonder in his voice.

"Yep."

He bent close. His lips brushed hers. And he said, "I love you, Sadie Jane."

She bit her lower lip to keep from bursting into happy tears. "I love *you*, Tyler Ross."

"I want to spend my life with you. I want you to move in here—you and Olive and Boo."

"Yes."

"Soon," he said. "Please?"

"Yes."

"Sadie, I want to marry you."

Those words meant everything—a lifetime together, the love she'd looked for with such staunch dedication, hers at last. "I want to marry you, too." She asked, "You remember your boutonniere from Nic's wedding?"

He frowned, looking puzzled. She knew he had no idea what she was talking about. "Uh, boutonniere, yeah. I remember I had one…"

"You left it in my room at the Arrowleaf Lodge. I kept it for luck."

His eyes got softer. "Yeah?"

"I pressed it between the pages of our senior year-book, feeling foolishly sentimental. But at the same time, I just couldn't let myself give up hope that we might work it out somehow."

He took her hand, opened her fingers, and brushed a kiss in the heart of her palm. "Sadie Jane, will you marry me?"

They'd been together—*really* together—for a week as of last night. Never in her life would she ever have imagined she'd be saying yes this soon. Saying yes right now would be totally outrageous.

He looked at her so tenderly. "I get it. We just got together and I'm not even on my knees. I'll work on it, I promise. Next time I ask you, I'll do it right."

She gave him a slow smile. "Yes, I will marry you."

He blinked down at her. "Wait. What?"

She laughed. "Yes! I said yes."

He drew a slow, shaky breath. His fine mouth trembled a little. "Say that one more time…?"

"Yes."

Bending close again, he whispered her name on another ragged breath. "Sadie…" They kissed deep and slow. Like they had forever just to be together, here on this sofa on the day before Christmas Eve.

Eventually, he lifted his mouth from hers a fraction, just enough to ask, "Would you fly with me to Denver next week to choose your ring?"

"Yes." She reached up, hooked her arm around his neck and pulled those lips of his back down to hers.

For a long while, neither of them spoke. They shared a dozen kisses and then a dozen more.

And when he raised his head the next time, he said, "Em's going to be over the moon. She did say we should get married."

"Yes, she did." Sadie knew he was remembering that family meeting back at the beginning of November when everyone laughed at Emily's suggestion that Sadie and Ty should get together. "At the next family meeting, she's going to want to start planning the wedding."

"As long as it's the way *you* want it, Sadie."

"It will be."

"You sound so sure."

"Because I am. After all, Ty, I'll be marrying you."

* * * * *

*Watch for Jason James Bravo's story,
coming in March 2024, only from
Harlequin Special Edition.*

SPECIAL EXCERPT FROM

HARLEQUIN
SPECIAL
EDITION

Time to rewrite their story?

He'd always simply been her best friend. But when Noah Cahill moved back to town, bookstore owner Twyla Thompson knew something was different. Was it holiday nostalgia for the loss they both shared or Noah's surprising decision to reignite a dangerous career? Their solid friendship had been through so much, yet now Twyla grew breathless every time Noah was near. Why wasn't Noah—handsome, fun but never-one-to-cross-the-line Noah—showing any sign of stopping?

Read on for a sneak preview of
Once Upon a Charming Bookshop
by Heatherly Bell.

Chapter One

Twyla Thompson was thrilled to see a line out the door on the night of *New York Times* bestselling author Stacy Cruz's book signing. This was exactly what Once Upon a Book needed—an infusion of excitement and good-will and the proverbial opening up of the wallet during the holidays for a book instead of the latest flat-screen TV. Even if Stacy's recently released thriller wasn't exactly Christmas material, the timing was right both for her, the publisher and certainly Twyla's family-owned bookstore.

The reading had been short due to subject matter—murder—and Stacy took questions from the crowd. As usual, they ranged from, "How can I get published?" To "I have an idea for a book. Would you write it for me?" To "My mother had a *fascinating* life. It should be a book, then a movie starring Meryl Streep." Stacy was a good sport about it all since the Charming, Texas, residents were her friends and neighbors, too.

Twyla, for her part, would never dream of writing a book. She barely had time to read everything she wanted to. Which was basically…everything. The heart of a bookseller beat in her and she recommended books like they were her best friends. Want an inspirational book? Read this. Would you like a tour de force celebrating the power of the human spirit? Here's the book for you. A little escapism with some romance and comedy thrown in? Right here. Want to be scared within an inch of your life? Read Stacy Cruz's latest suspense thriller.

The very best part of Twyla's day was getting lost in the worlds an author created. Her favorite books had always been of the fantasy romance genre, particularly of the dragon-slaying variety. She adored a fae hero who slayed dragons before breakfast. But honestly? She read anything she could get her hands on. Owning her four-generation family bookstore had made that possible. She'd grown up inside these four walls filled with bookshelves and little alcoves and nooks. She read all the *Nancy Drew* mysteries, Beverly Cleary and, when her grandmother wasn't looking, Kathleen Woodiwiss.

Twyla stood next to Roy Finch at the register as he rang up another sale of Stacy's latest book, *Vengeance*, that featured a serial killer working among the political power brokers in DC. Twyla had read it, of course. She could not deny Stacy's talent at terrifying the reader and making them guess until the last page. You'd never expect this from the married, sweet and beautiful mother of a little girl. She was as normal a person as Twyla had ever met.

"Nice crowd tonight," Mr. Finch said. "Too bad Stacy doesn't write more than one book a year."

Too bad indeed. Because while hosting yoga classes and book clubs, and selling educational toys had sustained them, it would no longer be enough. For the past two years, the little bookstore, the only one in town, had been in a terrible slump. Her grandmother still kept the books, and she'd issued the warning earlier this year. Pulling them out of the red might require more than one great holiday season. Foot traffic had slowed as more people bought their books online.

"I've got a signed copy of Stacy's latest book for you." Lois, Mr. Finch's fiancée, set a stack of no less than ten books on the counter by the register. "And I grabbed a bunch of giving tree cards."

The cards were taken from a large stack of books in the shape of a Christmas tree Twyla set up every season. Instead of ornaments, tags indicated the names and addresses of children who either wanted, or needed, a book for Christmas.

"We can always count on you, sweetheart." Mr. Finch rang her up.

It was endearing the way residents supported the Thompson family bookstore. They might have been in this location for four decades, but they'd never needed as much help as in the past two years.

Mr. Finch, a widowed and retired senior citizen, volunteered his time at the shop so Twyla could occasionally go home. For a while now they hadn't been able to afford any paid help. Her parents were officially retired and had moved to Hill Country. Their contributions amounted to comments on the sad state of affairs when a bookstore had to host yoga classes. But the instructor gave Twyla a flat rate to rent the space, and she didn't see *them* coming up with any solutions. They didn't want to close up shop. Of *course* not. They simply wanted Twyla to solve this problem for the entire Thompson family by selling books and nothing else.

"I don't know what I'd do without either one of you," Twyla said fondly, patting Mr. Finch's back. "Or any of the other members of the Almost Dead Poets Society."

Many of the local senior citizens had formed a poetry group where they recited poems they'd written. It had all started rather innocently enough—a creative effort, and something to do with all their free time. Unfortunately, they also liked to refer to themselves as "literary" matchmakers. Literary not to *ever* be confused with "literally." They'd failed with Twyla so far, not that they'd ever give up trying. Last month they'd invited both her and Tony Taylor to a reading and not so discreetly attempted to fix them up.

"You're both so beautiful, it's a little hard to look at you for long," Ella Mae, the founder of their little group, had said. "Kind of like the sun!"

"The double *T*s!" Lois had exclaimed. "Or would that be the quadruple *T*s?"

"Quadruple, I think," Mr. Finch said.

"You won't even have to change the initials on your monogrammed towels!" Patsy Villanueva clapped her hands. "I mean if it works out, that is."

"But no pressure!" Susannah held up a palm.

Twyla didn't own anything monogrammed, let alone towels, but she'd still exchanged frozen smiles with Tony. They'd arranged a coffee date just for fun. Unfortunately, as she'd known for years, Tony batted for the other team. He even had a live-in boyfriend that the old folks assumed was his roommate. It was an easy assumption to make since Tony was such a "man's man"—a grease monkey who lifted engines for a living. And he hadn't exactly come out of the closet, thinking his personal life was nobody's business. He was right, of course. But…

"You really *should* declare your love of show tunes, Tony," she'd teased.

"I'm not a cliché."

"Well, you *could* get married."

"I'm not ready to settle down." He scowled.

Still, they'd had a nice time, catching up on life post-high school. He'd asked after Noah Cahill, and of course she had all the recent updates on her best friend. In the end they'd decided she and Tony would definitely be double-dating at some point.

When Twyla could find a date.

This part wasn't going to be easy because Twyla had a bad habit. She preferred to spend her time alone and reading a book. Long ago, she'd accepted that she wouldn't be able to find true love inside the walls of her small rental. But accepting invitations to parties and bar hops wasn't her style. She wanted to be invited, really, but she just didn't want to go. An introvert's problem.

This was why she'd adopted a cat. But, she worried, if she didn't get a date soon, she was going to risk being known as the cat lady.

"That's the last copy!" Stacy stood from the table, beaming, holding a hand to her chest. "My publisher will be thrilled. I honestly can't *believe* it."

"I can." Twyla began to clear up the signing table. "You're very talented and it's about time people noticed. I just wish you'd write more books."

"So do I, but tell that to my daughter." Stacy sighed. "She's a holy terror, just like her father. Runs around all day, throwing things. I'm lucky if I get in a few hundred words a day."

"That's okay." Twyla chuckled. "We can't exactly base our business plan on how many books you write a year."

Stacy blinked and a familiar concern shaded her eyes. "Are you…are you guys doing okay? Should I maybe ask my publisher whether they can send some of their other authors here for a signing?"

As a bookseller, she knew everyone in the business was suffering, and publishers weren't financing many book tours. Stacy did those on her own dime, hence the local gig. Twyla didn't like lying to people but she liked their pity even less. She constantly walked a tightrope between the two.

"As long as we have another great holiday season, like all the others, we should be fine!" She hoped the forced quality of her über-positive attitude wasn't laying it on too thick.

But Stacy seemed to accept the good news, bless her heart.

"What a relief! We can't have a *town* without a bookstore."

"No, we can't," Mr. Finch agreed with a slight shake of his head. "It would be a travesty."

One by one the straggling customers left, carrying their purchases with them. Not long after, Stacy's husband, the devastatingly handsome Adam, dropped by to pick her up and drive her home. Everyone said their good-byes.

Mr. Finch and Lois brought up the rear, wanting to help Twyla close up.

"You two go home!" She waved her hands dismissively. "I'm right behind you."

"I'll be by tomorrow for my morning shift promptly at nine." Mr. Finch took Lois's hand in his own.

"Are you sure you don't want to take a break? Take tomorrow off." Twyla went behind them, shutting off the lights. "You worked tonight."

"I'll get plenty of rest when I'm dead," Roy said, holding the door open for Lois.

"Roy!" Lois went ahead. "Please don't talk about the worst day of my life a second before it happens."

"No, darlin'." He sweetly brought her hand up to his lips. "I'll be around for a while. You manage to keep me young."

These two never failed to fill her heart with the warm fuzzies. Both had been widowed for a long time, and were on their second great love.

Which meant some people got two of those, and so far, Twyla didn't even have one.

Twyla arrived at her grandmother's home a few minutes later, having stopped first at the bakery for a salted caramel Bundt cake. She and Ganny usually met for dinner every Saturday night and she always brought dessert. Was it sad that a soon-to-be thirty-year-old single woman didn't have anything better to do on a Saturday night? Not at all. She had her cat, Bonkers, waiting at home. He was mean as the devil himself, but he'd been homeless when she adopted him from the shelter, so she was all he had.

Twyla also had at least half a dozen advanced reader

copy books on her nightstand waiting for her. There were also all the upcoming Charming holiday events she'd agreed to participate in because that's what one did as a business owner. Ava had told her about a rare angel investor offering a zero-interest loan to a local Charming business. On top of everything else, Twyla had to prepare an essay this month to be considered. It wasn't as if she didn't have anything else to do. Too much, in fact.

"Hello, Peaches."

Ganny bussed Twyla's cheek. Occasionally she still referred to Twyla by her old childhood nickname. Once, she'd eaten so many juicy fresh peaches from the tree in Ganny's yard that she threw up. It wasn't the best nickname in the world.

"How was the book signing?"

"A line out the door." Twyla followed Ganny into the ornate dining area connected to the kitchen and set the cake on the mahogany table.

Ganny had been widowed twice and her last husband, Grandpa Walt, a popular real estate broker, had left her with very little but this house. It was too big for Ganny, but she refused to leave it because of the dining room. It was big enough to accommodate large groups of people, which she felt encouraged Twyla's parents to visit several times a year.

"It was a good start to the month."

"Good, good. Well, that's enough book business talk for tonight." Ganny waved a hand dismissively. "I've got a surprise for you tonight. An early Christmas present."

"You didn't have to get me anything."

But a thrill whipped through Twyla because her grandmother was renowned for her thoughtful gifts all year long. It could almost be anything. Maybe a trip to New York City, where Ganny had promised to finally introduce her to some of the biggest booksellers in the country. People she'd met over a lifetime of acquiring and selling books. Twyla had wanted to go back to New York for years. She could still feel the energy of the city zipping through her blood, taste the cheesecake from Junior's, and the slice of pepperoni pizza from Times Square.

"Why wouldn't I give my only granddaughter the best present in the world?" Ganny smiled with satisfaction. "He should be along any minute now."

All the breath left Twyla's body. Just the thought of another blind date struck her with a sadness she had no business feeling during the holidays. Everyone in town was conspiring to fix up "poor, sad Twyla who can't get a man."

She could get a man, but she wasn't concentrating her efforts on this.

Please let it not be Tony again. And yet there were so few single men her age left in town. Hadn't her grandmother always told Twyla she'd do fine on her own? If she couldn't find the right man, she didn't need *any* man? Twyla had embraced this truth. She wanted the perfect man or no one at all.

"Life with the right man is wonderful. But a life with the wrong man might as well be lived alone. So many things in life can replace a spouse. Work, travel and books, to start with," Ganny had said.

Twyla, then, *could* lead a happy and fruitful life without ever being married.

"Oh, Ganny." Twyla slumped on the chair. "You didn't fix me up with someone, did you?"

"Of course not, honey!" She patted Twyla's hand. "But speaking of which, you're not going to meet anyone special if you don't get out more."

"I'm just like you. Books are my family."

It seemed to have skipped a generation, because though her father, Ganny's son, had loyally run the family bookstore, it wasn't exactly his happy place.

"Yes, but keep in mind I made myself go out and meet people. It wasn't like it is today. Certainly not. I used to have three dates on the same day. No funny business, of course, but your mother already told me things are different."

Twyla couldn't imagine going out three times in one day. She'd be lucky to go out once every three years. Okay, she was exaggerating. But still. Men weren't exactly lining up to date her. One of them had said she'd look prettier if she'd stop wearing her black-rimmed glasses. Twyla refused to go the contact lens route because if glasses stopped a guy from being interested in her, it wasn't the guy she wanted, anyway.

"Fine, I promise I'll go out! But please don't fix me up." Her friend Zoey had bugged her to go out with her and her boyfriend, Drew, and Twyla hadn't yet.

"No blind date. This is someone you actually want to see."

"I can't even imagine."

There was only one "he" she'd like to see, and he was all the way in Austin, at home with his girlfriend. Probably planning their wedding.

"That's it. I'm having dessert first." Twyla opened the cake box.

The doorbell rang and Ganny rose. "You stay here and close your eyes! Don't open them until I tell you to."

Oh, brother. It was like being twelve again. She clasped her hand over her eyes, but not before taking a finger swipe of salted caramel frosting, feeling...well, twelve again.

"Okay, fine. My eyes are closed."

Twyla heard the front door open and shut, Ganny's delighted laughter, but no other sounds from this "he" man. Nothing but the sounds of boots thudding as they followed Ganny's lighter steps.

"Can I open my eyes now? I would really like to have a piece of cake. Whoever you are, I hope you like cake."

"I love cake," the deep voice said.

Twyla didn't even have to open her eyes to recognize the teasing, flirty sound of her favorite person in the world. She didn't have to hazard a guess because she knew this man almost as well as she knew herself.

And Ganny was right. It *was* the best present.

Ever.

"Noah!"

Twyla stood and hurled herself into the open arms of Noah Cahill, her best friend.

Chapter Two

There were few things in his life Noah enjoyed as much as filling his arms with his best friend. He held Twyla close, all five feet nothing of her. Her dark hair longer now than it had been a year ago when he'd left Charming. Today she was wearing her book-pattern dress, which meant the store must have had a signing. The outfit was a type of uniform she wore for those events. She had a similar skirt in bright colors with patterns of dragons, swords and slayers.

God, she was a sight. The old familiar pinch squeezed his chest. He almost hadn't come home this Christmas, thinking it would be easier. There was already so much he hadn't told her when he normally told her everything.

Almost everything.

Then he'd narrowly missed death, or at the least a devastating injury, and everything changed in the course of days. He would not waste another minute of his life doing a job he no longer wanted to do.

"I thought you weren't coming home this Christmas!" Twyla said, coming to her tiptoes to hug him tight. Her arms wrapped around his neck.

Automatically and before he could stop himself, he turned his head to take in a deep breath of her hair. She always smelled like coconuts. He set her down reluctantly, but he was used to this feeling with Twyla. It was always this way—the push and pull always resulting in the distance he'd created due to guilt.

And loyalty.

"Things have changed."

"Noah isn't just *visiting*," Twyla's grandmother said, sounding pleased. "He's come home to stay."

Bless Mrs. Schilling's kind heart. She'd always been pulling for Noah, against any and all reason, even if he could have told her a thousand times it was useless. He was destined to pine after Twyla forever. What he wanted to have with her would never work and the door had been slammed shut years ago. Now the opening might as well be buried under rubble. Like the roof that nearly fell on him.

"You're here to stay?" Twyla brightened. "But what about your job in Austin?"

"I quit." He held his arms off to the side with a shrug. "It's not for me. Not anymore."

"It's *exactly* you. You've been an adrenaline junkie since you were a boy. How is it not for you?"

Yeah, best not to tell her about the roof that fell inches from him during a building fire. His entire squad had been lucky to escape with no fatalities. Three had wound up with minor injuries.

Noah could have sworn something, or *someone*, had shoved him out of the way. In that moment, with the heat barreling toward him and unfurling like a living thing, he'd felt his brother, Will, there in the room with him. Will, shouting for him to get out of the way.

His long-dead older brother was telling Noah, in no uncertain terms, to stop trying to be a hero. To, for the love of God, stop rescuing people and start living his own life. Noah had first worked as an EMT, and then later a firefighter in nearby Houston for the past few years. He'd saved some people and lost some, but "imaginary Will" had called it. No matter what Noah did, he'd never get another chance to save Will.

And he was the only save that would have ever mattered. Now it was high time to honor his life instead. Noah may have always felt second best to his much smarter and accomplished brother, but that feeling wasn't one encouraged by Will. His older brother had always had Noah's back. Even on their last day together.

"It was good, for a while, but it's time to move on."

"But—"

"Let's have some of that delicious cake." Mrs. Schilling urged them to take a seat at the table. "We have plenty of time to discuss all this."

"I never say no to cake." Noah took a seat, avoiding Twyla's gaze.

If he looked too directly at her, she'd see everything in his eyes, so at times like these he had a system in place.

Don't make eye contact.

Three serving plates were passed around and Twyla sliced off generous pieces.

"No matter what, we're glad you're home," Mrs. Schilling said. "Aren't we, dear?"

"Yes, of course. It's just such a surprise. So…unexpected." Twyla took a bite of cake.

Using an old trick, he purposely looked at her ear, to make it look like he was meeting her eyes.

"It's a career choice. I have a really great opportunity here."

"Where are you staying?"

It was a fair question since he'd given up his rental when he'd grown tired of the memories that haunted him here and moved to Austin to start over.

"I rented one of those cottages by the beach. Just temporary until I find a place. The place where I'll be living is far less important than what I'll be doing." Noah winked.

This was his biggest news: the culmination of a long-held dream. He'd squashed it for so long after Will's death that he'd nearly forgotten it. But in that fiery building, he'd *remembered*.

"What *are* you going to be doing?"

"Taking over a business here in town." He'd start with the easy stuff first.

"Wonderful!" Mrs. Schilling clapped her hands. "Obviously, I have always loved the entrepreneurial spirit. Why, it's the reason the Thompson family started Once Upon a Book."

"What kind of business? Fire investigation? Teaching safety? You would make a *great* teacher." Twyla smiled and took another bite of cake.

He hoped the news wasn't going to kill her like it might his own mother. But he couldn't live the rest of his life in fear. Or worse yet, accommodating the fears of others.

"No. I'm taking over the boat charter. Mr. Curry is retiring, and he's been looking for a buyer for a year or more."

When his news was met with such silence that he heard Mrs. Schilling's grandfather clock ticking, he continued.

"He actually wants someone local to take it over, so he'll work terms out with me. I have enough hours on the water, so I'll be taking the USCG test for my captain's license. I've obviously already had first aid training and then some. Until I get my license, I'll have Finn's help and he already has his license. Mr. Curry said he'd be around awhile longer, too, if we need help." He filled his mouth with a big piece of cake.

Twyla sucked in a breath, and Mrs. Schilling's shaky hand went to her throat. Other than that, Noah thought everything here would be okay. Nothing to see here. Sure thing. They'd all get used to the idea. Eventually.

Just give them a couple of decades.

"Are you serious?" Twyla pushed her plate of unfinished cake away.

Only he would fully understand the significance of the move. For Twyla not to finish a slice of cake meant that in her opinion, the world just might be ending.

"Yes, I'm serious. Ask yourself whether if anyone else said the same thing, you'd have this kind of a reaction."

"That's not even funny. You're *not* anyone else." She took a breath and whispered her next words. "You're Will's brother. You…you almost died out there, too."

"Now, Twyla…let the man finish." This from Twyla's grandmother, thankfully, the voice of reason.

She didn't let him finish.

"If this is my surprise, I don't like it." Twyla stood.

With that she walked right out of her grandmother's kitchen.

"Twyla!" her grandmother chided. "Oh, dear. Noah, I'm sorry. She's had a rough year. The bookstore isn't doing well, and—"

"Let me talk to her."

"Noah? Are you sure about this? If Twyla reacts this way, you can only imagine how your poor mother—"

"I know. *And* I'm sure."

He found Twyla outside on the wraparound porch's swing, bare feet dangling as she stared into the twinkling sky. Without a word, he plopped himself next to her and nudged her knee.

"Hey."

"Hey." She leaned into him, and he tamped down the rush of raw emotion that single move brought. "I'm sorry. I may have…overreacted."

She couldn't stay angry at him for long. Neither one of them could. Not since they'd been kids.

"You think? It's not that I don't understand the concern but everyone seems to forget I grew up boating. Will and I both did. I'm going to be careful and follow all relevant safety practices. Probably go overboard with them." He chuckled and elbowed her. "See what I did there?"

"Funny man."

"I just…can't pretend anymore."

Starting over had served its purpose. He'd lived in a city in which no one knew him as Will's younger brother. A new place where he'd excelled and never been second best. He'd tried to settle down into a stable relationship with Michelle. But he hadn't been happy even before the roof collapse.

"What are you pretending?"

"That I'm okay living someone else's life. I don't want to live in Austin. I want to live here. You do realize the ocean is not the only danger in life?"

"Sure, I'd prefer you do something normal like… I don't know, real estate? You'd make a killing. *Everybody* loves you."

Wind up the only surviving brother after a boating tragedy and you're bound to get a lot of sympathy. He was tired of that, too. Another reason he'd left town.

He grunted. "Real estate is not going to happen. Too much paperwork."

"Why now? Did something happen?"

While he could tell her, letting her realize that it wasn't only water that could kill a man, this didn't seem like the right time. Later, he'd tell her about the roof collapse. Later, he'd tell her about Michelle.

And everything else. Someday. Just…not now.

"I think Will would want this. And I want this. This was our dream when we were kids. We'd wake up every day and go fishing. Every day would be like a vacation."

"I know he would want you to be happy."

"*This* is going to make me happy. I'm tired of living for other people. You only get one life. This one is mine."

They both sat in silence for a beat. Will had been only eighteen when they'd lost him in the accident that nearly took Noah's life, too. Their family had never been the same. When Noah's parents divorced, his father left the state and now rarely spoke to Noah. His mother still lived in Charming and had never truly gotten over the loss of her oldest son. She'd laid her dreams at Will's feet, who had done everything she'd ever asked of him. He'd been the good son, the strong academic. Noah had been the classic bad boy, unable to live up to the impossible standard that Will set.

"Remember when you, me and Will would lie under the stars at night?" Twyla pushed her legs out to start swinging. "And Will renamed the Little Dipper 'Noah Dipper' after you, and the Big Dipper was 'Will Dipper'?"

"Yeah, even if 'Bill Dipper' would have sounded better."

Noah smiled at the memory. Will believed in the power behind words and used to play around with letters all the time. Mixing them up, creating new words. Like Twyla, he was a bit of a book nerd. The valedictorian in his graduating class of Charming High. He and Twyla had been so much alike it was no wonder that though Noah met Twyla first, it was Will who wound up dating her. His courtship with her might have been short and sweet, but at least he'd had one.

"He used to like renaming stuff. Combining two words together, shifting letters. Word play."

"Mine was easy. Twilight was hereafter renamed Twyla for short." She chuckled. "Totally made sense."

It had been a long while since they talked about Will. Remembered. He was that silent spot between them, keeping them apart but making Noah wish for nothing more than those good times.

"He had the biggest crush on you."

Of course, Noah had been the first to have the crush,

except *crush* might not have been the right word. He'd been astounded. He recalled literally gaping when he first laid eyes on Twyla helping her mother at the bookstore, dressed in a pink dress and matching shoes. Pushing her horn-rimmed glasses up her nose and giving him a shy smile. She looked like an angel to an eleven-year-old boy.

"We should do that again sometime," Twyla said. "Lie under the stars together."

He almost jerked his neck back in surprise. She'd never suggested anything like this before. It amounted to doing something together that they'd only ever done with Will.

It was like…reinventing it.

"Why?"

"Why?" She spoke just above a whisper. "Because they're still there. Still twinkling. Is it okay with you if I want to look at them again and see them in a different way?"

He reached to lighten the moment. "Rename them, you mean?"

"Anything. Of course, maybe Michelle wouldn't like it. You and I spending so much time together."

Ah, that's why she'd brought it up. She didn't know about his breakup with the woman he'd dated while in Austin. He'd brought her to Charming once, where she'd met Twyla and the family. She thought Michelle was still there between them, a safe buffer from getting too close to him. There was no point in telling her the truth. Let her relax in her false belief. Their guilt had kept them apart this long. What was another decade?

Noah would throw himself into work. His dream. He'd live his life the way he wanted to and reach for happiness wherever he could find it. Around every blind corner. Behind every rogue wave. Fake it till he made it. He was excited about the future for the first time since he could recall.

Life was too short and if Will hadn't taught him that, then certainly the roof collapse had.

"No, probably not. She wouldn't like it," he lied. "But I don't care."

Twyla took off her glasses and wiped the lenses on the edge of her shirt.

She didn't say anything to that—probably because they didn't usually talk about any of his girlfriends. It was better that way.

He changed the subject. "Is it true you're having problems with the bookstore?"

Twyla sighed. "Why do you think I want to lie under the stars like when I was ten? Yes, we're having trouble. What else is new?"

"I thought everything was better after the last holiday season. You always say December counts for ninety percent of your business."

"Welcome to the book world. A lot can change in a year. The ground is constantly shifting under my feet."

"Well, you can't close the bookstore."

"Everyone says that."

"We grew up in that museum. Reading dragon slayer books in those cozy corner nooks filled with pillows. I'll help. Just put me to work."

She smiled. "You're going to be busy if you insist on this madness."

"I'll figure out a way."

"Hey, does this mean you'll be at the tree lighting ceremony tomorrow?"

"Wouldn't miss it."

"Wait until you see the little book shaped ornaments we have for the tree."

She sounded excited and like her old self for the first time tonight.

"Let me guess. Dragon slayer books?"

"Among some others, of course. We can't ignore *The Night Before Christmas* and the other classics."

Sometimes, Noah could still see himself and Will sitting among the shelves of dusty books. They'd read quietly every afternoon after school because Twyla's parents didn't mind being an unofficial after school center. It wasn't until much later, when he and Twyla had been in the depths of their shared grief, that they'd found "the book." The one that had defined the years after Will. They'd take turns reading chapters. One week the book stayed with Noah and he'd read three chapters, and one week it was with Twyla. He'd write and post stickers in the margins of the book, which had technically belonged to Twyla.

Noah would comment: *That idiot deserved to be killed by the dragon.*

And Twyla would answer: *Sometimes the dragon chooses the right victim.*

They'd mark significant parts, but almost never the same ones. Noah was far more impressed with dragon slayer tools while Twyla loved the mushy stuff about love and sacrifice. The book came to belong to them both, since they'd literally made it their own. Noah had never done this with any other book before or since and he'd venture she never had, either. For reasons he didn't quite understand, they'd made this particular book, *A Dragon's Heart*, their own. They shared the words until the day Noah stole the book from Twyla. There was just no other way to put it.

He'd "borrowed" the book without returning it.

That, at least, was something he'd never tell her.

Chapter Three

The next day, having risen before dawn to drive to the docks, Noah watched the sunrise while he waited for Mr. Curry to arrive. The view was calming and soothing in the way a Gulf Coast native could appreciate. Gold mixed with shades of blue and painted the sky with morning. Noah found little more beautiful than a Gulf Coast sunrise other than a sunset accompanied by fireflies. Over the years, he'd been seeing less of them lighting up the coastal nights.

"You're early." Mr. Curry emerged from his brightly detailed pickup truck.

The truck itself was practically a Charming landmark. Granted, it had seen better days and could definitely use a paint job. But the etching of two dolphins meeting halfway, blending into sharp blue and purple hues still grabbed attention. The letters spelled *Nacho*

Boat Adventures and the phone number. Boat tours, fishing charters, diving excursions, water skiing, rentals. Group rates available.

A walking advertisement. Not that Noah would need to take out an ad because the business, decades old, was practically the apex of Charming tourism.

And if Noah was early, it was because he couldn't wait to get started.

He handed Mr. Curry a coffee cup. "Will you throw in the truck, too?"

"Let's talk inside." Mr. Curry put his key in the door of the unimpressive A-line shack on the pier.

Weather-beaten and somewhat battered, the outside could also use a makeover. So could Mr. Curry, for that matter, who had grown his white beard down to his chest and looked older than his sixty-five years.

"Are you doing okay?" Noah asked, watching him hobble inside.

"Ah, it's the arthritis. Makes me a grump most days. Don't take it personal." He took a swig of coffee, then held it up. "Thanks for this."

"No problem." Drinking from his own cup, Noah took in the shop he hadn't been inside for years.

A handwritten schedule of boat tours hung on a whiteboard behind the register. Surf boards were propped against the rear walls, hung near boating equipment like ropes and clips. The smells of wood and salt were comforting. Noah inhaled and took it all in. It was his burden to have never had a healthy fear of the ocean. And even after all he'd been through, he still didn't shy away from the memories of long summer days boating. Their father had taught both of his boys everything he knew, and they'd manned the captain's wheel from the time they were thirteen and fourteen. Two boys, a year apart. Irish twins, his mother called them.

"You should know. I'm moving." Mr. Curry interrupted Noah's thoughts.

"I know. That's why you're selling."

"Me and the Mrs. We're headed west to Arizona."

"Landlocked?" Noah raised his brow. This he had not expected.

"Hell, yeah. They got lakes. Need the dry and hot weather for my stupid arthritis." He went behind the counter and seemed to be fiddling around back there. "That's all to say that while I want someone like you to take over, I also need someone who's going to stick around. Do I make myself clear? I can stay on awhile and take some of those boat tours we've already scheduled for the real die-hards, but there's no turning back. No second thoughts. Of course, you could sell, but you see how long it's taken me. This isn't the greatest moneymaker in the world."

"I figured." Noah had some ideas of his own to increase business but best not interrupt the man's flow of thoughts.

"You won't get rich owning this business, but you will also never be poor."

"I'm in this for the long haul. I picture myself a grandfather, like you, finally retiring someplace dry because I have arthritis." Noah reached for some other older person's ailment and came up with nothing. "Or something."

"That's what I want to see. You, growing old in this town. Safe. Giving tours. Teaching. Because, well, you know…"

Noah let the silence hang between them for only a

moment. He knew where this would be going. Knew it far too well.

"I know," Noah completed the sentence. "And the accident still doesn't define who I am. Never did."

"My wife is going to kill me twice when she finds out who I sold to. I told her I had an offer from a local. That I'd offered financing to help the young man out. She thinks the idea is great. But she doesn't know it's *you*."

Noah sighed. He'd felt the protectiveness of this town come over him like a choke hold. It no longer felt like protection. It felt controlling. Unreasonable.

"It's time for all of us to move on."

"*If* you're sure." Mr. Curry crossed his arms. "Then this…is a done deal."

"I'm absolutely one hundred percent sure. I'm never going back to firefighting again. One roof nearly falling on me is enough."

Mr. Curry gaped. "Hot damn, son. You might be the luckiest man I've ever met. All right. Welcome aboard."

He chuckled, then went on to give Noah the speed version of the business he'd managed for two decades. It was all written down, of course…somewhere. Though good help was hard to find, Noah would have two staff members staying on through the transition. They were both part-time workers—teens who loved boating and were willing to be paid a microscopic salary for the pleasure of working for the new boss.

Concern hit Noah like a hot spike, but he forced himself to shake it off. Teenagers near water did not *automatically* mean danger.

"What do they do around here?"

"As little or as much as you want. Diana answers the

phone and takes the bookings. Sells the little equipment we have for sale and the surf boards." He waved his hand in the air. "Tee, that's the ridiculous nickname he goes by, is working on a boating license. You can fire them both as far as I'm concerned but they're good kids and for a while they'll know more than you will about how we run things."

He had a point.

"Be at the bank tomorrow morning and we'll sign the papers. Owner financing the first year. It's all in the contract." He then reached under the register and came up with a small box. "May as well take these with you since you're here."

Noah accepted the box. "What's all this?"

"Christmas."

Indeed, dozens of tree ornaments in the shape of boats announced "A Merry Christmas from Nacho Boat." They were for the tree lighting ceremony tonight. This meant a couple of things. After tonight, almost everyone in town would know Noah was the new owner of Nacho Boat Adventures.

He was on borrowed time before his mother heard about the contract he'd sign tomorrow morning.

But he told himself one more day wouldn't hurt anything.

Just before the tree lighting ceremony, Twyla closed up shop and drove her sedan the short drive to the boardwalk. She carried her basket full of ornaments for the lighting of the Christmas tree. This had always been the first Charming event at the start of the month, which kicked off the season festivities. This never failed to make her heart buzz with anticipation, even if the excitement was dulled tonight due to Noah's unexpected news. She didn't like the idea of him taking over Nacho Boat any more than his mother would. But, more than anyone else, she understood what it was like to live under the heavy weight of opinion.

Charming was a small town and its residents were similar to an extended family you loved to hate. Even if more than a decade had passed, she was still thought of as "Will's girl." Even though she and Will barely dated for a year before he broke up with her because he'd be going away to college. Of course, that never happened. He'd never made it to college. She was Will's *last* girlfriend and some people, Noah's mother included, saw her forever frozen in the tragic role. The reason, she understood, was that Will himself would remain forever eighteen.

Twyla, on the other hand, would be twenty-seven this year. Like Noah, who'd been trying to escape his role as town hero responsible for the biggest water rescue in Charming history, she'd been trying to move on from the role of grieving ex-girlfriend. She'd signed up for some of the dating apps and forced herself on the occasional date. She'd even expressed her interest in Adam Cruz when he'd arrived in town over a year ago. He'd been single for about two minutes, however, and then there went that opportunity.

Over the years, she'd dated men here and there that Noah interestingly always found fault with. Yet he'd never even tried to fix her up. Not even with his best friend, Finn. Noah would sing the guy's praises all the live long day but whenever he was single, Noah stopped talking about Finn. She and Noah had never been on dates together, keeping that part of each other's life separate. She never complained about guys to him, and he never complained about women. But as far as she could tell, Noah never had any issues with the female population, other than the fact that he'd never seemed ready to settle down. Michelle, someone he'd met in Austin, was simply the latest and Twyla wondered how long they'd last long distance.

Walking toward the boardwalk along the seawall, Twyla took in the holiday scene. As usual, the decor on the boardwalk was already in full swing. Many of the vendors would stay open through their mild winter, their shops decorated to the hilt with snowflakes, trees and more lights. Sounds from the roller coaster on the amusement park end of the boardwalk were as loud as on any summer night, only with residents and not many tourists. Families were out having fun, creating memories. She strolled along accompanied by the sound of seagulls cawing and foraging for food in the sand. Aromatic and delicious scents of fresh coffee, hot cocoa and popcorn competed. She would need some hot cocoa sooner rather than later.

Despite the lower tourism rate that tended to hit every business, winter in Charming was her favorite time of the year, when temperatures hovered in the low sixties and, on a good day, reached the high fifties. She loved sweater and boot weather. Finally, she could haul out her cowboy boots and wear them without anyone teasing her.

She waved as she passed the Lazy Maisy kettle corn store, selling their classic peppermint-flavored, red-and-green popcorn as they did every December, each worker dressed like an elf for the entire month. Strands of white lights hung from every storefront. A plastic model of Santa and his sleigh guided by a reindeer were suspended across one side of the boardwalk, cheery signs everywhere announcing a "charming" Christmas. Yes, thank you. Twyla would have a charming Christmas indeed.

Noah was back. Christmas would be even better now.

She had to keep telling herself that. Nacho Boat had a great safety record. Noah was bright and intelligent. He'd take all necessary precautions because he'd never want his mother to hurt again. For so long, they'd all walked on eggshells around Katherine Cahill. Twyla included. The woman had suffered enough, but Noah did have a point. His career as a firefighter wasn't exactly a desk job. At least here, they'd all be able to keep an eye on him. Keep him safe. Yes, she'd do that. For Will and for Katherine. But mostly, for herself.

"Hey, Twyla."

She turned to find herself face-to-face with Valerie Kinsella, a third-grade teacher and wife of one of the three former Navy SEALs who ran the Salty Dog Bar & Grill.

"Check these out. I think the ornaments are amazing this year. I found a specialty shop in Dallas with a great price." She handed the box to Valerie, who would mix it up with the others.

"You've outdone yourself as usual." Valerie smiled.

Baskets filled with all donated ornaments would be passed around to the residents, who each got to choose at least one to put on a branch. People were already gathering around the huge tree in the center. Ava Del Toro, president of the Chamber of Commerce, climbed up the temporary risers hauled over from the high school.

Meanwhile, this year's Santa walked through the

crowd, handing candy canes out to kids as the ornament baskets made the rounds. Twyla glanced in the crowd for Noah, since he'd texted her that he'd be there early and she should come and find him. At first, she didn't see him at all, and then noticed him talking to Sabrina, one of his old girlfriends. Most of his life, Noah had never failed to get the attention of girls, and later, women. It was the whole bad boy thing. He'd surfed, driven fast cars and even had a motorcycle for a nanosecond. Twyla hated motorcycles but she loved those boots Noah got to wear when he rode one. Even teachers liked Noah. He wasn't a stellar student, but he was funny and kind.

When he'd been hospitalized after the accident, there had been so many flowers in his room that it resembled a botanical garden.

Twyla watched now as Sabrina leaned into Noah, touched his broad shoulder and tossed back her long red hair. The familiar and unwelcome pinch of jealousy, this time on Michelle's behalf, burned in Twyla's stomach. Then Noah turned, saw Twyla and his smile brightened. He gave a little "see ya later" wave to Sabrina.

He walked over to Twyla, hands stuck in the pockets of his blue denim jeans. "Hey, Peaches."

She grinned, ready to tease him. "Um, I'd be careful. You're going to make Michelle jealous."

A flash of guilt crossed his eyes. "Yeah, about that—"

But he was interrupted by a loud Ava nearly yelling through the bullhorn in her hands.

"Welcome, everyone! It's time for the lighting of the tree! So! Fun! This year our tree is donated by Tree Growers of Bent, Oregon. Another Douglas fir. Before we hit the switch and light up the night sky, you'll each get to place an ornament on the tree. Just reach in the baskets we're all passing out. Find an ornament in there and put it on the tree! And don't forget the upcoming Snowflake Float Boat Parade, followed by the first annual literary costume event at Once Upon a Book. Come dressed as your favorite literary character and support the giving tree! One of you could win a gift card worth hundreds of dollars, which ought to help with all that holiday shopping."

Many turned to Twyla and smiled, giving her a thumbs-up. She'd love to claim the idea as her own, but it had been yet another one of Ava's creative brainstorms. The woman was a marketing genius when it came to town tourism and supporting local business. Before Noah's return, the costume event would have been the most excitement she'd have all year. She'd been planning for months, her own ideas swinging between Elizabeth Bennet and Hermione Granger. She hadn't yet decided, but she already had the long Jane Austen-style dress she'd found for a deep discount on eBay.

"Literary character." Noah winked and tipped back on his heels. "Does dragon slayer count?"

Her heart raced at the memory. Their favorite book. She'd misplaced *A Dragon's Heart* about a year ago, just before the move into a smaller rental to save money. Books tended to get swallowed whole in a bookstore and half the time she expected to come across it on a shelf. So far, she hadn't. Everyone, including Mr. Finch, was on the lookout. This particular copy was unlike any other, and even though the genre had grown out of popularity with most readers, Twyla liked to read the book once a year. She'd ordered another copy for that reason alone, but it could never take the place of the one she'd lost. Noah's handwriting was in the margins of that book, along with her own.

"You can come as anything you'd like. I'm just happy to have you."

She nearly corrected herself but then let it go. He knew what she meant. She didn't *have* him. Michelle had him. And though she wondered with every moment that passed what he'd meant when he said, "About that…" she refused to ask.

"I kind of look like a dragon slayer and I'm sure I can find a cool sword."

She chuckled. "You do *not* look like a dragon slayer and I'm fairly sure you already own a plastic toy sword."

"Are you calling me an overgrown child?" He narrowed his eyes, filled with humor and mischief.

"Maybe."

"Got to say, it's tough to hang out with someone who knows me so well." The basket came around to them and Noah dug for several long seconds, causing even Valerie to quirk a brow. "Ah, yeah. Here we go."

He held up the ornament depicting the cover of *Where the Wild Things Are*. "My favorite book. Still read it every night before bed."

"Bless your heart," Valerie said and waited while Twyla dug through the basket.

She picked out an elf from the Lazy Maisy store and together she and Noah went forward and placed the ornaments. Side by side like they'd done for years. Just like old times.

A few minutes later, the lights slowly went up the

giant tree, starting from the lower half and scrolling slowly to the top until bright lights beckoned.

Noah turned to Twyla. "Let the wild rumpus start."

Don't miss
Once Upon a Charming Bookshop
by Heatherly Bell,
available December 2023
wherever Harlequin Special Edition
books and ebooks are sold.

www.Harlequin.com

COMING NEXT MONTH FROM

(H) HARLEQUIN

SPECIAL EDITION

#3025 A TEMPORARY TEXAS ARRANGEMENT
Lockharts Lost & Found • by Cathy Gillen Thacker
Noah Lockhart, a widowed father of three girls, has vowed never to be reckless in love again...until he meets Tess Gardner, the veterinarian caring for his pregnant miniature donkey. But will love still be a possibility when one of his daughters objects to the romance?

#3026 THE AIRMAN'S HOMECOMING
The Tuttle Sisters of Coho Cove • by Sabrina York
As a former ParaJumper for the elite air force paramedic rescue wing, loner Noah Crocker has overcome enormous odds in his life. But convincing no-nonsense bakery owner Amy Tuttle Tolliver that he's ready to settle down with her and her sons may be his toughest challenge yet!

#3027 WRANGLING A FAMILY
Aspen Creek Bachelors • by Kathy Douglass
Before meeting Alexandra Jamison, rancher Nathan Montgomery never had time for romance. Now he needs a girlfriend in order to keep his matchmaking mother off his back, and single mom Alexandra fits the bill. If only their romance ruse didn't lead to knee-weakening kisses...

#3028 SAY IT LIKE YOU MEAN IT
by Rochelle Alers
When former actress Shannon Younger comes face-to-face with handsome celebrity landscape architect Joaquin Williamson, she vows not to come under his spell. She starts to trust Joaquin, but she knows that falling for another high-profile man could cost her her career—and her heart.

#3029 THEIR ACCIDENTAL HONEYMOON
Once Upon a Wedding • by Mona Shroff
Rani Mistry and Param Sheth have been besties since elementary school. When Param's wedding plans come to a crashing halt, they both go on his honeymoon—as friends. But when friendship takes a sharp turn into a marriage of convenience, will they fake it till they make it?

#3030 AN UPTOWN GIRL'S COWBOY
by Sasha Summers
Savannah Barrett is practically Texas royalty—a good girl with a guarded heart. But one wild night with rebel cowboy Angus McCarrick has her wondering if the boy her daddy always warned her about might be the Prince Charming she's always yearned for.

YOU CAN FIND MORE INFORMATION ON UPCOMING HARLEQUIN TITLES,
FREE EXCERPTS AND MORE AT HARLEQUIN.COM.

Get 3 FREE REWARDS!

We'll send you 2 FREE Books plus a FREE Mystery Gift.

For the Rancher's Baby — STELLA BAGWELL

Hometown Reunion — CHRISTINE RIMMER

A Baby on His Doorstep

A Cowboy Worth Waiting For — Melinda Curtis

FREE Value Over **$20**

Both the **Harlequin® Special Edition** and **Harlequin® Heartwarming™** series feature compelling novels filled with stories of love and strength where the bonds of friendship, family and community unite.

YES! Please send me 2 FREE novels from the Harlequin Special Edition or Harlequin Heartwarming series and my FREE Gift (gift is worth about $10 retail). After receiving them, if I don't wish to receive any more books, I can return the shipping statement marked "cancel." If I don't cancel, I will receive 6 brand-new Harlequin Special Edition books every month and be billed just $5.49 each in the U.S. or $6.24 each in Canada, a savings of at least 12% off the cover price, or 4 brand-new Harlequin Heartwarming Larger-Print books every month and be billed just $6.24 each in the U.S. or $6.74 each in Canada, a savings of at least 19% off the cover price. It's quite a bargain! Shipping and handling is just 50¢ per book in the U.S. and $1.25 per book in Canada.* I understand that accepting the 2 free books and gift places me under no obligation to buy anything. I can always return a shipment and cancel at any time by calling the number below. The free books and gift are mine to keep no matter what I decide.

Choose one: ☐ **Harlequin Special Edition** (235/335 BPA GRMK) ☐ **Harlequin Heartwarming Larger-Print** (161/361 BPA GRMK) ☐ **Or Try Both!** (235/335 & 161/361 BPA GRPZ)

Name (please print)

Address   Apt. #

City   State/Province   Zip/Postal Code

Email: Please check this box ☐ if you would like to receive newsletters and promotional emails from Harlequin Enterprises ULC and its affiliates. You can unsubscribe anytime.

Mail to the Harlequin Reader Service:
IN U.S.A.: P.O. Box 1341, Buffalo, NY 14240-8531
IN CANADA: P.O. Box 603, Fort Erie, Ontario L2A 5X3

Want to try 2 free books from another series! Call 1-800-873-8635 or visit www.ReaderService.com.